"You've got a lot of principles, for a bandit," Amalia told him, rubbing her thumb over her lips. "Have you ever stolen anything?"

"Do hearts count?" He raised a sardonic eyebrow, feeling his mouth twitch when she laughed. "Principled or not, you're not scared of being alone in the wilderness with a bandit?"

"I'm not scared of anything," she replied swiftly. "And besides…" The considering gaze she dragged over him made Julián's pulse race. She gave a minute shrug. "I'm match enough for you."

"Are you?" he asked, letting her see his amusement.

As much as he ached to prove her wrong, Julián thought he had better be prudent for once in his life.

"I don't want any trouble when your uncle comes with the ransom," he offered by way of explanation. "If someone were to think that I took advantage of you…"

Amalia couldn't hide her disappointment, and seeing how much she wanted him almost made him kiss her again.

Author Note

I grew up with stories about *raptos*—unmarried women being seduced by nefarious men who abscond with them into the wilderness to compromise them and thus force them into marriage.

It wasn't until I was in my twenties that I learned of an alternate explanation for this practice: mainly that it was sometimes put into motion by women as a way of imposing their own agency when their families didn't approve of their choices in partner. My imagination was immediately seized, and I started trying to come up with other reasons for why someone would orchestrate their own *rapto*—and thus Amalia's story was born!

I knew she had to be bold and fearless—and that Julián had the courage to match. The two of them took on a life of their own, and I've been scrambling to keep up with them ever since!

LYDIA
SAN ANDRES

Alliance with
His Stolen Heiress

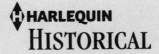

ISBN-13: 978-1-335-72388-8

Alliance with His Stolen Heiress

Copyright © 2023 by Lydia San Andres

Recycling programs for this product may not exist in your area.

For questions and comments about the quality of this book, please contact us at CustomerService@Harlequin.com.

Harlequin Enterprises ULC
22 Adelaide St. West, 41st Floor
Toronto, Ontario M5H 4E3, Canada
www.Harlequin.com

Printed in U.S.A.

Lydia San Andres lives and writes in the tropics, where she can be found reading and making excuses to stay out of the sun. Lydia would love to hear from her readers, and you can visit her at lydiasanandres.com or follow her on Facebook, Twitter and TikTok @lydiaallthetime.

Books by Lydia San Andres

Harlequin Historical

Compromised into a Scandalous Marriage
Alliance with His Stolen Heiress

Look out for more books from Lydia San Andres coming soon.

Visit the Author Profile page
at Harlequin.com.

To G.G.T., who would have been tickled
at having a romance heroine named after her.

And to my little sister, who is forever rescuing me.

Chapter One

San Pedro de Macorís, 1905

The sky was a pristine, unblemished blue, but something about the clouds hovering in the horizon made Amalia Troncoso think of rain as she alighted from her family's carriage.

It could not rain—not today of all days. Not after all the trouble she had gone to in planning this outing.

The patch of grass she landed on was still slightly slick with morning dew, so she turned back to offer her younger sister a hand.

"You can stop glaring at the sky," Lucía said, looking at Amalia with amusement as she grasped her hand. "It won't rain, you know."

Amalia cast another threatening look at the clouds in the horizon. "It had better not."

"As convinced as I generally am of your ability to take control of every situation, I think we'll have to draw the line at the weather." Lucía's giggles were hard to come by these days, and all the more precious for it. Amalia couldn't help giving the seventeen-year-old's fingers a brief, fond squeeze as she helped her down from her perch on the upholstered seat.

"That's what *you* think," Amalia answered her sister with a carefree chuckle that was not altogether genuine. For Lucía's sake, she would do far more daring things than attempt to glare rainclouds into submission.

Lucía joined the other young ladies gathered beneath an ancient *anacahuita* tree, to a chorus of eager greetings. A dozen lightweight wicker chairs had been arranged in the shade. The young ladies had likewise arranged themselves as picturesquely as if they were expecting their portrait to be taken. Bedecked in white and ivory frocks edged with delicate bands of lace, they looked like flowers among the lush tropical greenery.

Amalia smoothed down her own ivory-colored skirt. The slim column was paired with a square-necked blouse in the same shade, pale brown leather pumps and a straw hat ringed with silk flowers. It was not the ensemble she would have selected for a day spent traipsing around the countryside, but Lucía had been firm on the matter. The Troncoso sisters were not only fabulously wealthy, they were *always* fashionable, as well.

Given any choice in the matter, though, Amalia would have rather been pragmatic.

She'd also have preferred a nice wander through the narrow dirt paths that led to various sugarcane fields, or even a poke around the crumbling ruins of an eighteenth- or seventeenth-century estate that sprawled behind the tree. Unfortunately, there was no time for any of that today.

The maid that had accompanied them, riding alongside the coachman, was unloading the baskets containing their midday meal. Tucked into buckets filled with rapidly melting ice, the sparkling wine would have to be served quickly, before it grew warm. Amalia gave the young woman her instructions, then went to greet her sister's guests.

She went around the semicircle of chairs, bending to press her cheek against each of the guests, as was only polite. Though Amalia had been acquainted with them all for years, they really were mostly Lucía's friends. By the time Amalia dropped into the empty chair next to Paulina de Linares, Lucía had been drawn into the conversation and was chattering away animatedly.

The chairs had been arranged with their backs to the morning sun; the small amber earrings Paulina wore caught the light, looking like live embers. "It's good to see you, Amalia," she said. "I thought you would be joining us at yesterday's garden party, but Lucía said you were under the weather."

Amalia went blank for a second as she tried to remember the excuse she'd given for not attending. "Oh, yes," she said after a small pause. "I was so sorry to miss it."

Paulina smiled. "I hope you've recovered enough to attend the dinner I'm hosting tonight."

Amalia didn't squirm, but it was a near thing. Paulina had been trying to deepen their acquaintanceship into something more like friendship for weeks now, and though Amalia thought the young mother was very nice, she couldn't help the little flare of panic that sprang to life in her chest at the thought of getting too close to anyone.

Hoping that her smile didn't feel too forced, she said, "I was actually—"

The rest of her sentence was cut short by the thunder of approaching hoofbeats. The tangle of vegetation behind them quivered, then parted violently as a horse and rider burst through.

The horse was ordinary enough, brown and sleek with perspiration. Its rider, however…

Amalia stared up at the masked man in the saddle. Bristling with weapons, his sleeves rolled up to exhibit a pair of gleaming, sunbaked arms corded with muscle, he looked like—

"A bandit!" shrieked one of the young ladies.

The man in question inclined his head in acknowledgment, raising his pistol in the direction of the coachman standing on the other side of the clearing.

"A pleasure to make your acquaintance," he drawled, the cockiness in his tone turning the pleasantry into something slightly mocking. Swinging a long leg over his saddle, he dropped easily to the ground, contriving to keep his pistol pointed toward the coachman. "As loath as I am to break up your little party here, I've some business to conduct. I should very much appreciate your assistance."

Amalia's nerves might have failed her at that moment, if Lucía hadn't made a frightened whimper.

Brushing off Paulina's restraining hand, Amalia rose from her seat and took a step that put her between the bandit and the young ladies. "What is it that you want?" she demanded in strident tones.

Over the kerchief covering the bottom half of his face, the bandit directed a look at Amalia that made her knees quiver. "You."

Something more powerful than a shiver racked Amalia's body at the simple syllable. Almost without thought, she took a step forward, as if her body was responding to his command. Lucía let out another noise.

Amalia cast a quick look toward her sister. "I'll be all right, Lu," she called, making her voice as firm as she could. "Don't you dare worry about me."

Out of the corner of her eye, Amalia saw a wild-eyed Paulina reach for a tree branch. Did she really think she could fight off a pistol-wielding bandit with a *branch*?

"I wouldn't do that if I were you," the bandit drawled, lifting his other hand to point a second pistol at Paulina. Even in the dappled shade of the *anacahuita* tree, the sunlight glinted threateningly off the muzzle.

Amalia's pulse quickened. "Please don't. I don't want any of them hurt."

Keeping his pistols trained on their targets, the bandit sauntered toward Amalia with infuriating cockiness. He closed the distance between them with two strides of his powerful legs.

A shockingly hard arm came around her midsection, and Amalia almost gasped at the touch as he drew her against an equally solid chest. For the space of several breaths, all Amalia was aware of was the sensation of her body pressed tightly against his—she had never stood this way with a man, not even while dancing. That she couldn't see his expression made it all the more…

Her brain supplied her with the word *exciting*, but Amalia refused to consider it. There was nothing exciting about *this*. She should have been nervous, or at the very least annoyed at this abrupt and unsolicited embrace.

The bandit lowered his head to hers, and Amalia almost shivered as the edge of his kerchief brushed the curve of her ear. "Aren't you going to struggle?" he asked, his voice rich with amusement.

Surprise followed by irritation swept over Amalia. Before she could give him a swift kick in the knee, the moment was broken in a sudden explosion of violence.

Caught in the frisson running through her, Amalia wasn't quite sure what had happened. All she knew was that the muscles bulging against her tensed, and suddenly he was whipping around, barely pausing to take aim before he released a shot that sliced through the bottles of champagne her maid had laid out on a table.

Shrieks, screams and the sound of shattering glass pierced the air. The Troncosos' coachman, who had clearly been attempting to edge toward the spot where Amalia was being held by the bandit, threw up his arms to shield his face from the flying shards.

The bandit took advantage of the commotion to burst into action. Within moments Amalia was on his saddle and he was swinging himself behind her, his thighs and arms making an inescapable cage around her. She couldn't have gotten away if she wanted to and, well...

She didn't want to.

It wasn't only because the bandit had turned his horse toward a path too narrow for the coachman to pursue in their cumbersome carriage—in the time it would take him to unhitch a horse and give chase, Amalia and her captor would be long gone. They were racing at a speed that left Amalia breathless, the path so narrow that branches and vines tugged at Amalia's hair and clothes. Only the bandit's unyielding—and not altogether unwelcome—grip around her prevented her from tumbling into the tangle of vegetation.

Amalia supposed she should have found it terrifying, but in truth, it was actually rather...exhilarating.

It was—

Amalia didn't so much hear as feel the bandit's roar, gusting at her ear. She glanced back, uncomprehending, and caught a glimpse of a pair of flashing dark eyes before he threw his torso on top of her, making a sheltering cage of his body.

A moment later she felt the overhanging branch they had just narrowly avoided, scraping off her hat. Amalia's gasp was swallowed by the wind, but she could hear his breathless laughter in her ear as they rushed on, even faster than before.

The thundering of hooves grew more frantic, and Amalia's heart was galloping to match. Neither slowed until they reached the end of the path and burst out into a clearing. Amalia hardly had time to notice the small wooden shack nestled among the trees before she found herself being unceremoniously dumped from the saddle.

To the detriment of her already damaged ensemble, she landed on her bottom on a patch of dirt. The bandit dismounted with considerably more grace—and without sparing her a glance.

Indignation propelled Amalia to her feet, though her knees felt like they had been replaced with rice pudding.

The wind—not to mention the loss of her hat—had pulled long tendrils of hair out of the confines of her hairpins. Making an ineffective attempt to smooth them back, Amalia drew herself up to her fullest height.

"What the devil was that?" she asked the bandit furiously. "No one pursued us. There was no need to—to imperil our lives in such a way."

"I thought you would appreciate a little excitement, Your Highness," the bandit said, flicking a look at her as he finished hitching his horse to a nearby post. With more delicacy than she would have thought him capable of, he plucked a single leaf off her shoulder and let it flutter gently to the ground. "Isn't that why you hired me?"

Julián Fuentes had made a lot of mistakes in his wretched lifetime, but this surely had to be the worst.

His pulse was roaring in his ears when he removed the kerchief covering the black bristles on his chin and jaw, and used it to mop up the perspiration trickling down his brow.

The ride itself, and even the little interlude in the clearing, had been exciting enough. It had cleared the cobwebs, in any case.

This woman, however...

Barely ten minutes in her presence and already he was certain that he was no match for her.

Her lacy white clothes were littered with leaves and broken twigs, and thanks to his ungentlemanly removal from the saddle—necessary before she realized that it wasn't in fact his pistol that was digging into the small of her back—she also sported a long smear of dirt down her skirt. Coupled with the glistening flush on her cheeks, and the wild curls tumbling from their pins, she was quite possibly the most striking woman Julián had ever seen.

"In any case, you were supposed to wait until I was away from the group," she huffed, trying and failing to brush the dirt and grass clinging to her once-pristine skirt. "I wanted witnesses, not potential victims!"

Julián raised an eyebrow. "Victims? No one came to any harm."

"No thanks to you," she snapped. "What did you mean by flinging that pistol around? The last thing I wanted was for anyone to get hurt."

"Someone would have if I hadn't done what I did—your uncle's coachman looked like he was about to do something incredibly foolish. Now, when he faces your uncle, he'll say truthfully that he did try to rescue you from my clutches. That will keep him from getting into trouble, just as my shooting the bottles kept him from getting seriously hurt."

"I— Oh." She gave him a grudging nod. "I suppose that was quick thinking on your part."

"Mmm…" Giving his horse a final scratch between the ears, Julián made sure there was enough water in the trough before marching toward the shack.

It wasn't home by any stretch of the imagination, but for the past couple of nights, the dilapidated wooden structure had provided him with shelter. Which was more than he could say for his own family.

He had cast off his shirt and had plunged both hands into the full basin before realizing that she had followed him inside. Unbothered by her presence, Julián splashed the lukewarm water on his face, feeling rivulets run down his bare chest when he turned back to her.

He couldn't help but notice how she tracked them with her gaze, all the way down to where the water pooled on the waistband of his trousers, before biting her lip and flicking her eyes toward his face.

"I'm afraid I don't think much of your hospitality," she said, lifting her chin.

"You hired me for a *rapto*, Your Highness, not hospitality."

Julián had burst out laughing when she'd approached him with her idea. He'd been lurking in the street outside the large house where she lived with her uncle, wearing borrowed clothing he thought would help hide his identity, when she'd stormed out the front door, almost stumbling over him in her haste. Julián hadn't said a word, but she'd caught him crouching behind the family carriage and gotten entirely the wrong idea about who he was, and he'd only had a split second to decide whether or not to go along with it.

Julián reached for the tin mug on the shelf above his table and lightly tossed it in her direction, half expecting her to fumble. She caught it neatly, however, and held it out in that imperious way that Julián was still trying to decide was charming or irritating.

Either way, something about the way she seemed so determined to hold on to her composure made him burn to knock her ever so slightly off balance. That may have been why, instead of pouring her water from the clay jug, he unstoppered one of the bottles on the shelf.

She sputtered at the first sip. "What in the world is this?"

"Aguardiente," he said, hiding a smirk.

"Ardiente is right," she muttered, before adding with exacting politeness, "Might I trouble you for some *agua* of the nonburning variety? If it wouldn't be too much trouble, of course. I wouldn't want to inconvenience you in any way."

Thriftily disposing of the remains of the alcoholic beverage by knocking back the contents of her cup,

Julián grinned at her. "I think I've made it clear by now that I am completely at your disposal, *señorita.*"

She had positioned herself in such a way that he had to reach past her to get anything off the shelf. Her lips parted when his arm brushed the frills on her blouse, a soft intake of breath stirring the heavy, warm air between them.

Although only a moment before, Julián was enjoying teasing her, the sudden, fierce wave of desire that swept over him was disconcerting enough that he almost dropped the water jug. It didn't break, merely struck the table with a solid *thunk.*

Forget knocking her off balance—he was making *himself* unsteady.

"Water," he said, swirling some around the mug and tossing it out the hole that served as a window before refilling the vessel. He held it out to her with a gentlemanly bow, adding mockingly, "With my compliments to Your Highness."

Her eyes narrowed, though Julián caught the gleam of humor within them. "That's Your Majesty to you," she said, and Julián had to admit that there *was* something majestic in her bearing, even in her disheveled state.

He obliged her with a booming laugh, which served to dispel some of the tension crowding thickly between them.

She flashed him a smile, then turned to look out the window hole, holding herself slightly less tautly.

"It will probably be a few hours until your uncle receives the ransom note and gathers the money," Julián pointed out. Belatedly remembering his half-naked state, he pulled his one clean shirt off the nail it hung from and slid it over his shoulders. "You might want to occupy yourself with something more entertaining than looking out the window."

Why in hell did everything he say today sound so lascivious? Or did it just sound that way to his ears because he was still not quite recovered from the sensation of her lithe body pressed against his, the sweet scent of her hair threatening to overpower all his senses? The temptation to draw her close again and bury his face in the soft skin of her neck was almost more than he could bear.

If Julián knew how to read people—and he did—Miss Amalia Troncoso, eldest niece of Francisco Troncoso and heiress to a fortune so vast it made him dizzy, was also burning with desire.

Before she had a chance to remark on his less than felicitous turn of phrase, Julián elaborated. "Seeing as how I'm fairly new to banditry, I hadn't really realized how much of an appetite one could work up by snatching maidens. Am I mistaken in thinking that you must be hungry, too?"

"Famished," she admitted, and Julián would *not* mistake the faint flutter of her lashes for anything more than a simple change in expression.

"An early lunch it is, then. I think I have some crackers around here..."

Most of the coffee he'd brewed that morning was still in the percolator. Julián peered dubiously into its inky depths, then poured it out anyway, and plucked a large, round cracker from a covered plate.

And then he turned around.

For lack of a better seat, she had perched on the edge of his cot and was removing the few pins that still remained lodged at awkward angles in her dark hair. Julián watched her long, lustrous curls tumble down her shoulders, grasping, for the first time, just what it would mean to share these extremely close quarters with her until her uncle turned up with the ransom.

It had been a long, long time since he'd seen a woman at her toilette. Long enough that the sight of her fingers dragging slowly through her thick locks was doing unspeakable things to his self-control. He didn't just want to tangle his own fingers through her hair, tugging lightly until he dragged a gasp out of her. He wanted to spread it over her bare shoulders, tracing the soft whorls with his fingertips and—

Julián's heart was pounding. There was no way he was going to be able to keep from disgracing himself. His only course of action, unbefitting his status as a fearless bandit though it was, was to flee far, far away.

Thrusting the coffee and cracker in her general direction, Julián muttered something and strode to the door, meaning to find a less hazardous occupation outdoors—like standing on his saddle while his horse leaped over fallen logs.

Even before he reached the opening, however, he could see the first few droplets that had begun to darken the patch of dirt in front of the shack. Julián swore under his breath. Two more strides, and the light patter had turned into a proper tropical deluge, trapping the two of them inside.

Together.

Chapter Two

What in the world had Amalia gotten herself into?

She had heard dozens of stories about *raptos*. It was always evil scoundrels snatching innocent young women from their homes and taking them deep into the wilderness, or two lovers getting around their families' disapproval by pretending that one of them had kidnapped the other when in reality they had run off together.

She'd never heard of someone organizing her own *rapto*, but there was always a first time for everything, and Amalia Troncoso never left anything to chance.

She sat on the bandit's bed, her hairpins in a little heap on his shabby blanket, watching as he rummaged through the various cans and lidded jars on the table that seemed to serve as his washstand and makeshift kitchen.

From the relative barrenness of the shack, she could only assume that it wasn't his permanent residence. If the scatter of food on the table was any indication, though, he had spent at least one night here. Amalia couldn't help the tendril of curiosity unfurling inside her. Where *did* he live? And if it was true that he was new to banditry, unlikely as that seemed after his little display with the pistols, what profession had he been engaged in before turning to a life of crime?

The man may have looked every inch a bandit, but he was very well spoken and clearly educated. She tried to picture him sitting behind a desk, wearing spectacles like her uncle's bookkeeper, and almost laughed out loud. Not an accountant, then, nor yet a lawyer. Amalia gazed thoughtfully at his back. It was respectably covered by a clean shirt, but the sight of his sunburned chest was engraved in her mind. A man of property, perhaps, one accustomed to galloping the length of his lands under the punishing sun. Maybe he was trying to outrun some sort of tragedy. A dark loss.

Much to her annoyance, Amalia *was* hungry. Nibbling at the slightly stale cracker, she thought longingly about the baskets crowded with delicacies that her maid had packed for the outing and wished she'd had the presence of mind to pack a little basket for herself and stash it somewhere. Though of course, it wouldn't be too long before Tio Francisco sent someone with the money. Once she had it, she'd not only be able to buy herself as lavish a meal as she wanted, she'd also be able to afford something she and Lucía had longed for for years—security.

Then again, Tio Francisco was ever wary of thieves and didn't keep much money around the house. The amount Amalia had instructed the bandit to ask for in his ransom note would require her uncle to visit the bank. The rain would probably delay him even further.

She must have sighed, or made some sort of sound, because the bandit cast a glance at her.

As soon as it began to rain, he had retreated toward a stool in the corner with his own mug of tepid coffee. He had been staring deeply into its depths, his earlier cockiness faded into a less brash thoughtfulness.

"Everything all right?" he asked. His black hair was long enough to curl around his ears, and he seemed to have a habit of raking it back with his fingers. Without the benefit of a comb and pomade, that was only a temporary measure—within moments a rakish lock would flop back over his forehead, and the entire thing would begin again.

It was almost as distracting as the sight of his bare chest, and considering the latter's extremely chiseled quality, that was saying something.

"Oh, yes," she answered lightly, if a few seconds too late. "Just…thinking."

"About all the frocks you'll buy with your share of the ransom?"

"Frocks?" Amalia frowned. She had far more important things to put that money toward than frocks—her and Lucía's freedom, for one. Tio Francisco had taken over their care when their father died, almost fifteen years before. He had made sure the sisters never lacked for anything, but he had kept them both on a tight leash.

"I'm assuming it's not food or shelter you need," the bandit went on. "And unless you've some very serious gambling debts—"

"I don't gamble," she told him censoriously. "And women have more uses for money than adding to the contents of their wardrobe. You don't know anything about me, or my life—"

"So tell me."

"I beg your pardon?"

He leaned forward in his seat, his empty mug dangling from one strong finger. "What trouble could a pampered miss like you have possibly gotten into to justify staging abductions and consorting with scoundrels like myself?"

A pampered miss, was she?

"I'm not in any sort of trouble," she said tightly. "Before my father died, he made his brother, my uncle Francisco, the custodian of my sister's and my inheritance. I'd always thought it was only until we reached our majority, but it appears I was mistaken. Several weeks ago I was informed by my uncle that my father was so apprehensive of my sister and I being taken in by fortune hunters, that he wrote it into his will that my uncle should have control of our holdings and properties in perpetuity."

Julián's eyes gleamed in the dimness of the hut. "And he doesn't intend to relinquish that control?"

Amalia shook her head. "For years, I thought he was just really concerned with carrying out his late brother's orders. He's made everybody believe that he's this selfless, altruistic paragon of virtue whose only preoccupation is to keep Lucía and me safe from people who want to use us for our money. But the truth is, he just wants an excuse to keep his greedy paws on what's rightfully ours—and the only way he can do that is to shackle us to him. Or to whichever suitor makes him the best offer."

Her hands clenched around the dented tin mug, so hard her fingertips felt bruised. "My father was so busy protecting us from fortune hunters, he didn't realize his brother was the worst one of all. Sometimes I wonder if he would have done the same thing had my mother been around to talk reason into him. Or if he would have trampled over her opinion, too."

As wonderful as her father had been to her and Lucía, Amalia had always known him to be the sort of man who had a deep need to be right at all times.

Amalia hadn't realized how loud her voice had gotten until she reached the end of her speech and heard the raindrops thudding against the shack's cane thatch roof. It was desperately unfair that she had to resort to schemes like this one just to have some measure of independence. She and Lucía had all the frocks they could ever want. But that wasn't *all* they wanted.

"Lucía wants to study music abroad," Amalia said, past the sudden raspiness in her throat. "And I should love nothing better than to take her."

"I just want frocks, myself," the bandit said so offhandedly that Amalia gaped at him for a moment, before she dissolved into laughter.

In the process, she upset the mug she'd been holding, dribbling the dark dregs of her coffee over her much-abused skirt. With a raised eyebrow, the bandit offered her the kerchief he had discarded, which she used to blot at the stained fabric.

"I may have to purchase one or two myself, after all this," she said when she had recovered. "Seeing as I have completely destroyed this ensemble."

His tanned, calloused hand landed on her arm, and Amalia looked down in surprise to see that he had crossed the dirt floor to crouch in front of her. "Count on me to do whatever it takes to get your money back from your uncle," he said with quiet intensity, his eyes gleaming in the dim room.

As close as she'd been pressed against him earlier, she'd had her back to him. It was only now that she saw the thin scar running through one of his eyebrows.

She'd thought him a man of property? No—he was a bandit through and through.

And she had placed her trust in him, at least temporarily.

Trust was not something Amalia gave easily. In her experience, people were rarely worthy of it. She wasn't certain if this man was, at least not yet. But the sincerity shining in his eyes made her want to believe in him like she hadn't any other man.

It felt…dangerous. Trust Amalia to run full tilt toward it, foolhardy though it may be.

His fingers closed around the thin, delicate skin of her wrist, and Amalia almost gasped at the startling intimacy of being touched on the exact spot where her pulse was thrumming.

"I— You—"

All thought seemed to have vanished from Amalia's head. All, save for one—she didn't want him to let go.

Boldly, she placed her hand over his. He couldn't have known what she was longing for, but something compelled him to brush a kiss over her knuckles. He must not have shaved in days, and the bristles that lent him a roguish air scraped delightfully against her skin.

Her breath caught, her fingers reflexively squeezing his. And then Amalia did something she had never even contemplated doing before.

She lowered her face and pressed her lips against

his, feeling almost like this was part of the adventure she had embarked on.

She had expected his kisses to be as rough as his hands. She had expected…any number of things, but certainly not the exquisite, delicate gentleness with which he parted her lips with his own.

Amalia shouldn't have been surprised by her own boldness. After all, it had taken a great deal of it to even think of this scheme. Amalia was nothing if not filled with grit and valor. This wasn't even the first kiss she had ever shared with a man, just the first she had initiated…and the first that left her aching for more.

Until now, this moment, she had never allowed herself to stop thinking and scheming and let herself be carried aloft by pure sensation. Her body rocked with shivers as he followed the kiss with another, and then another and then…

He laid a ring of kisses around the base of her neck, right where the necklace she usually wore would rest if she hadn't removed it that morning. Amalia congratulated herself on her foresight, though it had been nothing more than prudence that had prompted her to put away her jewelry before haring off into the countryside with a bandit.

On the whole, it had not been a bad idea—the removal of the jewelry nor the haring-off part. Nor the bandit.

There had probably been an easier way to go about this whole business. But Amalia had to concede there was one distinct benefit to this particular plan, and it was currently pressing a kiss just below her ear.

Amalia had been a favorite at balls. She had kissed a man or two. But those kisses were nothing like these—

and those other lips couldn't come close to comparing to the rightness of his. There was something truly wicked about his lips when they curled into a smile. But when they were pressed against hers? It was nothing short of thrilling.

Julián was playing with fire. He knew it, and what was worse, he didn't care.

He was no stranger to wanting what he couldn't have—sometimes it seemed like he'd spent half his life surrounded by all kinds of riches and finding little interest or enjoyment in any of it. Amalia was just one more item on that long list.

Her skin tasted as sweet as it had smelled when he'd held her against him earlier. He reveled in it, his lips ranging over her neck, then her eager, welcoming mouth, then back again.

If Julián had been able to draw a breath long enough to speak, he would have cursed the current fashions for making skirts so slender. Kneeling in front of her, pressed against her legs, he would have done anything to have her open them wide enough to accommodate him.

That thought, more than anything, was what made him pull away.

As well as the crashing realization that she didn't really know who he was, or what he was after, or why he had been so willing to agree to her request.

Julián had never intended to pass himself off as a bandit—but when Amalia had unknowingly provided him with the perfect cover to investigate his father's shady business dealings, he had seized it. It had been an impulse, and a poorly thought out one at that. Even now Julián wasn't all that sure what he thought he'd accomplish by it.

All he knew was that her uncle was also embroiled in the situation, and that the whole thing was linked to the end of his last relationship, a messy split that Julián now knew had been engineered by his father. It was doubtful that Amalia even knew what was happening, but it occurred to Julián that when her uncle came with the ransom, maybe Julián could extract something besides money from him—information.

He knew what his family had done, but not why.

Julián would find out what had led his father to destroy his relationship with Concepción. And then he would make things right with her—if that was even possible anymore. It was certainly too late for him. His heart had shattered the moment she'd sent him away from her doorstep, and even though almost a year had passed since then, his chest still ached with the emptiness of those first weeks without her. The memory of it surged over him now, overwhelming in its intensity.

"We should stop," he told Amalia now.

She murmured something incomprehensible against his mouth, holding his face between her hands. Her lips had been rubbed red by his beard, and Julián couldn't resist soothing the scrape with the ball of his thumb as he stepped away.

"Must we?" she asked.

Her having concocted this scheme was already proof enough that she didn't have much of a care for her reputation. Though to the other people at the gathering she had ostensibly been an unwilling participant, Julián knew that everyone would assume he'd had his

way with her. Especially if the truth of who Julián really was ever came out.

All that considered, perhaps it shouldn't have been
surprising that she'd be not just willing, but eager, to
pursue the dangerous path they were on. If she was
about to return home to find her reputation ruined,
why not actually do what she would be accused of
having done? Had he been in her position, he would
have thrown caution to the wind and himself into bed.

Maybe it was just Julián being his usual contrary
self, but if anyone was going to be throwing herself
into *his* bed, he would have rather it be because she
wanted him, not because he was merely convenient.

As the notion came into his mind, Julián was uncomfortably reminded of all the women he had bed-
ded precisely for that reason. He had never been in love
and as far as he knew, none of his dalliances had ever
been in love with him. That was how he'd preferred it.

So why did the prospect of doing the same with
Amalia ring so hollow?

Julián laid a final kiss on the corner of her mouth.
"We do," he said, and all his saintly self-denial earned
him was a frown.

Disengaging himself, he retreated to the stool in
the corner. Outside, the rain continued to pummel the
shack's thatched roof. Julián was grateful for the sound,
if only because it drowned out his ragged breaths.

What the hell had come over him? Sitting there
panting like he'd tried to outrun a locomotive, from
nothing more than a series of kisses.

Hearing about her uncle had moved him into offering his protection—not something he'd ever done before. But he felt it roaring over him at the thought of

her trying so valiantly, and so desperately, to look after her sister. Julián hadn't met Amalia until the day she'd approached him with her plan, but he'd been vaguely aware of the Troncoso sisters, heiresses to one of San Pedro's largest fortunes.

He could never have imagined that they had been dealing with a tyrant of their own. Just as he had.

"You've got a lot of principles, for a bandit," Amalia told him, rubbing her thumb over her lips. "Have you ever stolen anything?"

"Do hearts count?" He raised a sardonic eyebrow, feeling his mouth twitch when she laughed. "Principled or not, you're not scared of being alone in the wilderness with a bandit?"

"I'm not scared of anything," she replied swiftly. "And besides…" The considering gaze she dragged over him made Julián's pulse race. She gave a minute shrug. "I'm match enough for you."

"Are you?" he asked, letting her see his amusement.

As much as he ached to prove her wrong, Julián thought he had better be prudent for once in his life.

"I don't want any trouble when your uncle comes with the ransom," he offered by way of explanation. "If someone were to think that I took advantage of you…"

Amalia couldn't hide her disappointment, and seeing how much she wanted him almost made him kiss her again.

"Why would you care what San Pedro society thinks about you?" she asked.

"I don't," Julián returned. "I care about the Civil Guard and their pesky little habit of tossing delinquents into prison. Which is where I'll be headed if anyone thinks I've touched a single hair on your virginal head."

"I thought you were an outlaw."

"I might be, after today."

"In any case, they're all bound to think the worst." She gestured at her torn, dirty clothing, then began scooping up her hair once again, returning it to its former orderly state.

"I'd just as soon not prove them right." *Them* in this instance being not the townspeople, but his father and cousin. Not that he was inclined to elaborate. Before she could open her mouth to ask him any more questions he'd rather not answer, he beat her to it. "Why are *you* so unconcerned about everyone thinking you've been…liberal with your affections?"

She made a noise that sounded distinctly like a snort. "Keeping my virtue intact doesn't serve my plans," she said. "In fact, the only person it serves is my uncle and whichever dolt from a wealthy family he's scheming to marry me off to. I am hoping that being abducted will do enough damage to my reputation to keep him from getting any more ideas, at least long enough for me to leave town, but if it's not enough of a deterrent…"

Julián had never heard a woman speak so frankly and with such pragmatism about so delicate a subject, but as shocking as it was, he had to admit that Amalia wasn't wrong. "Are you saying that you would willingly trade your virtue to keep your uncle from attempting to arrange a marriage? What if you meet someone and want to marry *him*?"

"Oh, I'm never getting married." Her tone was as final as the metallic snap of a key turning inside a lock. "Not willingly. And not for anything foolish, like love. After all, my father loved us. My uncle claims to. And that didn't stop either of them from locking Lucía and me in gilded cages. What would stop a husband, even a loving one, from doing the same? And besides, a husband would expect to be obeyed," she said scornfully. "Marriage would only make him think he had the right to control me, and I've had quite enough of that."

Julián could not bring himself to believe that was even possible. Whoever tried to control Amalia Troncoso would surely find it as easy as trying to control a bolt of lightning.

"What if you married a man with so much property of his own that he would never have any need of yours?" he asked.

"That would only be exchanging one captor for another." Amalia was full of conviction, her face mobile as she explained the reason for this belief. "My father settled a very large sum on my mother when they married. In theory, she was to have complete control over her own expenses, and to manage it as she saw fit. In practice... He was always questioning her decisions. Did the household really use up that many pounds of flour a week, and couldn't she find a less expensive brand of chocolate for breakfast? She would pore over her account books, anxious that she had made a mistake or not noticed that someone was overcharging her. I'd hate to live that way for the rest of my life."

"Not everyone's like that, you know," Julián said. "Some of us are shockingly neglectful with our money."

Amalia shrugged. "Why take the chance?"

Julián shifted in his stool, wincing slightly as he stretched out his cramped legs.

"Are you uncomfortable? There's plenty of room on the bed if you want to sit here," she said, patting the empty stretch of mattress next to her. "I promise I won't take advantage of you."

"Oh, no, Your Highness. I intend to stay far, far away from those sweet lips of yours." Julián leaned back against the wooden wall, crossing his arms and regarding her with mingled regret and amusement. "I'm not about to let you seduce me."

"Oh?" She cocked her head, a small smile playing right where he'd laid his last kiss. "I thought I already had."

Julián felt his lips spreading into a grin. She really was like no other woman he had ever met.

Chapter Three

Night was falling.

Amalia and Julián had managed to keep their hands off each other. Mostly because he had gone outside as soon as the rain eased, and Amalia had taken a long, lonely and unsatisfying nap on the cot that smelled faintly of him.

And still, her uncle hadn't come.

Of all the potential downfalls in her plan, it hadn't occurred to Amalia that he might refuse to pay the ransom, or to rescue her at all.

Standing in the doorway to the shack, Amalia watched the shadows lengthen as light leeched from the sky. Julián was mostly in shadow, cursing under his breath as he tried to light a fire beneath the brick cooking ring with wood that had to be soaked. Amalia's lips twitched at the sight, but the apprehension sweeping over her in a cold wave did not allow a smile to bloom.

Julián gave the crumbling bricks a swift kick, then, looking mulish, seized the pot from the ring and began hauling it inside.

Amalia moved aside to let him pass, but he paused

in the doorway, seemingly unperturbed by the weight of the iron pot. He cocked his head, his dark eyes raking over her.

"Everything all right?"

It was the second time he'd asked her that today—twice more than any of the men in her family ever had. Amalia started to nod as she always did, but it must not have been all that convincing. Julián set the pot down on the floor and placed a finger beneath her chin, lifting it until she was looking into his eyes.

"What's wrong?" he asked softly.

The concern in his expression was breathtaking. Amalia couldn't remember the last time someone had looked at her like this. She'd grown so used to being the strong one, the clever one, the one who found a solution for every problem. No one ever looked at her as though trying to determine whether or not they should offer comfort, or even help.

"I shouldn't have done this." Under the warmth of his concern, the words spilled out faster than they would have otherwise. "I shouldn't have tested my uncle's affection and risked my reputation and—"

"Amalia," Julián said. "The day isn't over. There's still time for him to comply with our demands. And let's not forget that he's a busy man—he might not have even seen the note yet. Maybe he's in the middle of some important deal. Has he mentioned something of the kind to you?"

Amalia frowned. "I wouldn't know. Tío Francisco isn't exactly forthcoming when it comes to all that. He doesn't even entertain his business acquaintances at home."

"That is curious," Julián said softly, adding when

Amalia's brow furrowed tighter, "You don't know that he's given up on you. In fact, for all you know he might be gathering an entire troop's worth of soldiers and preparing to storm our impenetrable fortress."

He gestured at the wooden walls around them, which Amalia would call neither impenetrable nor a fortress. She couldn't help but laugh.

For a ruthless bandit, Julián could be extraordinarily kind.

"All right," she conceded. "I'll try not to worry just yet. Although it looks like I may have cause to, seeing as you seem determined to burn our impenetrable fortress to the ground."

"I'm hungry," he explained. "It's been hours since the coffee and crackers and I did explain that banditry works up an appetite."

"I suppose I had better help you, then. Wouldn't want our fortress to go up in flames just because you don't know how to roast a *batata*."

As it turned out, neither of them were very adept at cookery. Amalia was used to meals appearing on the table, or on a tray in her bedroom, then whisked away as soon as she was finished by one of half a dozen people her uncle employed in the *quinta* that used to belong to her parents. Lavish meals in restaurants were also the norm, as well as vast arrays of delicacies at the house parties she and Lucía frequented.

All right, so maybe Julián hadn't been completely wrong when he'd called her a pampered miss.

Peeling a plantain left her hands as sticky as if she had dipped them into a pot of paste, but eventually the two of them managed to cobble together something that vaguely resembled a soup. Leaving it to simmer in the pot, Amalia retreated toward the basin, where she tried to scrub her hands to no avail.

"Let me try," Julián said. He dipped his kerchief into the water and rubbed the rough fabric over her palms, standing so close to her that his shoulders brushed hers.

His nearness was as overwhelming as it was intoxicating. It was shocking how Amalia had known this man for less than a day and already she craved his touch. Already, his hands on hers weren't enough. She longed to lay her head on his sculpted shoulder and tilt up her face until he could capture her lips with a dozen kisses.

When she caught sight of a smear of dirt on his forearm, it was only polite for her to return his ministrations. After taking the damp kerchief from him, she smoothed it over his muscles, sweeping along his corded forearm until she reached the edge of his rolled-up sleeve. She was raising the kerchief toward his face when he caught her by the wrist.

"I know I need a proper bath, but let's not get carried away," he murmured.

Amalia lifted her chin a fraction of an inch. "I'll have you know I am on my very best behavior."

"You had better be, Your Highness. I refuse to have *my* virtue compromised."

With a crooked grin, Julián slid away, going over to the pot to poke at the liquid bubbling within with a long, dented ladle. "I think it's edible," he reported.

"You don't sound terribly sure." Amalia took a moment to spread his kerchief on the table, though in this dampness it wouldn't dry any time soon.

"There's only one way to find out," Julián said and

scooped out a ladleful, which he presented to Amalia with a flourish.

"Coward," she said, laughing. She took the ladle from him and brought it up to her lips. A rich, salty, warm broth flooded her mouth. "Oh! It's not bad." She took another sip. "It's actually very good. A trifle garlicky, maybe, but good."

"Garlicky, hmm? All the better to avoid temptation. Maybe I should drop another few cloves in there."

"Don't you dare ruin it," she told him, tugging him away from the pot. "Go fetch the bowls—I don't think I can wait a second longer."

"Me, either," he said, and Amalia knew he wasn't just talking about the *caldo*.

Each holding a bowl, they retreated to their spots— Amalia on the cot and Julián on the stool with his long legs stretched so far into the room, his boots were almost inside the fire.

"Your uncle wouldn't have gone out of town, would he?" he asked, his pewter spoon flashing in the flickering light. "Maybe he was called away on business and that's why he hasn't received the note."

Amalia felt a flicker of surprise at his return to their earlier conversation. "It's possible, I suppose."

"Does he often have business outside of San Pedro?"

The surprise turned to suspicion. There was nothing subtle about Julián's interest in her uncle and his business dealings. She hoped it wasn't out of a desire to do Tio Francisco mischief when all this was over. She and Julián had settled on what she thought was a fair payment, but what would stop him from trying to extort more out of them at a later date?

"Why do you want to know?" she asked, unable to keep her eyes from narrowing.

"Just making conversation," he said easily. "If only to distract myself from the fact that I'm not eating roast pork and *moro de guandules*."

He laughed when Amalia wrinkled her nose. "What's the matter?" he asked. "You don't like *moro*?"

"I don't like *guandules*," she said.

"Not even with coconut?"

She shook her head. "Not at all. I like beans better—stewed ones over rice, not mixed in with it. Our housekeeper makes the creamiest beans."

"I'll have to get the recipe," Julián said, quirking an eyebrow. "What about dessert? What would you have?"

"Dulce de naranja," she said promptly. When made right, the sweet made out of oranges had just enough tartness and bitterness to make the flavor really complex while still being light and fresh. More often than not, Lucía ended up choosing dessert, and she always opted for something rich and overly sweet. "I don't suppose they make *dulce de naranja* in Europe, though."

"Maybe you can learn to make it," Julián remarked. "Are you as musical as your sister?"

"Heavens, no." Amalia made a face as she scooped a piece of plantain from the broth. "I can scarcely follow a tune. And I never learned to read music."

"Then what do you intend to do with yourself while she's studying music?"

"Buy pretty frocks," Amalia answered, and they both smiled reflexively. "I think there will be plenty to occupy me, wherever we end up. But honestly, that's the least of my worries. I just want her to be happy." She felt her mouth turning down at the corners as she contemplated Lucía. "She hasn't been, lately, and my heart breaks for her. Do you have any sisters of your own?"

"No siblings at all," Julián said, his mouth compressing into a tight line. "But my father did raise one of my cousins. I suppose you could say we grew up like brothers, but we're not particularly close. He and my father are," he added, almost offhandedly, then gave her a wolfish grin that didn't quite cover the pain in his eyes. "I'm the black sheep of the family, as is only befitting for a bandit."

"Don't tell me you took up banditry just to be contrary."

He laughed. "Something like that."

He didn't seem to be inclined to add much more, and they ate the rest of their meal in companionable silence. Afterward, Amalia braved another few sips of the *aguardiente* and felt her limbs grow languorous as the alcohol traveled down her chest. Giving up what little remained of her sense of propriety, she stretched out on the cot again, hardly noticing when Julián quietly removed the plate and spoon from her hand.

A low noise startled her awake sometime later. She rose up onto her elbow, peering intently into the gloom. The sound came again, and her stomach sank when she recognized it. Birdsong.

When she sat up, she could see the sky burning with the first glow of sunrise through the opening in the shack's wall. The night had gone by, and it was almost morning, and judging from the way Julián sat slumped on his stool, no one had taken advantage of the cover of night to storm their defenseless fortress.

Amalia's gaze met his, and even in the dimness, she saw the truth written all over his face. "My uncle's not coming, is he?"

* * *

Julián awoke with a foul crick in his neck and an even fouler disposition, directed toward the men in Amalia's family—namely, her late father and her uncle, who was just as late if in a different way.

He didn't know much about Francisco Troncoso, but what little he had been able to glean about him left a bad taste in his mouth. What kind of scoundrel could be this unfeeling—or careless—toward the very people he was supposed to look after? Amalia was no more a defenseless miss than she was a pampered one, but all her tenacity wouldn't have kept her safe if Julián truly had been a bandit and bent on getting more from her than information.

Nobody had ever depended on Julián, and he'd always been inclined to see that as a good thing. He could barely look after his own interests, let alone that of anyone else. As his father and cousin relished in telling him, Julián was a dissolute, irresponsible scoundrel with little regard for other people. And that may have been true, but if there was one thing he knew about himself, it was that he could never be this callous when it came to the safety of anyone under his care.

Anger started to build inside his chest, propelling him to his feet. Though he had expected Amalia to be likewise livid, or even indignant, she only looked worried.

"Something must have happened," she said and gnawed briefly on her lower lip. Julián could have done without the sight of her sitting up in bed, unbound hair tumbling every which way as she blinked sleep out of her eyes. Now that he had been witness to it, he was sure he'd be seeing it in his dreams. "Do you think it's possible that the ransom note went astray? Or maybe Lucía took sick."

"Is she sickly?" Julián asked. "Prone to sudden ailments?"

"No, but…" She shook her head. "I should go home. I could never forgive myself if something had happened and I wasn't there for her."

Her teeth sank onto her lower lip again. Julián grasped her by the chin. "You'll injure yourself," he said roughly, and her luscious lips parted with surprise. "It's a long way to walk. I'll take you home, if you really feel you need to go."

And if it turned out that her uncle wasn't the kind of rascal that would let his charge be snatched and this was merely his plan to ambush Julián on the road, well, Julián had gotten himself out of trickier situations.

Of course, most of those had involved slighted women, not guardsmen with pistols. The way some of them wielded their parasols, though—and, in one memorable case, a very old and valuable tome of poetry—Julián would rather take his chances with the Civil Guard.

"Are you certain?" Amalia asked, pushing a lock of hair off her face. "I wouldn't want you to get into trouble after all you've done to help me."

"I'll be fine."

He always was. For the most part.

Pushing away any more thoughts of ambushes, he poured a clean stream of water into the basin and left Amalia to make her morning ablutions while he went to saddle the horse. He was down to his last clean shirt, which would in any case have required him to visit the set of rooms he'd rented on the outskirts of town. His landlady had not only a genius for laundry, she was also discretion itself and never thought to question his erratic comings and goings.

Tending to his horse and readying him for the long trek into town didn't take as long as Amalia did to pull her hair and clothes into a semblance of order. The sun had begun to chase away the bluish shadows of early morning by the time she emerged from the hut. Her tumbling mane had been coerced into submission, probably with the aid of those half a million pins she'd extracted from it the day before, and the brown skin over her cheekbones looked scrubbed and faintly pink.

"Are you ready?" she asked, and Julián realized with a start that he had been staring.

"I've been ready for hours, Your Highness. Here, let me help you up."

But before he had finished cupping his hands into a makeshift foothold, she had hauled herself onto the saddle. "What are you waiting for?" Even her teasing smile couldn't erase the worried line between her brows.

He couldn't blame her. If he'd had a sister, he wouldn't have been able to breathe for the worrying. When younger, Julián had felt keenly his lack of siblings, but maybe it was for the best. Twenty-seven years of looking after only himself had been difficult enough.

A little too aware that he was showing off for her benefit, Julián pulled himself behind her with a single athletic bound. He began reaching around her for the reins, then realized she was already holding them in her small, finely articulated hands. She brushed him away, indicating that she didn't mean to let go, which was just fine with Julián, who had always been content enough to sit back and let someone else take the reins.

A light pressure from her knees and a soft murmur of encouragement was all it took for his horse to set off down the path. Julián wrapped his arms around her waist to keep them both steady.

Without the prospect of being chased by overzealous coachmen, riding pressed up against Amalia was an altogether different proposition than it had been the day before. This time he was able to notice that her head fitted just under his chin, her body tucked into his like they had been molded as a pair. This time there was no escaping her soft curves, or the talcum-sweet scent rising from the folds of her blouse.

Her back was perfectly straight, her muscles rigid, as she strove to keep the precarious sideways perch required by her slim skirts.

An image flashed into his mind—Amalia riding astride in one of those split skirts he had seen caricatured in a magazine once, the kind it was said American women wore for riding bicycles. The notion made him wobble atop the saddle, and he found himself gripping her tighter to keep from toppling over.

She cast a quick look over her shoulder. "Is everything all right back there?"

"Perfectly fine," Julián gasped.

It wasn't long before they burst out of the path, shady with overhanging branches, and into the main road. The morning sun was golden on the tall stalks of sugarcane as they passed through fields that were already bristling with cane cutters. Not too far in the distance, a black cloud issued from one of the great smokestacks that signaled the presence of a sugar mill.

There were far more of those in the region than Julián cared to count. San Pedro was sugar country these days, though plenty of the old cattle ranches still remained. There was the town, too, large and growing every day, with its bustling port and thriving commercial district. As far as he had been able to determine in a couple of weeks of sleuthing, the Troncosos' fortune lay mostly in shipping and imports, though there was also a great deal of land and some property in town.

Had he wasted his brief time with Amalia? He should have been able to glean more information from her instead of letting himself get swept up into the melodrama of her worries and smiles and kisses.

Then again, who would have been able to help it?

The kisses in particular, or at least reliving the memory of them, would be enough to carry him through this endeavor. Julián's father had made sure he learned his lesson about entanglements—the hard way. After the heartbreak of the past year, Julián would hardly welcome another love affair, no matter how tempting it proved. No matter how inflamed he was by the very thought of Amalia's luscious, generous, eager—

"This isn't an admission of defeat. My returning home, I mean." Amalia's voice broke through his reverie, making Julián realize that he'd been stroking her side with his thumb.

Luckily, it didn't seem like she could feel it through the boning of her corset.

"I wouldn't dare think so," he reassured her.

"It's only a temporary setback. A detour, if you will. I have only to think of another plan. So you needn't be worried about your payment."

Julián didn't care a fig about the money she'd promised him. But it *was* one way to keep her tethered to him until he could find what he was looking for.

"I'm not worried. I trust you to deliver it when you're able."

She twisted around. "Are all bandits this accommodating?"

"I'm not your average bandit," he told her.

"So it seems." A thoughtful pause stretched between them. "Do you think it might have anything to do with how new you are to the profession? Or is it your upbringing that makes you so unusual?"

Julián let out a laugh. "Have you been wondering about me, Your Highness?"

"I don't know if you noticed, but I haven't exactly had much to occupy me in the past twenty-four hours."

It was too bad she couldn't see his expression. Julián made up for that by lowering his head so that his breath ghosted over the back of her exposed neck. "What a short memory you have."

She may not have been able to feel his thumb stroking her side, but he was all too aware of the shiver that traveled over her body. As a distraction technique, his whisper had been all too effective.

The only problem was, she wasn't the only one affected by it.

Julián contemplated the damp little curl plastered to the back of her neck and thought about what would happen if he dragged his lips up and down the graceful column, all the while keeping her tight against him. Would she let out one of those shuddery little breaths like when he'd kissed her the day before? Or would she be as delightfully vocal as he suspected she could be, and intersperse a string of words with moans? Would she allow her eyes to flutter closed, or would she turn to fix him with her direct gaze?

Julián straightened up. He was *not* going to discuss his upbringing with this woman, but neither was he willing to work himself into a state to avoid it. "You're not exactly a regular sort of heiress, you know. At least, I've never heard of a debutante who consorts with bandits."

"Maybe they should start. I can speak highly of my experience so far."

"I'll remember that if I ever need a reference for my services," Julián said.

In the course of the next hour, the sugarcane fields gave way to the series of ramshackle buildings that announced they would be soon arriving in town. Before long Amalia was guiding the horse onto the road that wound alongside the Higuamo River. Over the roofs of the elegant masonry houses, Julián could see the smokestack of the Porvenir sugar mill jutting into the blazing blue sky, as well as the very top of the red-and-white firehouse at the center of town.

Had it been taller than a single story, the Troncosos' *quinta* would have had a lovely view of the river. Surrounded by a wrought iron fence and *coralillo* bushes in full bloom, the elegant white house was set back from the street. Graceful steps led up to a central front door, from which two wings extended, each bearing a porch ringed with Corinthian columns and crowned with the kind of ornate plasterwork that proliferated on San Pedro's newer buildings.

Unfamiliar as he was with the Troncosos' home, Julián was nevertheless immediately assailed by the strange stillness that hung over it. There were no housemaids sweeping the porch, no coachmen—or a coach, for that matter—idling out front. The shutters covering the many doors and windows that faced the street were all tightly closed, though they'd been hospitably propped open in every other house they had passed.

"Something *is* wrong," Amalia said tightly, giving voice to his thoughts. Barely waiting for the horse to stop, she leaped down lightly and took off running around the side of the house, disappearing from his sight in mere moments.

Julián swore as he scrambled to hitch his horse. Giving the reins an experimental tug to make sure his knot was tight, he sprinted after Amalia.

Chapter Four

Unused to being out in the sun without her hat and parasol, Amalia felt the heat in her face as she dashed through the front gate and around the side of the house. Her heart was hammering wildly inside her chest as, even in her haste, she noticed all the little things that alone would have been merely unusual, but together added up to a domestic catastrophe—the dirty front steps, the closed doors and windows, the fallen leaves littering the garden. The last might have been the most alarming, as her uncle employed a small army's worth of gardeners to keep the property looking perfectly manicured at all times. Those leaves would have never been allowed to remain scattered on the lush grass if Tio Francisco were around to see it.

She flung open the second gate that led to the kitchen yard, almost skidding to a stop when she saw one of the new housemaids, Ana. The young woman, evidently not expecting to be burst upon in such a fashion, dropped the pail she'd been carrying, and Amalia had to take a hopping step back to avoid the tidal wave of dirty water splashing her way.

"Where's my sister?" Amalia demanded, shaking water from the tan leather of her shoes. "Is she ill? Has there been an accident?"

"Your—no, miss. Not to my knowledge."

Amalia barely had a moment to feel relief as the slap of footsteps on the paving stones alerted her to Julián's presence. That, and the widening of the maid's eyes as she took in the sight of Julián and Amalia's disheveled appearance.

"He said you eloped," she blurted out, her gaze flitting from Amalia to Julián. "Don Francisco did, I mean. I was dusting in the parlor when a messenger came with a note. He said you had run away with a lover and was sending word that you were never coming back."

An incredulous snort popped out of Amalia before she had a chance to stop it. "A lover, me? When would I have had the time to find one?"

Julián made a discreet noise behind her, as if to remind Amalia of her attempt to do just that the day before. She flashed him an irritable glance, then turned back to Ana. "Where is everybody? I had a terrible fright when I saw the house all closed up."

Something like surprise flickered over Ana's expression. "Why, they've all left."

"Left...?" Amalia echoed, feeling as suddenly breathless as if the pail of water had been upended over her head instead of the ground.

Her tone must have been sharper than she'd intended, because Ana took a half step backward. "When your uncle got the note, he asked the housekeeper to pack up the house and—and your sister's things. By the time she arrived from her outing, we had packed all the trunks and were bringing them outside. I... I hope you don't mind my saying so, but your sister did not look at all happy at being made to leave."

"He kidnapped her?" Julián asked bluntly.

The maid looked suddenly frightened. "I wouldn't say that, exactly..."

"Why not?"

"Because he's her guardian," Amalia snapped, "and allowed to do whatever he wants without it being considered a crime. Did he say where he meant to go?"

"Not to me, miss." Ana hesitated for a moment. "But I did hear the coachman say something about taking them to the port."

The port. Amalia's head was spinning. That could mean any number of destinations, any number of countries or continents...

What the devil had happened while she'd been gone?

There was only one reason why Tio Francisco would spirit Lucía away with such haste—he must have found her someone to marry. Someone he knew Amalia would disapprove of. He had as much as admitted it the week before, when Amalia had accused him of trying to sell her off to the highest bidder. He'd said, in that wretched patronizing tone of his, "I'm afraid you wouldn't fetch a very high price, dear." But Lucía would. Sweet, biddable, seventeen-year-old Lucía, who wanted nothing more than to practice her music and giggle with her friends.

Julián caught Amalia by the shoulder before she could stumble. Firmly, he guided her toward the wood and rush chair that stood just outside the back door. The fibers creaked in protest when Amalia sank onto the rough seat, her face in her hands.

Her brilliant plan hadn't just failed—it had *back-fired*. Tio Francisco, who was shrewd enough when it came to business, had known to use Amalia's absence to his advantage. For all her scheming and planning, that was one thing she hadn't counted on.

In trying to improve her sister's life, had she actually ruined it?

Dimly, she realized that Julián had crouched in front of her and was tugging on her wrists. She raised her head and allowed him to grasp her hands firmly in his larger ones. "Everything is going to be all right," he was saying. His searching gaze found hers, and she squeezed his hands reflexively as she saw the concern and strength in his dark eyes. "We will find your sister, and we will make sure she comes to no harm."

Amalia jerked her head into a nod.

"Does your uncle have a study?"

Another nod, this one fractionally less dazed. "There's a small room off the parlor that he uses as an office."

Ana, who had vanished without Amalia realizing it, came forth now, bearing two glasses of water. "The house is locked up," she said, looking wary.

"That won't be a problem for me," Julián said, releasing Amalia's hands as he stood up to take one of the glasses from Ana.

As the haze of panic receded, Amalia realized that the girl had probably been entrusted with the care of the house and was rightly nervous that she would be reprimanded for the intrusion. She accepted the water and touched Ana's hand gently. "Please don't worry. I'll make sure you don't get into trouble with the housekeeper or my uncle."

Ana nodded. "Much appreciated, miss."

"Thank you for all your help." Amalia drained the glass, noticing for the first time how thirsty she was after the long, hot ride into town. Passing the glass back to Ana, she stood up and looked at Julián. "Let's go inside."

Under Julián's skillful hands, locked door after locked door fell open as he and Amalia traversed through the darkened house until they came to her uncle's office. The high-ceilinged room with its tile floors and whitewashed walls was lined with glass-fronted bookcases and a series of framed maps. The aroma of his cologne was still heavy in the air, as if Tio Francisco had merely stepped away for a moment and was sure to return and catch Amalia rifling through his desk.

Not that there was much to rifle through. A quick perusal of the desktop showed Amalia that the vast expanse of its leather blotter was empty, and so was the correspondence tray. Only a folded newspaper lay discarded in a corner.

"He must have put his papers in the drawers," she told Julián, tugging on a brass handle to confirm it was also locked. "Or taken it all with him."

He stepped up beside her. "Let's find out."

Sinking into Tio Francisco's heavy leather chair, Amalia sat back while Julián worked. Even through her anxiety, Ana's words kept replaying in her mind. *He said you were never coming back.*

So her uncle really had given up on her. He'd threatened it often enough, but Amalia hadn't really thought him capable of it.

She didn't know how effective his lie about her had been—the other girls at the outing had seen her being stolen away by a bandit, after all. The other girls and Lucía, who didn't know the truth of what Amalia had been plotting.

Something sour and bitter welled up inside her. Amalia's relationship with her uncle had always been rocky—that couldn't be denied. But for all the arguments they'd had, and all the times she'd stormed away to the sound of his long-suffering sighs, she had somehow, inexplicably, believed that he truly did have their best interests at heart. That his paternal act wasn't a complete lie.

How wrong she'd been.

Dwelling on it would get her nowhere. Amalia forced her thoughts back to the matter at hand.

"I wonder…" she said musingly, not realizing she had spoken out loud until Julián's gaze flicked up from the drawer he was attempting to open. "If Lucía had even a moment to come inside the house, she might have tried to leave me some hint of where they were going."

She sprang up from the chair and began to make her way to the front room. The pair of bergère chairs by the window that had once been her mother's had been covered with white bedsheets, turning them into hulking ghosts. The sight of them assuaged some of Amalia's turmoil—Tio Francisco would have taken all the furniture and decorations if he never meant to return.

Reflecting the chairs was an oversize mirror, toward which Amalia headed.

"We used to leave secret notes to each other behind the mirror," she said, running her fingertips around the heavy gilt frame.

Out of the corner of her eye, she saw Julián leaning

against the door frame, taking in the luxurious room with his usual inscrutable expression. Heaven knew what he made of it all—the cloisonné vases that were empty now, but which usually held massive arrangements of cut flowers, the lace drapery, the oil paintings her family had collected over generations, the burled wood secretary where Amalia sat in the mornings to answer invitations to all kinds of frolics. It was a far cry from the shack where they'd spent the night.

True to Julián's unflappable nature, even in his muddy boots and shirtsleeves, he looked at home among the trappings of elegance that provided the background for Amalia's life. He picked up a silver frame from one of the side tables, his lips curling up slightly as he looked down at a portrait of Amalia. The photograph had been taken two or three years before, when she'd dressed up as Spring for one of the many dances held by her and Lucía's social club. Her unbound hair had been painstakingly decorated with tiny silk flowers, dozens of them, and in gauzy white classical robes, she looked as ethereal as a nymph. Julián seemed to think so, too, judging by his smile.

Or maybe he was inwardly laughing at all the silly things society people did to pass the time.

Amalia's covert examination of him came to a swift end when her fingertips met with the crackling of paper. Holding her breath, she teased out the scrap, hoping against hope that it wasn't some leftover note from their childhood.

"You found something?" Julián asked, coming closer. "Want me to move the mirror?"

"I don't think that'll be necessary." Amalia crowed triumphantly as she pulled out a scrap of paper. It looked like it had been torn from an envelope, and there were only two words hastily scribbled on one side—Puerto Plata.

Amalia was almost weak-kneed with relief. Not another continent, then, or even another country.

"That's your sister's handwriting?" Julián asked, glancing down at the paper.

Amalia nodded. "I have to go after them," she said, and began to pace as she worked through another plan.

Puerto Plata was on the northern coast of the island, only a few days' travel from San Pedro on the southern coast. But traveling overland had always been a chancy proposition, even with the new railroad.

One thing was immediately apparent—there was no way she could do this alone. She had never left San Pedro and she knew next to nothing about arranging a voyage, in particular one that would most certainly end in a confrontation.

"I think our best chance is to get on the next ship headed there," she said out loud. Puerto Plata was a port city, much busier than San Pedro, so it would take a while to track down Tio Francisco. "Once we're there, we— Oh." Whirling to face Julián, she gave him an apologetic look for having assumed that he would abandon all his bandit-related pursuits to run off after her sister with her. "I know I have no right to ask you for anything else, particularly as I haven't the means to compensate you for everything you've already done— yet. So I will understand if you refuse."

Before she could get any further into her request, Julián swept into a flourishing bow. "Your Highness, I would be delighted to escort you to Puerto Plata."

The smile that broke through Amalia's inner turmoil

may have been tremulous, but it was genuine. "Keep being this gallant, and you'll find yourself pressed into service as an escort the next time the governor of the province has a ball."

His expression at the prospect made Amalia burst into outright laughter. "I'd take you to the ends of the earth, but I draw the line at wearing a set of tails."

"Well, lucky for you, Puerto Plata is only on the opposite side of the island," Amalia said, hoping her matter-of-fact tone was enough to hide the frisson that had gone through her at the first part of his sentence.

She started to turn away, saying something about looking up departure schedules in the newspaper she had seen on Tío Francisco's desk. Julián halted her with a soft touch to her arm.

He was an entire head taller than she was, but he captured her face between his hands and tilted it up so that she could look into his eyes and see that his jesting tone had vanished.

Framed by his long, calloused fingers, her face felt as hot as it had out in the sun. As hot as the desire curling through her. Her lips parted, but he didn't kiss her.

"I am at your service, Amalia," he said with such blazing intensity that she found herself burning to believe him.

The logical part of her brain won out in the end. Likely, all he wanted was a bigger share of the payment she had promised him.

"Your offer is much appreciated," she said briskly, drawing back, away from his warm fingers. "And please, be assured that I will compensate you for this as soon as I can manage it."

"Yes," he said after a moment's pause. "Compensation. That's exactly what I want."

She stood, eager to put enough distance between them to quell the irrational flutters in her chest. If she had any hope of finding her sister, she couldn't let herself be distracted by this man's words, however pretty they might sound. She wouldn't be at all shocked if he was trying to flirt in the hopes of getting more money out of her.

Her mouth firmed. This was a business arrangement, not a love affair, and Amalia could not let herself forget it.

Julián strode out of the Troncosos' house as fast as if he expected someone to chase after him. *I am at your service.* The devil was wrong with him? He'd known Amalia Troncoso for all of five minutes and already he was making a fool of himself, spouting declarations of allegiance as if he were one of the medieval knights in the storybooks he'd read as a child.

Julián was the furthest thing from a storybook knight, and Amalia must have known it.

To his bemusement, she had gone to a spindly legged secretary and fished out a necklace from a tiny wooden box. "It's not extraordinarily valuable, but it should be worth enough to exchange for two cabins on the next steamer."

A simple gold chain studded with amber and ending in a delicate pendant, it, in fact, was not all that impressive as jewels went. Only the slight tremble of her lips betrayed the fact that it must have held some sentimental value.

He'd tried to refuse, forgetting for a second that he

was supposed to be a ruthless bandit. But she'd insisted. "It's all I have," she'd said, squaring her jaw. "Tio Francisco put all of the valuables we inherited from our mother into some sort of safety deposit box at the bank that we can't access. And we've already established than when it comes to actual money, I'm as penniless as an urchin."

Sighing, Julián had held out his hand. "All right, then, I'll see if I can get a good price for it."

Pulling back slightly, she frowned. "I'd really rather do it myself."

"You're a suspicious little soul, aren't you? I won't run off with your necklace, if that's what you're worried about," he'd told her, then added, smirking, "It's not really worth my while."

It was the truth, too, though she couldn't begin to know the reason why. Hopefully, she'd take it to mean that he had stolen much more valuable things.

There wasn't much time to argue and Amalia knew it, though that didn't keep her from looking annoyed as she reluctantly handed over the necklace and watched as he tucked it into the pocket of his trousers.

"I'll try to be back in less than an hour," he had said. "With passage on the next ship and whatever money's left over after I hock the necklace."

Julián would be damned if he'd do such a thing. Unlike her, he had plenty of cash—the spoils that came from being the son of a railroad tycoon. All he needed was to go fetch it.

San Pedro may have been growing into a prosperous town, but it still wasn't all that big. It didn't take too long for him to reach his rented rooms. His landlady's small house was unfashionable, but he had the whole of the second story to himself, and a private entrance via a set of wooden stairs built into the side of the house.

He thundered upstairs, and within minutes had stuffed his shaving kit and several changes of clothing into an old carpetbag. Only when his bag was packed did he unbutton his shirt, exposing his perspiring chest to the balmy breeze filtering through the shutters—and the sheaf of documents he had pilfered from her uncle's study.

He had just eased open the drawer he'd been trying to unlock when she'd rushed off to check the mirror for notes. She hadn't noticed him glancing through the papers inside. He hadn't planned on taking anything, but when he'd spotted his father's name on one of the letters, he had shoved the whole bundle inside his shirt, tightly folded and tucked securely into the waistband of his trousers.

There was no time to go through them now, but Julián meant to scour them as soon as he had a free moment. He was starting to get the distinct feeling that there was more to the situation than he'd previously thought. For her uncle to have whisked her sister away to Puerto Plata, the city of Julián's birth and where his father still lived…

Julián wasn't sure what it meant, but he knew it couldn't be good.

Wrapping the bundle of letters in one of his shirts, he buried the bundle in the bottom of his bag. And then, after extracting a stack of bank notes from his hiding place in the rafters and tossing it in with his clothes, Julián set about transforming himself into a respectable gentleman—he might not have been a real bandit, but neither was he anything resembling respectable.

The worst part of the whole thing was that he'd meant it when he'd told her he was at her service, and not just because, at the moment, her interests aligned so closely with his. She wanted to get her fortune back from her uncle, and he wanted to interfere with his father's business just as his father had interfered in his relationship.

Julián had taken one look at the pain and determination in Amalia's eyes and he'd forgotten his promise to himself to avoid new entanglements. Because as dangerous as it was to do so, she made him want to forget. That should have been alarming enough to make him abandon this entire pursuit and refuse to give another thought to anything beyond dancing with pretty women and growing a mustache.

And yet...

Julián had been a good-for-nothing all his life. He had never done anyone a scrap of good. No one had ever needed him. Until now.

Chapter Five

They were in luck. A steamer bound for New York, with a brief stop in Puerto Plata, was scheduled to leave in precisely two hours. The harried clerk had almost laughed Julián out of the ticket office when he'd asked for two cabins, and it had taken a great deal of Julián's money and charm to secure the last remaining one. No matter. He was used enough to rough living—it would be no bother to let Amalia have the cabin while he found an empty spot on deck for himself.

The Julián who returned to the Troncosos' *quinta* was a different person than the bandit who had left that morning. In an exceptionally respectable black suit, and with his hair pomaded into submission, he looked...

Well, he still looked like a rakish scoundrel, thoroughly disreputable under the black-banded Panama hat, but in this ensemble, his proximity to Amalia would cause no suspicion.

He was not only in possession of two steamer tickets; after leaving the ticket office, he had managed to acquire a gleaming black carriage that was as genteel and respectable as his suit. As the coachman rolled to a stop in front of Amalia's house, Julián hopped down and tipped his hat.

"Buenas tardes, señorita," he said, stifling a laugh as Amalia, clearly startled at being addressed by this well-dressed stranger, returned his greeting with an automatically polite one of her own.

Then she recognized his face under the shadow of his hat's brim. Her lips parted in surprise. *"Julián?"*

"In the freshly bathed flesh."

She took a step toward him as hesitantly as if he had truly been a stranger. His breath caught as her fingers fluttered up to graze his jaw, which suddenly felt far more naked than the absence of a few bristles could account for. "You shaved," she said softly.

Why was his mouth dry all of a sudden? "I did," he said in a raspy voice. Julián cleared his throat. "Couldn't let you board the steamer on the arm of an unkempt ruffian."

Her eyes were shaded by her own hat brim, and by the long sweep of her lashes. "I liked the unkempt ruffian," she said, and her lips moved into a sudden curve. "And I find I also quite like this schoolteacher ensemble. All that's missing is a pair of spectacles."

"Yes, well, you don't look half bad yourself. Nary a streak of mud to be seen."

There was nothing practical about her traveling costume. The short-sleeved suit was a delicate pale pink, trimmed with braids and frills and buttons. From the neckline of the jacket peeked out a scrap of gossamer that Julián supposed was meant to be a blouse. Simple pearl earrings frosted the tips of her ears, behind which danced enticing little curls. Even her hat looked like something that had been made in a confectionary shop, decorated as it was with pink satin and miniature flowers.

Julián's compliment was by no means inspired, but she met it with a gracious nod. "Shall we go? It's a long ride to the docks."

Evidently, she hadn't realized that the carriage waiting less than a meter away was to convey them to their destination. "Do you really think I'd make you ride a horse in that getup?" Julián asked. He signaled to the coachman to take the valises at Amalia's feet, which the other man did promptly. "May I ask why you packed as though you're going on a pleasure cruise instead of a rescue mission?"

"We have no idea what the rescue mission will entail. Better to be prepared for all eventualities," she said, shrugging.

"Looks like you're prepared for a second great flood."

"I am nothing if not thorough." The smile she flashed him belied her haughty tone.

Julián offered her his hand, and she took it with the air of someone who had never gotten into a carriage without being helped up.

It was an open carriage, with a short canopy to keep the sun from broiling the tops of their heads. Julián asked the coachman to return them to the docks, then went around to the other side and leaped inside in a single bound to find Amalia frowning suspiciously as she examined the plush upholstery.

"Julián," she said, "why are we riding on the Gonzalezes' carriage?" At his uncomprehending look, she elaborated. "I recognized it by that little stain over there. The boys are fond of port and they have a dreadful habit of bringing their wineglasses along when we go on drives after dinner. There's a matching stain on my favorite evening gown," she added, looking aggrieved.

Julián hid a smile of amusement. "Oh, I borrowed it," he said airily.

"Borrowed?" She narrowed her eyes. "Are you using that word in the traditional sense?"

He shrugged. "If by that you mean that I convinced their coachman that I was the visiting Frenchman he'd been sent to pick up. But it should be all right. We're headed directly back to the docks, after all. By the time they discover my deception, we'll have boarded the ship."

"I can't say I approve of your methods, but I am grateful at not having to walk all the way there."

"I should think so, considering the five tons you're carrying in those valises of yours." Julián sat back, listening to the clatter of the wheels as they set off at a brisk pace. The Gonzalezes' carriage was a roomy one, intended for a family, which left plenty of space between him and Amalia.

Or that would have been the case, had she not been battling with the wind as it tugged artfully arranged ringlets out from under her hat. Well armed with hairpins, she held her elbows extended like a set of wings that grazed Julián with every bump and jolt of the carriage. Until a particular hard jolt sent her careening toward him, and the word *grazed* was no longer applicable.

"I'm so sorry," she said, pulling herself upright. "The

Gonzalezes' carriage has a lot to recommend it, but I don't think I can say the same for their coachman."

Julián didn't laugh so much as wheeze, rubbing the spot on his chest where her elbow had dug in. "It's fine," he said when he had regained his breath. "Here. Let me help you."

She hesitated for a second, peering out at the street they were speeding through. This close to lunchtime, there were no passersby to be seen. "I— All right."

Unpinning her hat and holding it on her lap, she turned slightly so that her back was to Julián. He disposed of her hairpins by easing them out and dropping them on her upturned palm, then raked a hand through brown locks that were as unruly and willful as she was. The sensation of them slipping against his rough palm was almost more intimate than the kiss they had shared the day before. A deep longing to caress those silky curls until they reached their destination almost overwhelmed Julián—but he knew better than to surrender to it. Grimly pushing it down, he made himself focus on the matter at hand.

Taking care to smooth back the shorter curls in the front that had most plagued her, he wound the long mass of her hair into an efficient twist at the nape of her neck and secured it with the pins he had removed. It wasn't a work of art by any means, but at least it would keep her hair out of her eyes.

"What do you think? Can I list hairdressing among my many accomplishments?"

"Well, you certainly can't add modesty to the list," she said, laughing as she returned her hat to its rightful place.

"I've never been partial to it," Julián admitted.

"Modesty, I mean. It's always struck me as insincere. If I'm good at something, why not take pride in it?" He was veering into perilously earnest territory, which required as sharp a left turn as the coachman had just made. Lounging back against the seat, he folded his arms behind his head. "Take my extraordinary talents in the art of dressing ladies' hairs."

He snuck a peek at Amalia and came away with the distinct impression that she was seeing clear through him and wasn't at all impressed.

"Why do you do that?" she inquired.

Julián was the picture of innocence as he looked down at himself. "Do what? I can assure you, Your Highness, I spend most days striving to do nothing at all."

She gave an impatient wave of her hand. "Act like a rascal when you and I both know you're not."

"On the contrary," he said softly, feeling the smirk slide from his lips. "I'm the worst kind of rascal you could ever meet. The sooner you realize that, the better it'll be for you."

If she had any sort of response to that, it was lost as the carriage reached San Pedro's bustling port. The rattle of carts heavy with barrels and crates and the din of men hurrying back and forth as they loaded freight into one ship's cargo hold and out of another was familiar to Julián's ears.

He would have never predicted that he'd be boarding another steamship so soon after his return from Puerto Rico, where he'd spent much of the past year. This time, at least, he wasn't running off with his tail between his legs and bitterness swirling in his heart.

This time he was on his way to seek all the answers he hadn't realized he needed.

This time he was going home.

The port was crowded with great merchant ships flying French, American, German and Haitian flags, their masts rising into the clear blue sky in a way that reminded Amalia of the mills past which she and Julián had ridden that morning. Instead of burnt sugar, though, the air around her was redolent with the scent of salt. The Caribbean Sea, undulating gently behind the steamer, reflected the intense blue of the sky.

Amalia's knees felt oddly liquefied as she walked up the gangplank, her fingers so tight around Julián's forearm that she would have worried about bruising him if all her attention hadn't been on the possibility of stumbling in her heeled pumps and plummeting to the water below. She hadn't normally a fear of heights, and was tempted to attribute this sudden lack of stability to Julián's having unnerved her with his gentleness in the carriage. She could still feel his fingers sliding through her hair, brushing her scalp and the back of her neck and sending tingles all down her body.

It was almost more than she could bear. And then to turn around just to witness his little display of unfeeling insouciance…

It reminded Amalia of why she refused to trust most men, but especially the young, handsome kind. Bandit or not, he was just like all the others.

Amalia shouldn't have cared. She *didn't*.

She stepped off the gangplank and onto the steamship, and the relative steadiness of the boards under her feet firmed up her knees as well as her resolve.

Disentangling herself from Julián's arm, she marched up to the uniformed officer who was checking off passengers against the list cradled in the crook of his arm.

When she gave him her name, he responded with a courteous, "Your checks, *señora*?"

Checks? Amalia stared at him, so nonplussed that she forgot to correct him. A woman had to be married to be called *señora*—though perhaps he'd mistaken Julián for her husband.

"Here are your luggage, berth and meal checks," Julián said smoothly, pressing several rectangles into her hand. "I'm sorry. I should have given them to you earlier."

It only took a few moments for the officer to confirm their tickets against his list. Then he beckoned to one of the men who stood to one side like porters or stewards.

"I'll show you to your cabin, *señora*, *señor*," the steward said. Clyde-Mallory was an American line, but the men who crewed the steamers on the southern route seemed to speak proficient Spanish.

"Cabin?" Amalia asked, turning to Julián.

"There was only one left," Julián murmured into her ear. "It's all right. I'll find accommodations elsewhere."

Amalia frowned, but said nothing as she followed the steward down a narrow hallway. Her bedroom for the single night it would take to go around the eastern coast of the island was about the size of the dressing room she and Lucía shared at home; it was, however, far better appointed than she'd expected. Paneled walls, a double bed covered in a gleaming satin coverlet and even a polished mahogany-and-marble washstand with an oval mirror.

"Your luggage will be up shortly," the steward said and withdrew, looking pleased at the sizable tip Julián had discreetly tucked into his palm.

Julián himself lingered by the door, his hands in his pockets. "I'll leave you to get settled in. I'll be out on the deck if you need me."

"The deck? Is that where you're planning to sleep?"

Julián shrugged. "Or in the lounge. There's bound to be one on a ship this big. It won't be the first time I've slept on a chair."

"Sounds comfortable," Amalia replied with studied blandness.

There it was, that infamous smirk of his. "You're sure you don't want to offer me a corner of that big bed?"

Placing a hand on his shoulder, Amalia maneuvered him to just outside the doorway. "Not if you were the last bandit left on earth," she said sweetly and closed the door in his face.

It wasn't long before her luggage was brought up by yet another crisply uniformed man. As he stacked the valises along one wall, she dug furtively into her handbag for a tip and, to her embarrassment, was only able to come up with a handful of copper *cheles*. The low-denomination coins must have been left over from the last time she and Lucía had convinced the housekeeper to part with a fraction of the marketing money for them to buy sweets for the household—a necessary ruse when their uncle generally refused to let the sisters handle money, and kept close track of everything they charged to his account at the various stores in town. Both Lucía and the housekeeper had an insatiable sweet tooth, so the arrangement worked to both their benefit.

To Amalia, there was no benefit at all in the whole thing. She'd have much rather earned those coins herself than have to scrabble or beg her uncle for them. In fact, she had been seriously considering abandoning her plan in its entirety and seeking employment in Europe when she managed to spirit Lucía there.

But of course, she would need money to do *that*. What an infuriating world this was.

There was also the matter of Julián's payment—the reason he had agreed to take her halfway around the island. Another man would have cut his losses and made do with the sum fetched by her mother's necklace. The fact that he hadn't must mean that he expected far greater recompense from Amalia. After all the trouble he'd gone to to help her, she would be damned if she didn't deliver it.

Dropping the few paltry coins into the porter's hand with a murmured apology, she closed the door behind him.

The shortness of their time aboard meant that there was no real need to unpack, save for her nightdress and something to wear at dinner. After laying out a fresh dress for the next day and putting her little wood-and-velvet toiletries case in the adjoining lavatory, Amalia ventured out to the deck.

The wind was blowing in earnest here. Amalia patted the back of her head to assure herself that all was in order, and found that Julián had done as good a job on securing her hair as he'd done undoing every lock in his path that morning. There seemed to be nothing his quick, clever fingers couldn't do.

Before Amalia could pursue that singularly intriguing line of thought, the man in question came into view, lounging against the railing as if it were the bar of some disreputable tavern.

Even in his sober black suit, Julián stood out from the respectable crowd strolling on the deck. A wolf in sheep's clothing was still a wolf, after all. What he wore didn't matter—his true nature was written on the long, powerful lines of his body and the rakishness of his smile as he turned to look at Amalia crossing the deck to where he stood.

Her step didn't falter, but it felt as though her heart did. With the exception of her younger sister, had anyone ever watched her approach with such unbridled welcome in their smile? Another pang went through her at the sudden realization that sometime in the next few days, whenever she finally found Lucía, she and Julián would probably part ways. And when they did... who would look at her with this much joy? With such wicked humor sparkling in his eyes? Who would caress her hair like it was made out of silk or spun gold?

She'd get used to doing without it, as she had all her life. Julián had only been in it for two days, after all.

"I knew you would change your mind about letting me into your bed," he remarked when she reached him, low enough to avoid being overheard by the other passengers.

"As I recall it, you were the one who declined the honor yesterday. Did no one ever tell you that life rarely gives second chances?"

A gull soared overhead, its shadow flickering in Julián's dark eyes. "No," he said. "No one ever did."

The shadow was gone before she could tell if it had been real or not. Mildly disconcerted, Amalia tried not to show it. "Well, even gently reared young ladies get tired of extending the same invitation multiple times."

The easy grin was back, though Amalia could tell it wasn't altogether genuine. "I'll have you know no one ever gets tired of inviting me into their bed."

She was not the most practiced flirt, and her heart jumped inside her chest when she stepped closer to Julián and trailed a fingertip over the line of buttons on his waistcoat. "And what exactly would you do if you were in mine?"

"Are you really sure you want to know?" he asked, capturing her hand like it was some sort of prey and keeping it captive in his.

The murmur of the crowd receded and for a long moment, all Amalia could hear was Julián's harsh breaths, underlaid by the restless rolling of the waves and the purr of the steam engines beneath their feet.

The tip of her tongue stole out and swept over her lower lip. His gaze dropped to track its progress with such scorching intensity, it was almost as if she was being kissed by him again. Her body remembered all too well how it had felt to be in his arms. As her heartbeat quickened and her limbs flooded with a warmth that had nothing to do with the sunlight bearing down on them, it was all Amalia could do to keep herself from straining toward him.

He seemed to be having the same problem.

His fingers grew tighter around hers. Not enough to cause her pain, but enough for her to know that he was as reluctant to let go as she was.

With his free hand, he brushed the curve of her jaw, following its contour all the way to the hollow behind her ear. Suppressing a shiver, Amalia leaned into his touch. It was almost worrying, this hunger she felt around Julián, this desperate craving for his hands, his mouth. She wanted to seize fistfuls of his shirt, or his hair, and pull her to him until there wasn't a breath of space left between them.

If he was a wolf, she wanted to be devoured.

"Sleep," Julián said, his voice rough. It took a second for Amalia to remember the question he was answering. Then his eyebrow quirked up, and he released her hand to scrape back his hair, and the tension that had been mounting between them was suddenly broken. "I haven't slept in a proper bed in days."

"Fair enough." She stepped back, feeling flushed from the sun and the laughter and the provocative turn of the conversation. "I could use a little rest myself. It's been…a most interesting couple of days."

And there were many more to go. Whatever Amalia had started by orchestrating the *rapto*, it was only just beginning.

She turned to look out into the port and the city beyond it. The familiar sights of San Pedro were rendered strange from this vantage point. Strange and beautiful. The oddly elegant lines of the port, the lines of houses trailing along the edge of the river and unfurling into two- and three-story buildings farther inland, the great smokestacks jutting into the sky…

The deck lurched beneath her, making Amalia stumble gracelessly against Julián.

He caught her by the elbow, his long fingers firm on the bare skin below the cuff of her short-sleeved jacket. "Steady there. You'll get your sea legs soon enough."

"Will I? I've never been on a ship before," she admitted.

"Never?" he asked, sounding surprised. "I thought society people spent their lives flitting off to Paris to order new frocks and up to New York for, I don't know, shoelaces."

"Not us. Tío Francisco always claimed to be too busy with work."

Skepticism was written all over the arch of his eyebrow. "But surely you have plenty of friends who plan house parties at their country homes or excursions to the seaside."

Amalia shook her head. "My uncle won't hear of us accepting any invitations that take us out of town, no matter how many respectable matrons are to be in attendance. He has a horror of letting us out of his sight—or among people who might have ulterior motives for befriending us." She frowned. "Or at least, that's what he claims. To hear him speak, half the people in San Pedro are after our money. In any case, I haven't been…anywhere."

"Did you want to?"

"It would have been nice to see the world. It *will* be."

The shudder of engines beneath their feet intensified and, within minutes, the ship started to move. Amalia's fingers tightened reflexively on the white railing, even though the metal was uncomfortably warm from the sun.

Julián glanced over, but remained where he was standing. "Well, you're going somewhere now."

"I am, aren't I?"

Keeping the sun from shining would have been easier than keeping her anxiety at bay. The city of her birth was receding into the distance, far quicker than she'd expected. Amalia found herself leaning forward, as if she could make the ship move faster through sheer force of will. Before long all she could see of shore were white beaches and palm trees rising out of great tangles of vegetation.

A sidelong glance at Julián, who had fallen silent, revealed that he was leaning against the railing with his eyes closed, his straight, longish hair buffeting in the wind. For a fleeting moment Amalia wondered what it would be like to unpin her own hair and join him. The other passengers around her would find it scandalous, certainly. Julián would get a kick out of it. And Amalia herself?

To her, it would feel like freedom.

Julián's eyes opened slowly and he turned to meet her gaze, the corners of his lips already curling into a smile in response to whatever he saw on her face.

And though she was fully aware of all the reasons why she shouldn't, Amalia tilted up her head and kissed him.

Julián sank into the kiss like his body had known it was just a matter of time until it happened again.

Like it had been inevitable.

His arm settled around Amalia's waist. She had risen to her tiptoes in order to reach his mouth, and with the engines rumbling underfoot, steadying her was only the polite thing to do. Mindful of the crowd around them, he didn't crush her against his chest or plunge his fingers into her firmly coiled hair. As for bending her over the railing and having his wicked way with her...

His arm tightened around her as he considered the possibility. Amalia replied with an encouraging little moan against his lips, and Julián applied himself to the task of making her do it again. Very lightly, he nibbled on her lower lip. Her hands, which had been cradling his face, slid down to clench on his lapels.

Even in a lifetime of being scandalous and improper, Julián had never done anything this self-indulgent. It felt damn good—then again, indulging always did. That was why he did it so often. Not to besmirch his family's name, as some of them liked to claim.

Amalia was an enthusiastic kisser, and a skilled one. Julián, who had made sport of every willing widow who'd crossed his path, had no patience for fumblers. Her mouth on his was hot and sure, and it tasted like the salt-tinged breeze whipping around his head and—

"Amalia Troncoso! Is it really you?"

Julián very nearly swore out loud as a tremulous feminine voice intruded into the kiss. In fact, he wasn't altogether sure he hadn't.

The gray-haired woman standing before them wore a smile that flickered on and off like a faultily wired electric lamp as she shifted her gaze from Amalia to Julián. Amalia composed herself enough for a polite greeting, but all Julián could manage was a baring of his teeth that made the woman blink uncertainly.

"And this must be your new husband," she said. At Amalia's look of surprise, she elaborated. "I hope I'm not speaking out of turn, but your uncle mentioned something yesterday about your having...eloped."

Amalia looked close to panic in the face of the older woman's scrutiny. Julián couldn't blame her—from his own experience, he knew how unpleasant it was to find out just how easily your own relations could cast you aside. And Amalia's uncle hadn't just failed to rescue her from a presumed bandit, he'd also thrown her reputation into the garbage pail.

"Oh, Doña María, I…" Amalia licked her lips, which Julián was pleased to notice were dusky from the pressure of his own mouth. "Well…"

Briefly compressing his own lips in a silent plea for patience, Julián extended his hand. "Julián Fuentes, Doña María," he said, echoing the name Amalia had just used. "Enchanting to meet you."

A flash of motion at the corner of his eye made him glance toward Amalia. Ah, of course. He'd never told her his last name. She didn't appear to recognize it as belonging to one of her uncle's business connections, though of course there was no real reason why she should. With each moment that passed, it was becoming more and more evident to Julián that Amalia had been completely shut out of her uncle's business affairs.

It didn't necessarily mean that this whole pretense had been in vain. If not for her, he would have never gotten access to her uncle's desk and the correspondence he had stolen from it. Hopefully, the contents of those letters would be enough for him to start piecing together his father's business with Amalia's uncle. And hopefully, *that* would give Julián some insight on why his father had destroyed Julián's relationship with Concepción.

Mollified by the civility of his greeting, the older lady seemed to gather impulse. She stepped closer and laid a confiding hand on Amalia's arm. "I told my sister yesterday—you remember my dear sister Carmen, don't you? Well, I told her yesterday that I didn't see how it could be at all possible that such a well-brought-up girl like yourself could have done something so scandalous. After all your dear uncle sacrificed to raise you girls."

Julián almost snorted out loud. "An elopement? There must be some confusion, Doña María," he said with scrupulous politeness, giving her one of the boyish grins that made older women fall into puddles at his feet. He took Amalia's hand. "Amalia and I have been engaged for a year. Only I've been in Puerto Rico on business for almost as long. It wasn't until several days ago that I was able to return and I'm sure you will understand, as did Don Francisco, that I simply couldn't wait a moment longer to be wed to my beloved."

He was laying it on a little too thickly, but the gray-haired woman was lapping it all up. "I did tell my sister that I was sure there was not even a hint of impropriety to the whole thing." She turned to Amalia, who was looking decidedly less delighted with Julián's prevarications. "My dear, you must be delirious with happiness. Won't you let me see the ring?" As an aside to Julián, she added, "I have yet to meet a newlywed who isn't excited to show off her wedding ring."

Amalia's fingers clenched around Julián's. "Oh, I'm afraid I—"

Watching her flounder was too painful to his inner bandit. Julián stepped in smoothly, reaching into the inner pocket of his jacket. "I have it right here, *mi cielo.* I put it away earlier—for safekeeping, you know. One can never be too careful when traveling," he explained to Doña María, who gave a vigorous nod in agreement.

The diamond ring he extracted from his pocket would have been impressive in the dull light of a single candle. On the deck of a steamer, with the faceted stones catching the sunlight and not a scrap of a shadow to dull its brilliance, it was...

"Astonishing," gasped Doña María, inching closer for a good gawk.

Ignoring her, Julián slipped the slender gold band onto Amalia's finger. She was very quiet as he did it, and when he lifted her hand for an impulsive kiss that wasn't entirely for the older woman's benefit, her eyes gleamed out at him from under the brim of her hat. She didn't look gleeful or even relieved. She looked troubled.

Julián lowered her hand, though he kept their fingers lightly linked.

The speculative gleam that had come into Doña María's eye at the appearance of the ring didn't fade as she lingered over their conversation, obviously trying to find out more about Julián and his business in Puerto Rico. As he really *had* spent most of the past year in Ponce, he found it no trouble to answer her many questions. Her many, *many* questions.

It was no use resisting the older woman's inquisitiveness. And in any case, from the dark looks emanating out from under Amalia's hat brim, Julián was fairly certain that they would not be returning to their earlier occupation.

Something about the ring had clearly troubled her, and Julián had no idea why. It was only a bauble—albeit an enormously expensive one. No matter. She'd talk when she was ready. In the short time Julián had known her, Amalia hadn't struck him as someone who would hold back on anything that was bothering her.

Sure enough, the moment Doña María was beckoned by her traveling companions and she was forced to abandon her line of inquiry, Amalia turned to Julián. "You got me a ring?"

Never had Julián's shoulder risen into a more casual shrug. "I had it lying around and I figured it might come in handy."

"I should give it back to you," she said, twisting it off her slender finger. "I would have liked to think that I'd prepared for all eventualities, but this was not something I imagined happening."

He held his hand up. "You can keep that for now," he said offhandedly. "In case we run into her again."

"I don't... I shouldn't feel comfortable wearing the spoils of banditry." She gave a little shake of her head, then said, "I know it's silly for me to object to it now, after I've spent all day benefiting from your, ah, skills, but I can't in good conscience wear what is most likely stolen property. Whichever poor woman you took this from—"

Julián's lips twisted into a smile. "The ring was my mother's, Your Highness. But you could say that procuring it was my first attempt at banditry, so you're not entirely wrong. And the least we say about how she came by it, the better."

That made it sound like his mother was an outlaw who rode around robbing people on moonlit roads. At least it made for a better story than the truth—the ring had been a wedding present from his father, who was so bloodthirsty in business that he put real bandits to shame.

Julián watched Amalia's eyes widen.

"You haven't said much about your family," she ventured.

"And I don't mean to. My father and cousin are both

scoundrels—and so am I. My mother deserved better. She was…happiness itself. The kind of person who could find fun in the dreariest of days." And the only person who could coax laughs out of his father. Julián couldn't remember the last time he'd heard his father express any kind of joy. "She loved taking me on all kinds of outings, always somewhere different. Except on Friday afternoons, when we always went to her favorite hotel for lunch. We would sit in the courtyard and compete over who could come up with the silliest jokes or the worst riddles."

The entire household had lost its color when she died. Julián's father, never the warmest of men, grew more absorbed in his work than ever, leaving Julián to deal with his cousin on his own.

"Has she been gone long?" Amalia asked, looking sympathetic.

"She died when I was six. Railroad accident," he added curtly. Before she had any brilliant ideas about trying to comfort him, he turned from her and folded his arms over the railing. "It was a long time ago. I don't remember much."

A few minutes passed before Amalia spoke up again. "I lost my mother to a fever. I was older, though— twelve."

Old enough to have gotten to know her. Julián didn't know which was worse. The few memories he had of his own mother were bad enough—how much worse would it be if he could remember her better?

"I'm sorry," he said, softening his tone.

Julián had spent enough time batting away inconvenient swells of feeling that he was fairly accomplished at it by now. He'd built an entire fortress to keep them out. But as hard as he tried to shore up his walls, something about Amalia knocked down all his defenses.

He wasn't used to feeling so off balance, at least not where women were concerned. Amalia was not the only one to probe into corners of his life that he'd rather not even think about, but whereas he'd been able to satisfy the others with shallow explanations or distractions, he had a feeling that this tenacious heiress would not be put off so easily.

Julián kept his gaze on the waves cresting in the distance. He didn't have to look to know that Amalia was giving him one of her piercing looks.

"Will you kindly stop scrutinizing me and just ask whatever it is you want to ask?"

If she was surprised by his bluntness, she didn't show it. As if she'd only been waiting for an invitation, she promptly said, "If you've never broken the law, and you don't go around stealing exquisite jewelry from women, what is it that you actually do?"

Julián turned to look at her; at her dark eyes, ringed by impossibly long lashes; at the well-formed lips that fit so well against his own. He was as drawn to her as she so clearly was to him, but he'd be damned if he'd let her break through what remained of his walls.

With a gesture that bordered on impudent, he chucked her under the chin and wasn't surprised when she pulled away, her back rigid. "That, Your Highness," he said with a smirk, "is none of your business."

Chapter Six

Amalia returned to her cabin to freshen up before dinner. The second the door closed behind her, she divested herself of her jacket, hat and shoes, and cast a longing glance at the neatly made bed. Surely, she had plenty of time to lie down for a few minutes. Unused to being on horseback for so long, her thighs ached from the long ride into town that morning. All the muscles in her upper back, too, seemed to have clenched tightly in response to the day's stress.

The water in the lavatory's basin was as refreshing on her face as the thin layer of cold cream she applied to her nose and cheeks. After undoing the buttons of her blouse, she loosened her corset and shuffled barefoot back into the bedroom.

She let out a sigh of pure, contented bliss as she lay on top of the quilted satin bedcovers and stretched out her bare feet. The mattress was almost as good as the one she had back home, and the down pillows were fluffier than the pink-tinged clouds outside her cabin's tiny window. Curling up onto her side with one of the delightful pillows tucked into the crook of her neck, Amalia fell into a deep sleep.

When her eyelashes finally fluttered open, the blazing sky had turned black and her pillow was awash in moonlight. Groggily, she propped herself up on her elbow. A glance at the clock on the paneled wall told her that she'd slept clear through dinner. It was so close to midnight that she might as well finish undressing and try to fall back to sleep—heaven knew she needed the rest. But she was so hollow with hunger, she was sure it would keep her awake for hours.

Amalia put herself back together, making sure to add a dab of violet-scented toilette water behind her ears before venturing out of her cabin in search of a steward or someone who might be able to find her something to eat.

It was galling. Amalia never left anything to chance and she hated to rely on anyone else. If she'd been thinking clearly, she would have asked Ana to pack her some *cazabe* before leaving. That it hadn't occurred to her made Amalia wonder what else she had missed in her haste.

Brass sconces placed at intervals down the quiet, empty hallway shone their weak light on the carpet as Amalia made her way to the grand staircase. At its foot were the social areas—namely, the lounge and dining room—that she and Julián had explored earlier that afternoon, after their kiss had been interrupted by Doña María and he'd rebuffed her attempt to satisfy her growing curiosity about him.

It served her right—however intriguing she found Julián, she knew better than to probe into his private life. Just because she'd invited him into her business didn't mean she had to go poking into his. And in any case, as she had to keep reminding herself, it wasn't like she would ever see him again when this was all over.

A good thing, too, because merely being around him made her act as flighty as a leaf dancing in the wind.

Amalia didn't know what had come over her earlier. It was one thing to kiss a man, even a bandit, in a secluded shack where there was no chance of being spotted. Doing so on the deck of a ship, in full view of all the other passengers *and* one of the biggest gossips in San Pedro? Even with all those people around them, she had been a hair's breadth away from losing her head entirely.

It wasn't just bold; it was reckless. And that was something Amalia couldn't afford to be, not with so much on the line.

Still, she was finding it hard to muster up sufficient repentance for her impulsive gesture. The searing memory of his lips on hers was cause alone, never mind the way he'd held her, steadying her as if he knew that feeling his mouth on hers made her limbs quiver as if they'd been turned to flan.

Even now, as she traipsed through the steamer's darkened interior, she was aware of a slight tremble in her knees.

The dining room's double wooden doors were locked, but there was a lamp burning in the lounge opposite, so Amalia changed courses. Through the panes of glass set into its doors, she could see the richly appointed room, paneled like her cabin, and filled with sumptuously upholstered armchairs and gleaming lamps with fringed silk shades.

Julián lay in an elegant sprawl in one of the armchairs, his head pillowed on his folded jacket, unaware of the steward striding toward him.

"Excuse me, *señor*," the steward said, shaking Julián's shoulder. "I'm afraid you can't sleep here."

Julián's head jerked up, and he was halfway off his seat before Amalia could draw in a breath. From where she stood, it looked like it took him a moment to recognize the other man as a steward. When he did, a blink was all it took for him to shed his bellicose expression for an apologetic smile.

"I'm sorry," he told the steward, running a hand through his messy hair. "I'm afraid my wife and I had a little disagreement and she was adamant about my not returning to the cabin. You must be used to such things, I imagine. Is there a place for exiled husbands to pass the night?"

"There isn't one. You'll have to return to your own cabin," the steward said firmly.

"It's all right, darling," Amalia said, striding into the light. "I have come to forgive you."

Relief flickered over both the men's faces, but not for long. Facing the steward, Amalia said, "I hate to bother you, *caballero*, but I was wondering if there was a way for me to get a bite to eat."

"Not until breakfast, *señora*. The galley is closed this time of night."

She'd been afraid of just that. Amalia's hollow stomach sank. "And there's no way..."

The steward started shaking his head before she had even finished talking. "They lock the doors when the dinner service is over. I could bring you a pitcher of water, if you like, but..."

Amalia glanced at Julián, who was busily folding his jacket over his arm. She had no doubt that he could have charmed or wheedled the gray-haired steward into finding her something to eat, but Julián didn't offer so much as a pleading look. It was the suspiciously bright glint in his eyes that made her tell the steward, "That's all right. Thank you, anyway."

He replied with a polite murmur, stepping away but not leaving the lounge. Evidently, he wasn't about to risk having anyone else fall asleep there. Under the steward's watchful gaze, Amalia took the arm Julián held out to her and followed him to the staircase.

They were almost out of sight of the lounge's glass-and-wood doors when Julián jerked his head to one side. "Come this way. I know a shortcut."

It turned out to be a plain service door leading to an even plainer set of metal stairs. Their footsteps echoed in the enclosed space.

Amalia peered down, feeling a rush of excitement. "We're going to sneak into the kitchen, aren't we? The galley, I mean."

"What makes you think that?" he asked, raising his eyebrows in mock outrage at her suggestion.

"Because you're an expert at unlocking things and I'm *famished*. Did you go in to dinner?"

He nodded. "I knocked at your door twice, but you didn't answer. I should have saved you a roll or something. This way."

They turned into a nondescript hallway, narrower than the ones above and much plainer, save for the visible rivets and pipes running along the closed doors. One more turn and they reached a set of double doors with round windows like portholes set into each side.

"This is it, I think," Julián said in a low voice, reaching into his jacket as he bent over the lock. "I did a little exploring of my own after we parted."

In the dim lamplight, his wink was a mere flicker. It was enough, however, to make Amalia's chest fizz and pop with champagne bubbles. To quell it, she tapped her foot soundlessly against the floor in imitation of one of the lively tunes her sister enjoyed composing.

He glanced at her over his shoulder. "Are you having second thoughts?"

Amalia shook her head. "Wondering how you learned to pick locks."

"As with all my skills, it's the product of a misspent youth," he answered, flashing her a smile.

"You spent your youth breaking into locked rooms?"

"Breaking out of them, actually. For a handful of years, my cousin Victor found it great fun to lock me in my father's office, which we were prohibited from entering. My father would find me hours later and roar at the intrusion." He shrugged. "Eventually, I learned how to let myself out. Victor tried to lock me out of the house on more than one occasion, but I could climb trees before I learned to read, so that was never a problem." He paused. "Except for the time a branch snapped and I broke my arm."

Julián had said so little about himself that Amalia was tempted to hold her breath, lest the sound remind him that she was still there. Still, she couldn't help but ask, "How old were you?"

"Seven or eight or so." He must have read the horror in Amalia's expression, because he shrugged. "Little boys are beastly like that. Ahh, here we go."

After another second of careful maneuvering, the

mechanisms holding the door shut sprang free. As it swung open, Amalia reflected that she'd have undoubtedly done the same if she'd been the one receiving such attention from his skillful hands.

The thought flooded her with heat as she crossed the threshold. It was soon replaced by a more prosaic sort of hunger as she took in the gleaming moonlit surfaces. If she had expected the remains of the dinner banquet, she was sorely mistaken. There wasn't so much as a grain of salt to be seen.

The ghost of every onion and bulb of garlic that had ever been chopped in the cramped galley hung in the air in a thick, savory miasma that made her stomach rumble in earnest.

Julián didn't seem fazed by the cupboards, which had been fastened shut with metal latches. Amalia peered over his shoulder as he swung open one door and studied the neat metal canisters lining the shelves.

"There's nothing to eat," she said in dismay.

"There will be," he said with a confidence Amalia found unwarranted, given his struggles with the plantain soup the night before. "Take a seat, Your Highness, and leave the cooking to me."

"A seat?" Amalia echoed, looking doubtfully at the stoves and cupboards.

Strong fingers grasped her waist and she found herself being swung atop the pristine work surface.

"How's that for a throne?" Julián flashed her a wicked grin before turning around to continue rooting through the canisters. "How does a Spanish *tortilla* sound? I think I can manage that."

She raised an eyebrow. "Can you?"

Julián's arms were laden when he stepped away

from the cupboard, kicking the door shut behind him. He'd found a covered plate crammed with rolls, several eggs, a green pepper and a potato. Amalia seized a roll and began nibbling at it.

He reached behind her for a bowl and began cracking the eggs with surprising proficiency. "As it happens, I was taught by a beautiful girl from Sevilla I used to…be acquainted with. Here," he added, handing her the bowl and a fork. "Beat the eggs while I chop the potatoes."

Amalia set the roll aside and dipped the tines into one of the yolks, swirling it around. "I suppose you're acquainted with a great many beautiful girls from Sevilla," she remarked.

"Quite a few."

"Oh? Are they aware of each other's existence?"

He made quick work of the pepper, chopping it into thin strips. "All my paramours know what they're getting into. I have dalliances, Amalia. A great many of them. It's fun for both parties, and when it stops being fun…" He shrugged. "We both move on. I've never cared to form attachments."

"I didn't realize it was possible," she said. "To be intimate with someone without growing attached, I mean. Somehow, I'd imagined…"

He grunted. "Yes, well, plenty of people can manage it. Some even prefer it."

Amalia thought she might. To let herself succumb to temptation without the fear that her heart would betray her and she would find herself trapped. It sounded like the sort of pragmatic arrangement that would suit her just fine.

The dull thud of the knife striking against the wooden

cutting board ceased for a moment as he cast a sideways glance at her and frowned at her lackluster egg beating. "You'll have to put more energy than that into it, Your Highness. Like this."

Instead of taking the bowl, his fingers closed around hers, warm and strong and sure as he guided her hand into a brisk pace. His touch was as intoxicating as a second glass of Veuve Clicquot. Or a third or a fourth.

Heat bloomed in Amalia's cheeks. She could feel it rising from where their hands touched, all along her arm, curling over her shoulder and neck like the ghost of a touch. She had left off her hat and jacket, and the delicate silk organza of her blouse felt like too flimsy a barrier.

Then again, she would have felt the same if she'd worn a suit of armor. She didn't know what it was about Julián that made all her barriers feel as thin as her blouse.

His mother's ring—if that was what it truly was—still glinted on her finger. The large diamond at its center, and the two smaller ones flanking it, flashed in the low light as their tangled hands moved faster and faster, until his fingers tightened suddenly around hers.

"Devil take me, but I should really like to kiss you again," Julián said roughly.

With trembling fingers, Amalia set the beaten eggs aside. Her heart started to pound. "Why don't you?"

His lips found the hollow behind her ear. It was yearning, she realized. The curling warmth that flared to life whenever Julián was near. Sometime in the past two days her body had begun longing for his touch, and the few embraces they had shared were not enough to satisfy that craving. She wanted more.

She needed more.

Amalia found Julián's lips, thinking that he kissed like he moved—with deliberation, with confidence that bordered on arrogance and with a great deal of grace. He was holding her lightly by the waist, as he had earlier, only now his hands were proving more adventurous as they roamed to the small of her back and explored the hard edges of her corset.

The questing touch thrilled her. She could have no more asked him to stop touching her than she could have asked the waves to stop their ceaseless rolling or her heart to stop beating.

Dimly, she realized that her own fingers were gripping the edge of the work surface. She loosened her grip and wound her arms around his neck instead. This time she was the one who was pulling him close, desperate to feel the hard, lean lines of his body against her.

Looking at Amalia felt like falling.

Julián had tumbled from his perch on a high branch once. For a bare handful of seconds, falling had been as exhilarating as he'd imagined flying would be.

Then he'd struck the ground. As the sickening pain spread from the arm he'd broken and through the rest of his body, he'd dazedly promised himself that he would climb every tree in the grounds until he was good enough at it that he would never fall again. And he had. He'd become so damn good at climbing he'd spent half his boyhood escaping his cousin Victor's torments by shimmying up the slim trunks of palm trees.

Maybe swearing off women had been a wrong idea.

Maybe what he needed was to treat them like palm trees—make a game of how many he could climb.

Indulge in their bodies without letting his treacherous heart get involved in the matter.

He had a feeling that Amalia, with all her talk of never wanting any part in the farce that was love and marriage, would agree. If nothing else, she seemed to like the indulgent part just fine.

Three kisses—four now, maybe five, who the devil could keep count?—and they had already found a rhythm to it, ravenous and urgent and no less thorough for all that.

He could feel the lushness of her curves even through her corset's stiff boning. Julián's hands roamed over her hips, her rib cage, right up to the spot where her corset gave way to yielding skin. The scrap of a blouse she wore was thin enough that he could feel her warmth as well as the slight shudder in her breath when he pressed a kiss to the hollow of her throat, just above the prim little ruffle that ringed her collar.

If their earlier encounters had been driven by reckless impulse, this time Julián was scrupulously deliberate. A proper seduction—and one he could control.

He pulled away, just enough to look into her eyes. Even in the galley's dim light, their brown depths seemed to dance with laughter and glints of gold. The curves of her lips, as generous as those beneath his hands, stilled as he caught her gaze and held it, letting his own fill with the desire coursing inside him.

"I want to unwrap that blouse like the bow on a present," he murmured, dragging the tip of his finger over the delicate fabric covering her collarbone. "Open it wide and sink into you like you're something rare and expensive that's been saved just for me." He outlined the swell of her breasts with the back of his hand. "I want, Your Highness, to make you feel like the gift that you are."

The shudder in her breath wasn't slight anymore. Julián let his lips curl into a smile as he took in the effect his words had on her. Yes, Amalia was enjoying the indulgent part just fine.

"Do you want me to keep going?" he asked, returning his hand to her waist.

"You had better," she commanded raggedly and licked her lips.

"In deed, or in words?"

In response, she fisted her hand in his shirt and dragged him down. Her mouth opened beneath his. When his tongue delved into its warmth, she kissed him back just as deeply. And when he reached for the tiny, cloth-covered buttons marching down the back of her blouse, she helped him undo them. The blouse fluttered to the floor, as ethereal as a cloud, and Julián was finally free to revel in her breasts. They pressed against the thin cotton of her chemise as if straining toward him. What could he do but ease the slender straps off her shoulder and bare her skin to the balmy air—and to his merciless mouth?

Quite a few hours had passed since he'd shaved that morning, and he made sure to scrape his bristles over her tender skin. With something that sounded like a breathless curse, she parted her legs as far as her skirts allowed her and pulled him even closer.

Yes, this was more like it. No tender murmurs, no declarations of love, no telling her that he was at her service. Just seduction, and an eager and willing response.

She leaned back, all the better to expose her chest and the long column of her throat. Julián devoured her, his mouth ranging over her silky skin, tasting salt and brine and the underlying sweetness of her and feeling her body shudder with each ragged exhalation.

Julián didn't intend to let her catch her breath.

"Pull up your skirt," he said, tracing light circles on her tight nipple with his thumb.

He should have known that she wouldn't care to give in to commands, no matter who issued them and why.

"Pull it up yourself," she managed to retort through something that sounded like a cross between a gasp and a moan.

"Are you always this contrary?"

"I try," she started to say, but her words were swallowed by another gasp as his fingers closed gently around her other nipple.

"You are a maddening woman, you know that?" He nipped softly at her smooth shoulder. "Maddening and beautiful and fearless. I've wanted to do this from the moment I saw you."

She opened her mouth, likely to make another smart remark. As much as he wanted to hear it, he wanted her mouth more. He covered it with his, skimming his hand up the silk stockings covering her shapely calf and feeling her skirt rise in its wake. And then, unable to resist, he pulled back enough to watch as the velvet ribbons at the top of her stockings were revealed.

Placing a kiss on the slice of bare skin between the ribbons and her drawers, he grasped a length of pink velvet and pulled. It did feel like unwrapping a present, the anticipation of it building in his chest as he uncovered her inch by inch.

Call him impatient, but he had never been one to bask in anticipation. Julián, if nothing else, had always been a man of action.

He started by kissing the crook of one knee, then the other. Her thighs were warm and firm and obligingly pliant as he stroked his way higher and higher. His questing fingers found the edge of her drawers and he lifted an eyebrow in inquiry.

Her eyes widened at the intimate touch. "What…are you proposing to do?" she asked breathlessly.

Julián straightened up. "I should like to touch you. Kiss you, too. Would you like that?"

Whatever scrap of doubt there had been in her eyes vanished at his question and was replaced by that defiant look he was beginning to recognize as one that appeared whenever she was contemplating doing something society would consider improper. "I won't know until you try it, will I?"

She nudged him with her knee, looking regal enough to suit his name for her. He didn't need more urging. Hiding a smile, he found her wet heat again. He knew just how to touch her to make her squirm—his fingertips light but sure, stroking up and down the seam of her drawers.

Amalia's breath hitched, and her hand shot out to grasp Julián by the forearm.

He stilled immediately. "I can stop if you want me to."

"Don't you dare," she all but growled. "You mentioned something about kissing?"

He had indeed. "Lift your hips so that I can pull down your underthings."

Bracing his palms on the work surface on either side

of her, Julián applied himself to his task. Her fingers twined in his hair, and the pleasant tugging in his scalp reminded him why he'd never liked cutting it shorter.

He couldn't see her face, but he didn't have to. He could feel her pleasure in the quivering of her thighs, the unsteady breaths gusting from her mouth, the tightening of her fingers on his hair. He could feel it when she began to move against him, cautiously at first, then with more and more abandon, until her legs were clenching around him.

It wasn't anything he hadn't done with at least a dozen other women. There was no reason for why it should feel so different this time, only it did. And whether that was due to Amalia herself, or to this past year wreaking some sort of change in his character, he wasn't altogether sure.

All he knew was that he didn't like it.

Feeling dazed, Julián gripped her thighs until the shuddering stopped.

"That…" she started, and then stopped to let out a low moan as her body shook with another tremor. Her knees were parted, her breasts bare above her corset, and he was filled with the sudden urge to take her back into the circle of his arms and brush her trembling lips with his own and—

Devil take him, he had to get a hold on himself.

Julián straightened up, flicking her a practiced grin. "I take that to mean you liked it?"

She made a noise in her throat that sounded distinctly enthusiastic. It took her a moment to regain her breath long enough to ask, "What about you?"

"I liked it, too, Your Highness."

"No, I meant—do you want me to return the favor?"

She was looking at him with those frank brown eyes, with none of the blushing or stammering he'd have expected from a pampered heiress.

"I'm fine," he lied, turning away. His own arousal was straining painfully against his trousers, and though he would have liked nothing better than to plunge inside her, he was no longer as confident in his ability to keep a safe distance.

He left her to put herself to rights and went back to the cupboard for the bottle of cooking sherry he'd noticed earlier. He pulled out the cork and took a steadying swig—and then another, until he'd drained nearly half the contents. Only then was he able to smooth out his expression and turn around.

Looking markedly more rumpled than when they'd wandered into the galley, Amalia was nonetheless fully covered and biting down on a roll. Julián ignored the pang of disappointment and went straight to the eggs they had abandoned.

"Have some sherry," he said, reaching for the sliced green pepper that had gotten knocked halfway down the work surface. "It'll dull the hunger until the food is ready."

She put a hand over his with enough pressure that he glanced at her with surprise. "Everything all right?" he asked.

"Is it? You look remarkably unenthused for someone who claimed to enjoy what we just did. If you're having second thoughts…"

Her gaze was sharp on his. Of all the heiresses he could have gotten embroiled with, he had to go and choose the only one who could lay him bare with a single look.

She would see through any of his practiced smiles, too, so he opted for something that was close enough to the truth. "I'm not. I just didn't expect to enjoy myself quite so much." He let go of the pepper and went to press himself against her legs to convince himself as much as her that he hadn't been as affected by their encounter as his racing heart wanted him to believe.

Her arms slipped around his neck. "So you're not wishing I was a beautiful woman from Sevilla?"

"There was only ever one of those, and she's long gone from my life." Julián let out a careful breath and was surprised to feel that the pain he'd carried for the past year had faded from a knife wound to a thorn in his side. "I wouldn't trade you for the Queen of Spain, Your Highness." It was the kind of line he might have employed on any number of casual acquaintances, but it had a ring of truth when he said it to Amalia.

Maybe the shock of it was wearing off, but he didn't feel as overwhelmed as he had a handful of minutes ago. "I know we've known each other for a very short time. But when all this is done—"

She pressed her lips against his. "Don't make me any promises. Just…kiss me again."

He was only too happy to oblige. Somewhere in the back of his head, he was aware that he'd promised her dinner; that they were at risk of being discovered; that he had a bundle of letters hidden in the small of his back that he had taken from her uncle's house.

He had retrieved it from his carpetbag earlier, and had read through most of them in the lounge while Amalia napped. From experience he knew that his father couched important details regarding his business in what to an outside observer would look like personal correspondence. Julián knew how to read between the lines, though, and he thought he had a good idea of what his father and her uncle were trying to do.

He would tell Amalia the truth of who he was soon enough. When there weren't so many sharp things close at hand.

Julián teased her lower lip with the tip of his tongue, unsurprised but definitely pleased by the unrestrained fervor with which she responded.

A brief noise made him pull away abruptly.

Amalia's small sound of protest was overlaid by the sound of the fork clattering to the floor.

"Wait…" Julián murmured, putting out a hand to stop her as she hopped down from her perch to retrieve it. "Do you hear something?"

Amalia stiffened. "I don't—" she began, but was interrupted by a heavy tread outside the galley doors.

A moment later an authoritative voice pierced the silence. "Is there anyone there?"

Putting a finger to his lips, Julián seized the sherry and the rolls and beckoned for her to follow him to a second door set at the opposite end of the galley. As it closed behind them, he glanced back and saw the steward from the lounge peering into the darkened galley and frowning when he saw the scattered remains of their would-be dinner on the work surface. Then his gaze shifted, and he caught sight of them creeping out. "You, there! What are you doing here?"

Amalia's hand closed around Julián's arm. "Run!"

Chapter Seven

Julián hadn't been well behaved a single day in his life, but getting into trouble had never been this much fun.

He pelted after Amalia as she raced up a different service staircase than the one they'd descended earlier. She was running as fast as if there was an entire legion chasing after them rather than an elderly steward who, Julián suspected, had given up pursuit halfway up the stairs.

"Did you see his face?" she panted, flashing him a grin as she slowed down. "Oh, I haven't run this fast in years. Haven't run at all, as a matter of fact. Being a proper young lady can be so boring."

"I wouldn't know," Julián replied breathlessly. "I haven't been proper a day in my life."

"I can't say I object to that," she said, turning a corner and pausing to smile up at him. He was suddenly breathless again, for an entirely different reason. "I've never had much use for propriety myself."

They were almost at her cabin, and she was clearly as loath as he was to part for the night. A more prudent man would have insisted she go to sleep, mindful that the following day was bound to be a strenuous one as they arrived in Puerto Plata and started the search for her sister. Julián was even less prudent than he was proper, and he was prepared to linger in this corridor until daybreak if it meant getting his fill of her hungry mouth and luscious curves.

Julián took a swig from the bottle of sherry he'd swiped from the kitchen. "Ever been improper in the corridor of a steamship?" He dipped his head lower to speak into her ear and found himself unable to resist brushing the delicate curve with his lips.

"Someone might see," she murmured, but she didn't pull away.

"Or they might not. It's dark and everyone's asleep."

"Except for the steward."

"Mmm..." He found the hollow behind her ear. "He's had enough shocks for one night, hasn't he?"

He slid his free arm around her and she let out a soft noise as she nestled deeper into his embrace, tilting her head up so that he could kiss his way down her neck. He was so busy savoring the taste of her skin that he almost didn't notice when she stiffened.

He glanced up sharply to see what had alarmed her and immediately tensed as he spotted a man in a brown suit leaning against the wall, several paces from her door.

The man had been making a pretense of leisurely perusing the newspaper he was now folding, but his hard, darting eyes gave him away. That, and the fact that it was well after midnight and the steamer held far more comfortable places for an insomniac to pass the time.

"Evening, *señor*," the man said, and it sounded mild enough.

Too bad his tone didn't match the coiled menace in his limbs.

Julián had spent too much time in taverns and gaming halls to not recognize the other man for the ruffian that he was. The only question was—what the devil did he want with them? Robbery? Wouldn't surprise him, not after the way Julián had foolishly flashed his mother's ring for all to see.

Or did the ruffian have something more sinister in mind? Heaven only knew Julián was embroiled in enough intrigue to make the latter a more likely proposition.

He strove to keep the wariness out of his voice as he returned the man's greeting. *"Saludos."*

Julián was still holding the bottle of sherry by its neck. He forced himself to relax his grip, though every instinct screamed at him to wrap his fingers around the bottle as if it were a club, in case he had to wield it as one. From experience he knew all too well that wielding a bottle as a club should be left for a last resort—there wasn't much a person could do with broken glass save for seriously injuring someone else, and the last thing he wanted was to put Amalia in the middle of a nasty brawl.

He'd much rather put her inside her cabin, where she'd be moderately safe, or at least behind a locked door, but they'd have to go past the ruffian. Julián might have tried it, had the man not unpeeled himself off the wall and sauntered their way, too casually to be anything but suspicious.

Julián considered reaching behind him for Amalia's hand. That would tie up his free hand, though, and under the circumstances it would be better for her to remain out of bottle-swinging range. Maybe he could maneuver her around—

He didn't sense the other man at his back until pain was blazing between his shoulder blades. He staggered, reeling, and another blow caught the back of his head, hard enough that he saw stars. Julián whirled, or tried to, but the first ruffian had reached him and was pummeling him with large, grimy fists.

Julián swung back and missed. It was laughable how he'd thought that a lifetime of brawling in taverns—and quite a few elegant hotels—had prepared him for the rigors of banditry. This man was a true professional, landing one vicious punch after another, each calculated to inflict the most damage. Julián's second attempt to punch back was deflected with a flick of the other man's arm, like someone swatting an annoying mosquito.

Between blows, Julián caught a glimpse of Amalia trapped in the grip of the man who'd struck his back. Her face was ashen, her brows twisted with pain.

"Let her go," Julián croaked, throwing up an arm to deflect one of the fists barreling unerringly toward his jaw. The sherry bottle, he noticed dimly, had fallen to the carpet and rolled just beyond his reach. "Whatever you might want with me, just—"

Don't hurt her, he wanted to say. But it was too late—they already had, and it was his fault.

He should have known this would happen. Nobody

got to be around him without getting hurt—in every sense of the word.

"Take her in there," the ruffian said to the man who was holding Amalia, nodding at the door to her cabin. "No use waking up half the ship."

Amalia didn't hesitate to show her displeasure with that decision. As Julián fended off another blow, she let out a furious cry and did her best to yank herself out of the scoundrel's grip. He only laughed and gripped her tighter, in a horrible mockery of the embrace she and Julián had just shared.

Julián's blood boiled. Bellowing out his rage, he rushed at the scoundrel—and stopped abruptly at the sound of breaking glass. A glance behind him confirmed that the man who'd been striking him had gotten hold of the sherry bottle and he apparently had no compunction over using it on Julián.

"No heroics," he said. "Or Miss Troncoso gets a nice new carving on the side of her face."

At the sound of Amalia's name, realization crashed upon Julián. They hadn't come for him at all—it was her they were after.

Fury at his own helplessness rushed over his limbs, but he forced himself to remain still as the ruffian shoved him against the corridor's striped wallpaper. "What do you want with her?"

"Nothing that concerns you." The man turned to his associate, jerking his head. "Into the cabin, quickly."

He had a key out, which Julián realized opened the cabin next to Amalia's. How the devil had they arranged it? How had they *known*?

The man who'd grabbed Amalia started to drag

her inside. Julián tensed, willing for their attention to waver for even a second. There wasn't time to formulate any sort of plan—the most he could hope for was a moment's distraction during which he could launch himself at them and give Amalia a window in which she could run and hide or fetch the steward...

Amalia must have seen his determination, because she stopped struggling. "They won't hurt me," she said calmly from the doorway of the cabin. He met her gaze, frowning, and almost missed the slight widening of her eyes. "Not if they've been sent by my uncle. They might hurt you, though, so please—"

The rest of her words were drowned out as the henchman holding her let out an unearthly howl and yanked his arms from around her to grab at his side. Julián didn't waste any time in swinging around to slam his fist into the other ruffian's eye. He had a moment to drive his foot into the man's knee and watch in satisfaction as he went down, yelling, before Julián was following him to the floor, grabbing for the sherry bottle.

Holding the jagged remains by the neck, Julián pressed them into the side of the bastard's neck, his other forearm pressing down hard on the man's collarbone.

"Maybe you'd like to reconsider telling me what you want with Miss Troncoso," Julián said, more politely than the ruffian deserved.

Spitting out curses, the man jerked his head to one side. All that did was make the sharp glass slide against his skin, shallowly enough that blood didn't spurt, only trickled down over Julián's fingers.

There was no time for more. All down the corridor,

the doors to the other cabins were popping open and passengers, befuddled and irate at having their night's rest interrupted by a brawl, were beginning to venture out of their cabins.

It wasn't long before the startled passengers were joined by a handful of stewards trying to find out what had happened while simultaneously attempting to usher those not involved back into their cabins, to little effect. The two ruffians, now injured and unable to flee, seemed prepared to try and brazen it out.

And apparently, so was Julián.

"What happened?" Julián snapped at the crew, as haughty as an aristocrat not just in his manner, but in the way he squared his shoulders to take up more space in the narrow corridor. "My wife and I have just been assaulted. That's what happened."

Amalia, who had long since tucked the eggy fork she'd used to stab the ruffian into her skirt's pocket, clung to Julián's arm. It wasn't a pretense, or at least not entirely—she was more shaken than she would have cared to admit, and her legs were undecided as to whether they would continue to hold her up. It was damned infuriating. Amalia had never been the swooning type and she didn't intend to start now.

Straightening her spine, she started to step away but was forestalled as Julián briefly pressed her hand against where it was trapped between his biceps and rib cage. Amalia's first instinct at this silent command was to yank her hand out of his grasp and tell him in no uncertain terms that she didn't need his help. But she did need it, didn't she? She might have been able to make her way to Puerto Plata alone, but she would have never been able to overpower those brutes without his help.

It had been brutal having to stand there motionless, watching the ruffian deal him blow after blow as Amalia waited for the right moment to strike. And yet, had it not been for him, she would have been locked up in some cabin, entirely at their mercy.

Next to her, Julián was spinning a tale about taking a midnight stroll around the deck. "When we realized how late it was, we decided to return to our cabin— and that's when we were set upon by these scoundrels. They didn't bother to hide their evil intent, so I was forced to defend my wife and myself."

Amalia didn't try to conceal the revulsion in her expression at the memory of those rough arms wrapped around her waist. Safe against Julián, she glared at the ruffian, then switched her gaze to his companion, who was once again wearing that vaguely smug smile as he raised his hands as if attempting to look harmless.

"My associate and I were hired by the girl's uncle to rescue her from this brigand," he said. "Who abducted her from the family home and is attempting to—"

"That's a damned lie," Julián said furiously.

The man extracted something from his pocket. "Then you would say you aren't the author of this ransom note?"

Amalia had to struggle to control her expression as she felt Julián freeze beside her. She'd only caught a glimpse of the note, but even at a distance, it looked very much like the one her uncle must have received the day before. She'd asked Julián to write it in case her uncle recognized her handwriting, though she was the one who'd dictated its contents.

"I have a note from her uncle, too, in which he asks me to do whatever necessary to return the young lady," the ruffian said, waving another folded piece of paper.

The chief steward turned to look at Amalia and Julián, eyes narrowing suspiciously.

Amalia stepped forward.

"I have most certainly not been kidnapped," she began with as much scorn as she could muster.

"I should say not!" A diminutive figure wriggling its way through the crowd was revealed a second later to be Doña María, in a wrapper and braided hair. "How dare you impugn this man's character?" she demanded, bristling with indignation. "He happens to be the son of one of the most prominent families on the island and my dear Amalia's beloved husband."

Amalia very carefully did not look at Julián. He must have made quite an impression on the elderly woman for her to mount such a vigorous defense on his behalf.

Looking apologetic, the chief steward tried to get a word in edgewise, but Doña María talked him into submission until he was forced to promise that he would have the ruffians confined to their cabins.

"Considering what I've seen of your security measures, I'd feel much safer if you tossed them overboard." Julián exchanged a glance with one of the men in the crowd. "When I booked our passage, I was under the impression that the Clyde-Mallory lines valued the safety of its passengers."

A rumble of agreement among the other passengers made the chief steward hasten to appease them all. He did his best but the commotion didn't show any signs of subsiding, and a select few were beginning to complain loudly about interrupted sleep. Finally, the chief steward held up his hands.

"I can offer you all my assurances that this matter will be dealt with by the proper authorities as soon as we make port. In the meantime, these gentlemen will be escorted into one of the crew cabins downstairs."

"Post a steward to stand guard at each end of this corridor and I might be persuaded to believe you. At the very least, it will make everyone in this section of the ship sleep easier."

The crowd voiced their vehement agreement, and the chief steward had very little option but to concede to Julián's demand. So assuaged, the passengers dispersed as the ruffians were hauled away.

Amalia felt the tension leave Julián's biceps, though when she glanced up, his expression remained unchanged from the impassive mask he had worn for the past quarter of an hour. The mask stayed in place as he guided her toward her cabin, waiting as she reached into her pocket for the keys.

Stepping inside after her, he inspected every corner of the cabin and the adjoining lavatory, going so far as to get on his hands and knees to look under the bed. When he was satisfied that there was no one lurking under the dust ruffle, he turned the lock on the thick cabin door. The slim piece of metal seemed awfully fragile to Amalia, who would have considered asking him to pile all the furniture in front of the door if most of it hadn't been fastened in place.

"You're staying?" she asked him.

"If it's all right with you. I'd rather not leave you alone with those two still on board and with the key to the cabin next door." He nodded toward the bed. "And

I don't much relish spending another night in a chair, however little there's left of it."

Amalia grasped him by the collar. "I wouldn't have let you leave even if you'd wanted to. You're hurt, and tired and I'm—"

She cut herself off swiftly. Amalia had never admitted to being scared out loud, and she wasn't about to start now.

Julián seemed to understand. He ignored the last part of her sentence and smiled, wincing slightly as the gesture pulled at the cut on his lower lip. "You know me, Your Highness. Always at your command."

He said it lightly and Amalia, already overwhelmed by the tangle of feelings inside her, answered in kind.

"Well, then, I command you to sit down and let me clean those cuts." He sank into the armchair. Gently, she pressed her fingertip to the corner of his mouth. "You'll have another scar, I think."

He shrugged and put his hands on her hips. "It'll only make me handsomer."

She ought to have found it irritating, the remark and the practiced smile that accompanied it. Only this time it didn't sound as insincere as it had in the carriage, mostly because she was beginning to see beyond his flippant tone to the pain and worry shading his dark eyes.

That he didn't care to let her see it didn't mean it wasn't there.

She cupped his face in both her hands, turning it to both sides to get a full look at the damage. A split lip, a wicked bruise beginning to spread over his temple and around his eye, a swollen nose…all incurred in her defense.

"I think I've seen him before," she said, releasing his face and going into the lavatory. She dampened a towel with water from the jug and returned to find him pulling off his necktie and undoing the button at his throat. "The first man, the one with the newspaper. On the deck, but also— I think he's an associate of my uncle's. The kind that deals with unpleasant matters."

Julián nodded grimly. "I wouldn't put it past him to have left word for you to be restrained if you turned up."

"He knows I would go after Lucía. Whatever his plans for her, they must be important enough that he was willing to go this far to keep me away."

"You don't think he'll—"

"He won't have me hurt, if that's what you mean. Not physically, in any case. I have no illusions about the strength of my uncle's feelings toward me, but he's never been inclined to violence."

Julián grunted as Amalia pressed the dampened cloth to his lip. "Depends on how you define *violence*. I'd argue that ruining your reputation by telling everyone you ran off with some man could be considered as violent."

She felt her lips twisting with wry amusement. "It was vindictive of him, yes. He's always hated that I'm not some pliant, impressionable girl he can mold to his will." Amalia refolded the bloodstained cloth and patted Julián's temple with a clean corner. "Honestly, having everyone think I'm married is not the worst that could have happened. It'll mean more freedom. And it means he won't find it as easy to marry me off to one of his business associates. It's the last thing he intended, but I think he might have done me a favor."

"Favor or not, I'd still like to strike the bastard when we find him."

His use of the word *we* sent a dart of relief through her. It wasn't that she thought he would back out of their agreement, but surely any rational person would think twice about getting embroiled in a situation after being pummeled like he had.

"Oh, he's done plenty to deserve it," she assured him, brushing back his hair to wipe the cloth over his forehead. "Though I did aspire for a little more subtlety." She sighed. "I just hate knowing that I worried Lucía as much as I did over a scheme that didn't work."

"You didn't consider telling her the truth?"

Amalia shook her head. "I didn't want to risk it, in case the plan failed and my uncle suspected she was involved."

He grazed her wrist with his fingertips. "We'll get to your sister soon, and she'll be able to see with her own eyes that you're fine."

"We will," Amalia said, trying as always not to let the smallest scraps of fear and doubt cloud her certainty. It was either that or carry her anger like a heavy mantle over her shoulders and let the weight of her uncle's greediness make her bitter.

She ran the damp towel over the back of Julián's neck. His eyes fluttered closed and he lowered his forehead to press it against Amalia's midsection. "That feels good. Nice and cool."

The back of his neck was dark from the sun and oddly vulnerable. Amalia rubbed the cloth over his overheated skin, watching his hair curl with the damp. How was it that this felt so much more intimate than what they'd done in the galley? She rested a cautious hand on top of his warm head.

She could feel each individual beat of her own heart, echoing through her body. Surely, Julián heard it as well. Could he tell how it quickened every time he was near? She'd been inclined to think that it was merely a response to the thrill of adventure and the relief of finally doing something to better her and Lucía's situation. But maybe…

Maybe it was something more.

The thought should have terrified her. It might have, if it didn't feel so right.

Chapter Eight

Julián lay on his back, watching the sky grow lighter by degrees.

Amalia was on her side with her back to him, her long curls flung over the pillow and his chest. Just before she'd fallen asleep, he had plunged his hands into her hair as he'd wanted to do in the carriage and released it from its pins just to watch her tight curls cascade down to the small of her back.

He picked up one of the strands and pulled it lightly, watching as the curl straightened, then bounced back into its original coil as soon as he let go. Would he be able to spring back, too, whenever he and Amalia parted? Or had the past two days changed his shape for good?

As much as Julián wanted to pretend otherwise, there was no doubt in his mind that they *would* eventually part. Maybe she'd agree to a dalliance, for a time. But eager as she seemed to further their acquaintance, there would come a time when her interest in him would fizzle and go out like a sputtering candle. Just as it always did.

He would find someone else, in time. There were plenty of women in the world who would be willing, even eager, for their turn in Julián's bed.

The only trouble was none of them would be Amalia Troncoso.

Amalia stirred beside him, and Julián realized she hadn't been as deeply asleep as he'd thought.

"Did you get any sleep?" she asked drowsily.

"An hour or so, maybe. It's early still—it'll be a few hours yet till we dock. You should try to get some more rest."

"I'm all right." Her sleeve was a pale flutter in the gloom as she raised a hand to cover a yawn. Julián could feel her legs flexing against his, even though he'd been prudent enough to wear his trousers to bed.

Prudent, Julián. What a laugh.

Julián tightened the arm she lay on, pulling her close enough for him to place a row of kisses on the nape of her neck. Her squeak of surprise was thoroughly enjoyable, as was the irritated little huff she let out when he stopped.

For a while they lay in silence as the sun inched its way up the sky. Amalia's body was a solid weight at his side, firm in some places and pleasantly yielding in others.

"You fit well in my arms."

It must have been the blaze of exhaustion that made Julián say such a thing out loud. Amalia must have been as surprised as he was by the sudden break in the silence, because she stiffened suddenly.

He forced out a low laugh, loosening his hold on her. "You needn't worry about being ravished, Your Highness. I'm too exhausted to have my wicked way with you."

Not that he wasn't burning to. But first, there were precautions he had to take and secrets that needed to come out into the light.

"I wasn't worried," she felt the need to point out. "In case you hadn't noticed, I very much enjoyed your earlier attempt at ravishing."

He'd noticed all right, and the memory of it was making his body reconsider his statement. "Then what's the matter?"

"Earlier, when you said you never form attachments. Does that mean you've never been in love?"

"Love? Never heard of it, Your Highness," he said lightly. "Why do you ask? Are you thinking you might want to give it a try?"

"Never," she replied promptly. "I don't want any part in that sort of thing. But we're not talking about me right now."

Julián had never been the sort to bare his heart. It wasn't pleasant, or even productive, and his few attempts at sincerity had always been met with uncomprehending coldness from his father and sneering from his cousin. Here in the near dark, however, with Amalia curled against him, her cheek pillowed on his arm…

"I thought I loved someone once," he found himself saying, unable to muster up another deflective, lighthearted reply. "And I was foolish enough to think she loved me back. Maybe she might have, if circumstances had been different—I have reason to believe that she and I were both lied to, in a deliberate attempt to break us apart."

For a long moment Julián listened to the sound of Amalia's even breaths.

"Then again," he said, even more softly than before,

"I wouldn't blame her if love was the last thing on her mind. I'm not…" He paused and breathed through the shame and grief blooming in his chest. "I'm not the kind of man who's easy to love."

There was a rustle of starched sheets as she turned over to face him. The jaunty little curtains at the cabin's window did little to block the faint sunshine beginning to press against the panes. The pale glow of dawn touched her features as gently as he would have if he'd been able to unclench his hands from the crisp sheets.

"Do you really believe that?"

"I'm not a good man," he said, more harshly than he'd intended. "I'm a damned blackguard, a scoundrel, and everyone who gets close to me ends up getting hurt."

"Yes, yes, I remember. The worst kind of person, right? Well, let me tell you something." She leaned closer until the tip of her nose was almost brushing his, her breath trailing over his lips like a sultry breeze. "I don't think you're as bad as you like to pretend you are."

"And you don't know me as well as you think you do."

A year ago—maybe even a week ago—he would have found it necessary to avoid those eyes that seemed to pierce him through even in the faint light. Now, however, he met them with matching intensity.

"Don't I?" she asked.

He didn't back down from the challenge in her gaze. "You don't know me at all, Your Highness."

"I know that you came all this way here with me when you didn't have to."

"What makes you think I'm not just interested in the money?"

She raised her shoulder in a slight shrug that made her prim little nightdress slip off her shoulder. Julián couldn't resist pressing his lips to the smooth skin it revealed. "What does it matter if you are?" she asked. "I doubt bandits do a lot of things out of the goodness of their hearts. That's not all you care about, though. If it were, I don't think you would have put yourself at risk defending me from those two men."

"I may have just been protecting my investment," he pointed out. "I've wasted a lot of time and effort on you not to see this through to the end."

"You had every opportunity to pilfer valuables from the house when you were there," Amalia said. "And the knowledge that not only was it unattended save for a single maid, but that none of the locks are a match for you. You could have stayed behind and burgled its entire contents." She stroked the patch of hair at the center of his chest, her fingernails pleasantly sharp as they scraped his skin.

"You make a good case for me," he said softly.

"And yet, I can see you don't believe me."

He wanted to, with such a swift and fierce desperation that he found it hard to keep from swearing out loud. "I've always been a worthless, reckless scoundrel. My own family hasn't much use for me—why would anyone else?"

"I have use for you." Amalia lifted herself up on her elbow as if to emphasize her point. "But that's not why I— Why I don't believe you're a scoundrel. You don't have to be useful in order to be a good person—or worthy of love."

Julián's throat felt tight. "I thought we both agreed that we want nothing to do with love."

"I don't," she said quietly. "What I'm trying to say is that maybe your girl from Seville had more affection for you than you realized. You aren't difficult to love, Julián. Not for those who partake in such things."

Amalia may have been bold and fearless, but she had led a very sheltered life and knew so little of the world. Still, she spoke with such conviction that Julián was almost convinced. Almost. Twenty-eight years of hearing his father listing, in unsparing detail, all the ways in which Julián had failed as a son and as a man and as a businessman were not that easy to overcome.

Her hand was venturing lower, and Julián was finding it hard to remember why he shouldn't flip her over and repeat everything he'd done to make her pant the night before. Reluctantly, he captured her hand in his and held it tight.

"You're not the only one who has family troubles, Your Highness. I—"

There was a loud rap at the door, too demanding to have come from a steward. Julián was instantly on alert, springing to his feet and reaching the door in a couple of long strides.

"Yes?" he asked sharply.

"Good morning, my dears," came Doña María's voice through the thick wood. "Will you be coming in to breakfast? They opened the dining room early, on account of no one being able to rest with those two ruffians on board. I sent my nephew down to save us all seats at the same table, but I'm afraid there's a rush and—"

"We'll be there in a few minutes, Doña María," Julián called, deciding it was better to appear a little rude

than to open the door and scandalize the elderly lady
with the sight of his bare chest.

There was a muted creak behind him and then Amalia was pressing herself against his back, her breasts
round and soft through the thin fabric of her nightgown.
"Minutes?" she murmured, nuzzling his shoulder.

He turned. "Wouldn't want to disappoint the nice
lady."

"Then we'd better hurry," Amalia said and dashed
into the lavatory.

There was nothing Julián wanted more than to give
chase, but a man needed to know his limitations. Following her into the lavatory would only result in his
insisting on brushing the nightgown off her shoulders
to watch it glide down her body. He wouldn't be able
to resist reveling in her skin, licking droplets of water
off her curves as she bathed, diving into the deep cleft
between her breasts and refusing to resurface for hours.

Forget breakfast—they would probably miss their
chance to disembark in Puerto Plata and find themselves
halfway to New York before he found the strength to
pry his lips away from Amalia's.

There would be time enough for all that later.

Thanks to Julián's noble restraint, they made it into
the dining room only forty minutes after Doña María
had knocked on their door. The space was more beautiful flooded in morning light than it had been the afternoon before. The intense rose glow of the sky was
reflected in the copper pots that held fishtail palms,
and on the cut-crystal vases from which sprouted tall
sprays of pink and red ginger flowers, hardy blooms
that would withstand the days until the ship reached

its final destination. Damask drapes and silk-shaded sconces reminded Julián of some of the higher-end hotels he had visited on the European continent.

The walls here were paneled, too, only these were carved so intricately they were a match for Amalia's frilly shirtwaist. She had unearthed another thoroughly impractical ensemble from one of her valises, this one consisting of a shirtwaist laden with lace and a pale green skirt that was saved from looking dull by the lustrousness of the fabric. A darker green sash threaded through with a buckle cinched her in at the waist and made Julián crave to measure the tight circumference against the span of his hands.

After greeting Doña María and her young nephew, Julián pulled out a chair for Amalia. The soft, clear glow of early morning suited her as well as moonlight had. It made her curls gleam and her rich brown eyes sparkle, and it made the gold ring she still wore shine like a beacon, guiding him home.

The devil take him. This was more than mere infatuation. This was—

He caught Doña María's eye as he sat, and the knowing look would have made him blush if he was capable of such a thing.

Instead, he gave her a shrug and the kind of faintly sheepish smile he imagined would come naturally to a newlywed.

"You're smitten, aren't you, *mijo*?" she asked from across the table.

"And happy to be," he replied airily, unfolding the linen napkin and spreading it over her lap. Beside him Amalia was exchanging pleasantries with the nephew, a boy who couldn't have been older than fifteen or sixteen. "Doña María, I haven't had the opportunity to thank you for coming to my defense last night. We—"

She dismissed his gratefulness with a wave of her heavily ringed hand. "I should have hated to see your honeymoon ruined over such a thing. My dear sister had a terrible time of it on *her* honeymoon and she's every bit as upset over it twenty years later as she was that day. I don't believe I asked yesterday—are you on your way to New York as well?"

"I'm afraid we're disembarking later this morning, once we make port in Puerto Plata."

"Of course, of course," the older woman said. "That's where your people are from, aren't they?"

Julián was spared having to answer by the appearance of a waiter with a coffeepot in one gloved hand and a carafe of ice water in the other. He poured them each coffee from the silver pot, which Julián noticed was etched with the same Clyde-Mallory symbol printed on their tickets and the breakfast menu. Julián made a production out of adding cream and sugar to Amalia's coffee before attending to his own and re-marking, as he did, upon the extensive list of jams and marmalades printed on the crisp menu.

He kept the table entertained until the waiter returned with their eggs and sausages and another acquaintance of Doña María's joined them at the table and seized the older woman's attention with a very long and involved story about a mutual friend of theirs. The nephew was drawn into the conversation, too, leaving Amalia free to turn to Julián.

"Were your eggs all right?" he asked, nodding to her plate, which she had cleared with impressive speed. "You can have my toast if you want. And look, they have orange marmalade—it's no *dulce de naranja*, but I think you'll like it."

She shook her head. "Thank you, but I couldn't eat another bite." Leaning a little closer to Julián, she said, "I keep looking around as if I expect to find those men from last night lurking in the corners. I think I'd rather return to the cabin and get our things together—it won't be long before we make port and I'd like to be ready to go as soon as possible."

Julián seized the linen napkin on his lap and laid it beside his plate. "Let's go and pack."

There was barely an hour left until Amalia would cease to be Julián's new, if fictional, bride, and she intended to take advantage of every single minute of it.

Unfortunately for her, the chief steward found Julián before they reached the cabin. With an apologetic smile and a squeeze of her hand, Julián walked her to the cabin and made sure she had locked herself in safely before going with the older man.

He had placed his things neatly back into the old carpetbag he'd brought, but the clothes Amalia had worn the day before were strewn around the small cabin. She picked them up, folding them into inexpert bundles that she stuffed back into one of the open valises.

As she shook out the white organza blouse and tried to work out how to put it away without crumpling it beyond ruin, she couldn't help but think of the delicate ease with which Julián had removed it the night before. He'd clearly had plenty of practice. He also hadn't seemed to think much of their sharing a bed, though of course they'd both been too tired to do much other than sleep and talk.

Maybe that was normal to the kind of life he led, but it had been the first time that Amalia had ever lain next to a man. The awareness of his proximity had burned through her all night, even in her dreams, the cotton of her nightdress so thin it might have been made out of spun clouds.

And then waking up with her body still snug against his, sharing confidences as the day brightened around them…

She had always expected such intimacy to rob her of something—instead, being with Julián gave her strength. It made her feel powerful. Like the sort of person who galloped through narrow country roads, dodging branches and defending herself from ruffians and chasing maidens in distress halfway around an island.

Like the kind of person strong enough to create an entire new future for herself and for her sister.

The thought of Lucía was like a little shock of ice water against sun-warmed skin. Whatever her feelings for Julián, she couldn't let herself forget the real purpose for this journey. Her sister's safety came first.

But once that was assured…

Then Amalia could let herself dream about what might come later, and who she would share those moments with.

When Amalia had finished packing and Julián still hadn't returned, she went out onto the deck and stood looking past the railing, as she had upon their departure. During the night they had left behind the bright, placid waters of the Caribbean Sea and crossed into the fiercer, darker Atlantic Ocean. She was just in time to watch as the steamer made its way into the intense blue waters of the Puerto Plata bay. At the entrance to the half circle, to Amalia's left, were the sturdy brown walls of what looked like a colonial-era fort, topped with crenellations and surrounded with palm trees.

"That's the customs building."

The scent of Julián's shaving soap was faint enough in the overpowering salt tinging the air that Amalia wouldn't have perceived it had he not stepped in close to her. Even though they'd been parted for less than an hour, the desire to seek out his skin with hers flared as intensely as if they had been separated for weeks. Amalia gave in to it after a slight pause, and twined their fingers together.

Pressing his shoulder to hers, he extended his free hand to point at something in the distance. "And over there, behind those trees, is a pretty little park with a two-story gazebo right in its center. Just the place to while away a lazy afternoon."

"You've been here before," she said, twisting around in surprise.

"I was born here, Your Highness."

At some point along the way the nickname had stopped sounding faintly mocking and had become almost affectionate.

"We should get ready to leave as soon as the gangplank's lowered," Julián continued, before she could react to the scrap of information he had volunteered.

Julián raked a hand through his hair, and Amalia realized he wasn't wearing a hat. The bridge of his nose was already reddened by the sun. "The chief steward and the captain both gave me their reassurances that the ruffians will be taken into custody by the Civil Guard as soon as I make a formal complaint against them. But there's every chance that your uncle is having this port watched as well, and I'd just as soon not get pummeled again."

"No argument from me there," Amalia said and smiled as Julián pretended to be astonished. "My things are packed—I'm ready to go."

But not quite ready to leave him, though now that they were so much closer to reaching Lucía, Amalia could feel herself growing impatient to get her search started. Julián seemed to share her mood—he was restless, almost twitching with impatience as he gathered their luggage and waited by the door to the gangplank.

He exploded into motion the minute their feet struck solid ground. He'd asked a steward to run down ahead of them to fetch a carriage, tipping him handsomely. This allowed Amalia and Julián to lose themselves in the crowd descending from the ship before quickly getting into the waiting carriage. If there were any more ruffians waiting for them, Amalia was moderately sure they had avoided them.

"Where will we start?" Amalia asked as the coachman guided them away from the bustle of the port.

"We'll leave your things at a hotel I'm acquainted with." Julián took her hand to stroke the back of it with his thumb. The movement made the faceted stone on Amalia's finger glitter in the sunlight.

He hadn't asked for the ring back. Amalia knew she should say something about it. She didn't understand what was holding her back. She wasn't interested in marriage—of that much she was still certain. When Julián had told her that he found it easy to engage in physical affection without being ensnared in feelings, she'd been intrigued. As far as she could tell, their interlude in the galley hadn't sparked any inconvenient feelings or emptied her head of important thoughts. She hadn't simpered or giggled or heaved any dreamy sighs. If anything, she felt more powerful and sure of herself.

So why this reluctance, then?

Impatiently, Amalia twisted the ring off her finger and thrust it toward Julián, noticing immediately how weightless her finger felt without it. "Before I forget, here's your mother's ring. There's no need for it anymore."

Julián hesitated. "Keep it for now," he said. "Just in case we find ourselves needing to continue the ruse."

Amalia slipped the ring back on. And there was no denying it—it did feel right.

Chapter Nine

The coachman took them straight to the Hotel Europa, a three-story building with wrought iron balconies and shuttered windows twice Julián's height.

"Will you wait for me here?" he asked Amalia as the coach rolled to a stop beneath the striped awning at the hotel's entrance. "Just for a few minutes—I cabled ahead before leaving San Pedro and I want to make sure everything has been arranged as I asked."

If it hadn't been for the urgency to find her sister, Julián would've been tempted to act like a true bandit and steal away with Amalia—tell the coachman to turn right around back to the port and whisk her into the next ship headed for Europe, where they could both forget their names and responsibilities and devote themselves solely to the pursuit of losing themselves in each other's bodies.

Sometime during the previous night, in between listening to her soft exhalations as waves of pleasure rocked her body and whispering confidences in the half dark, the world he used to know had shattered around him and been remade. And at the center of this new world was Amalia, as bold and fearless as he had always longed to be. His mission, which had seemed so important a few days ago, more than paled in comparison.

Julián waited for Amalia's nod before reaching for her. Softly, he ran the pad of his thumb over the sweet curves of her upper lip, wondering why those slopes and valleys made his chest ache with longing. He dove into its depths for one kiss, and then another, but that did nothing to quell the deep well of need yawning inside him.

So he flashed her a crooked, breathless smile and said, "I'll come back for you in a minute or two."

He leaped lightly out of the carriage and he strolled inside with a friendly nod to the crisply uniformed bellhop standing in the rectangle of shade cast by the awning.

The strength of his desire for Amalia didn't make him panic—not quite yet, at any rate. He was well aware that he was a little too infatuated. That *infatuated* wasn't even the right word, because the thing that had been building between them was too large to be contained by the words in his insufficient vocabulary.

Only the knowledge that Amalia didn't want to be bothered by love or commitments kept Julián from fully losing his head.

A good thing, too, because he needed his wits about him, especially now that he was back in Puerto Plata. He wasn't sure what they would find when they tracked down her sister, but he had a good idea of what awaited them. And of Amalia's reaction when he confessed the truth of why he had come all the way here with her.

The sooner he explained, the better. Maybe she'd

agree to come upstairs with him for a few minutes of uninterrupted conversation so that—

Halfway to the front desk, Julián collided against an elderly gentleman who all but struck Julián upside the head with his silver-tipped cane as he yelled something about brigands.

"My apologies, *señor*," he murmured, steadying the man with a quick grip of his elbows.

It wasn't until Julián heard his own name being spoken out loud that he recognized the older man as an acquaintance of his father's. Instead of a simple greeting, the older man launched at once into an anecdote about the time when he was set upon by bandits.

Julián would have found it interesting at any other time, but the last thing he needed at the moment was to get drawn into a long and involved conversation. He was trying to think of a polite way to extricate himself from it when the older man said, "Oh, but I shouldn't keep you. I'm sure you're eager to get back to your father." He gave Julián's shoulder a kindly pat. "Go on. I know how much Reynaldo dislikes being kept waiting."

Dread as cold as ice swirled through Julián. "He's waiting for me?" Puerto Plata was large as towns went, but gossip spread with astonishing speed and his father had a network of informants to rival any emperor's. He'd figured everyone would know soon enough that he'd returned—he just hadn't expected it to be this fast.

"In the courtyard. Isn't that why you're here? For the party?"

Julián let out a word that made the man's mouth drop open. Without pausing to apologize, he bolted back the way he'd come from.

He had to get Amalia out of here. Immediately, before

anyone in his family saw her and guessed that she was there with him.

Before she herself stumbled into the truth of all he'd been keeping from her.

The coachman was leaning against the carriage's back wheel, legs crossed as he touched a match to a crude wooden pipe. He glanced up wildly when Julián came barging toward the carriage.

"Don Julián? Is something wrong?"

Julián didn't stop to answer him. He wrenched the carriage door open and stared frantically into the plush—and empty—interior.

Amalia was gone.

No more than a minute or two after Julián left, Amalia was tumbling out of the carriage and into the hotel's lobby. She had never been able to bear being told to sit and wait quietly, and she had no intention of ever complying with such requests, however well intended they might be.

The lobby was spacious and more luxurious than she'd anticipated. A stretch of terra-cotta tiles gleamed unbroken from the entrance to a wooden counter equipped with a brass bell and mahogany-and-brass pigeonholes that Amalia assumed were for mail or keys. Birds of paradise in glazed pots, stained-glass sidelights on the doors and graceful fretwork arches so intricately carved they looked like the lace edging on Amalia's shirtwaist, provided a background to the bellhops in their sharply tailored uniforms and dark blue waistcoats.

A seating area to the right held a grouping of love seats and armchairs. Amalia's gaze flitted from a trio of little boys setting up a game of marbles beside a side table to an older gentleman who seemed to be waving his silver-tipped cane at Julián. She couldn't see Julián's face, but the conversation seemed to be taking an intense turn.

Curiosity would have prompted her to sidle closer, had Amalia not caught a glimpse of a figure that looked curiously familiar, disappearing through an arched colonnade that surrounded some sort of outdoor space.

Was that—? Surely, that couldn't be her sister.

Her heart suddenly hammering wildly inside her rib cage, Amalia didn't hesitate in bounding after the girl.

It wasn't until she had gone through that she realized that the large, brick-paved courtyard had been set up for a party. The white bougainvillea spilling from the second- and third-floor balconies, twined with trailing vines, looked festive enough on its own without all the added decorations. The half a dozen trees in the courtyard, all of which were ringed with the same red brick of the floors, were as strung with garlands as the female guests were with ropes of pearls and amber.

At the far end a tiled fountain was flanked by two long tables that appeared to be blooming with Castilian roses and lacy ferns in silver vases. More silver gleamed on the white damask tablecloth—trays and salvers piled high with imported apples and grapes and all kinds of party food.

Amalia glanced away from the *pastelitos* and ham *croquetas* and the delicately frosted cakes. To the right, on a small stage underneath one of the balconies, musicians in evening wear played a lively waltz. None of the elegantly clad couples were dancing, though. They stood in loose clusters around the courtyard, holding champagne flutes as they chatted. The figure Amalia had followed to the courtyard didn't seem to be among them.

And even though it was more than likely that the girl hadn't been Lucía after all, merely a product of Amalia's wishful thinking, and though Amalia was aware that finding her sister wouldn't have been so easy, she could feel disappointment flooding through her at the notion that she had lost her sister yet again. It was an irrational thought, but one Amalia couldn't seem to shake off.

Lucía wouldn't have been involved in any of this if it hadn't been for Amalia. She couldn't help but think that if she hadn't tried so hard to defy her uncle's authority, he wouldn't have seen Lucía's docility as a reason to use her for his plans instead of Amalia.

Swallowing back her guilt, Amalia turned to make her way back to Julián and begin the search in earnest. That was when she saw her.

Lucía, dressed in an ivory cotton voile frock with a high neck of floral lace that made her swan-like neck look fragile. Two men stood at either side of her—Tío Francisco to her right, expansive as he held court over a small group, and a younger man to her left, who contributed the occasional aside to the gathering. He must have been as charming as his smile indicated, because the group obliged him with frequent laughs.

When Amalia had pictured this moment, she had seen herself charging in like a knight on a white horse and wrestling her sister away from a wicked villain, not a party.

Then again, Amalia knew how oppressive some parties could be.

Lacking the armor and the white horse, Amalia opted to glide toward the shadows behind one of the columns where she could avoid being spotted until she was able to capture Lucía's attention.

It didn't take long before Lucía's attention wandered in the direction of Amalia's hiding place, which showed how engaging the conversation must have been.

Her eyes widened, though she stopped short of gasping. Quickly composing herself, she made her excuses to the group and began walking toward Amalia. Instead of stopping when she reached her sister, though, Lucía continued straight through the arched colonnade.

Amalia waited a beat, then followed her sister into what turned out to be the hotel's dining room. Breakfast evidently over, the ample space was empty and dark. It had already been set up for the midday service, with fresh linen tablecloths and polished silver cutlery. Amalia had just enough time to catch a glimpse of the carnations in the small silver vases at the center of each table before Lucía had launched herself at her, sweeping her into a long, tight hug.

"Are you all right?" Amalia demanded when she was finally able to pull away, holding her taller sister by the shoulders.

"Me? Are *you*? The last time I saw you, you were getting ki—kid—"

Lucía dissolved into tears and Amalia gathered her close again, murmuring soothing things into her ear. But Lucía was no longer a child with a scraped knee, and when her sobs subsided she had plenty of questions for Amalia.

There wasn't much of a chance for Amalia to answer them, though, because the door to the hotel's dining room swung open and their uncle strode inside, followed by the younger man who'd been standing with them.

"Lucía, there you are," Tío Francisco said irritably. "What do you mean by abandoning your guests? We—"

The astonishment in his face when he caught sight of Amalia was almost comical. He stopped so abruptly, the other man narrowly missed walking into his back.

Amalia had to stifle the impish urge to wave hello. "Tío Francisco," she said as neutrally as she could manage.

Her uncle stopped, licking his lips and darting a look at the man next to him. "Amalia. I'm so glad that you've made your way back to us," he blustered. Though he'd had a few moments to compose himself, he couldn't quite conceal the virulent glower flickering beneath his bonhomie. "And just in time to join in the celebration."

Amalia's arm was threaded through Lucía's; it was impossible to miss the sudden tension in her sister's body at the word.

"Celebration?" Amalia asked sharply.

"Surely, that's not an unfamiliar concept," the stranger said.

Above the starched white collar was a face that Amalia would have called handsome if she hadn't taken an instant dislike to the sardonic tilt of his eyebrow. He had ruddy skin and pomaded black hair that had been combed back so carefully, she could see the ridges where the comb had passed through.

Something in his demeanor reminded Amalia faintly of how Julián had looked when he was demanding to the chief steward that the men who'd attacked them be hauled away.

"Who the devil are you?" Amalia snapped. She knew she was being unforgivably rude, but she didn't much care. Whoever this man was, he was clearly in cahoots with her uncle.

Something like amusement flashed over his face. "I'm Lucía's fiancé."

The word clanged unpleasantly through Amalia, as if someone had rung a bell directly over her head. It was exactly what she'd feared—Tio Francisco was trying to marry off Lucía and he'd taken advantage of Amalia's absence to hasten it along. She'd known he was planning something, but upon this confirmation, scalding anger welled up in her chest.

Before it had a chance to come pouring out, the outline of a man filled the open doorway.

"Victor."

She almost didn't recognize Julián's voice, filled as it was with barely restrained loathing. Then her brain registered what he'd said. "You know this man?"

"Know me?" The man's sardonic tones matched the expression on his face when he raised an eyebrow and drawled, "He's my cousin."

Chapter Ten

Julián didn't deny it, and why would he? It was clear from a single glance that the man he'd called Victor was telling the truth.

Beside her, Amalia heard Lucía gasp. "You're the bandit!"

Amalia herself couldn't say a word. Shock waves were reverberating through her as her gaze traveled from one man to the other, cataloging the similarities in their appearance. Both were devastatingly handsome, with angular noses and firm jaws. She could see it. Take away Julián's bristles, substitute the rusty black suit for a more sharply cut one… In Victor, though, the sharp humor that made Julián's dark eyes warm translated into something that made her blood run cold.

"All this time…" Amalia said slowly, pausing to gather her thoughts. "You knew I was trying to save Lucía and you were working with them all along?"

"No. *No*, Amalia."

"Were you planning on delivering me back to my uncle? Or to your father? Or—" Amalia thought back at all the subtle questions he had asked her about her uncle's business. "Or was it information you were after? Some juicy tidbit you could bring back to your father to finally make him notice you?"

Her words must have cut close to the truth because Julián looked suddenly and carefully blank.

"You have no idea what you're saying," he said, looking every inch the aristocrat.

Amalia's stomach—or maybe her heart—sank as she recognized the snobbish tones as the accent he had used while trying to get the ship's chief steward to lock away the ruffians who'd assaulted them.

Doña María had been right when she'd called him the son of a prominent family. She'd known all along who Julián truly was. Only Amalia, absolute fool that she was, had been in the dark.

She swallowed past the knot in her throat, willing for it to turn into anger.

All the little things Julián had let slip about his family were notching into place. His mother's outrageously expensive ring, which still encircled her finger. What he'd said about his father's office, which had made Amalia assume his father to be some sort of bookkeeper or clerk.

And then there was the cousin, who used to lock him in it. Whatever Julián had claimed about little boys being wild, she had privately thought that the cousin must have been unspeakably cruel to do such a thing. As she looked into Victor's face, she found it easy to match her mental image of that awful boy with the man standing in front of her, his smile intact even as his gaze raked over her and took in her shock—and the ring on her finger—with something like calculation.

Amalia would have rather expired on the spot than

give him the upper hand by being the first one to turn away, but her attention was drawn to the door as yet another person made his unexpected way into the dining room.

"The return of the wayward son." The crisp voice belonged to someone accustomed not only to issuing commands, but also of being heeded without question. It belonged to a barrel-chested man, whose neat gray mustache and thick eyebrows did little to hide the cold assessment in his eyes as he took in Lucía's tearstained face as well as Julián and Amalia.

Amalia would have known this was Julián's father just from the way Julián's jaw tensed, so hard she was sure it must be aching. Her own jaw firmed as she made herself look away, unwilling to catch his eye even for the most fleeting of seconds. Not until she could properly vent her fury at his deception. He must have known that she was reeling with shock, but he wasn't trying to apologize, or even explain. Knowing him, he was probably congratulating himself on a successful performance.

Half the things to come from his mouth had probably been lies, but Julián had been honest about one thing—he was most definitely a scoundrel.

"I'd apologize for whatever he's done, Francisco, but I'm afraid that taking up that particular habit would use up all my time," Julián's father continued. Not so much as a greeting passed between the eldest Fuentes and his son.

Tío Francisco responded with an unconvincing chuckle. "Not at all, Reynaldo. As it happens, we were just making introductions. It appears that my dear niece has become acquainted with your son."

"Ah, yes," Don Reynaldo said. "My son does have a most unfortunate habit of making acquaintances with every pretty young woman in the vicinity."

The reprimand in his voice was obvious, but all it did was make Julián smirk. "I wouldn't call it a habit so much as a talent," he said.

Forcing herself to look as if she hadn't just been shattered, Amalia looked past Julián to his father. "Actually, I was just being introduced to your nephew. Victor, was it? I can't say it's a pleasure to meet you."

Victor laughed with as much delight as if she'd offered him a compliment instead of a rude comment. "I was warned that you were spirited."

"Did they tell you I was curious, too?" she shot back. "Mostly about how my sister found herself whisked off to a new city and in possession of a fiancé in the space of two days."

A cold look from Don Reynaldo was apparently Tio Francisco's cue. "What I'd like to know is where *you* have been for that time," Tio Francisco said with a creditable attempt at a fatherly scolding. "Your claim to care about Lucía would be much more believable if you hadn't abandoned her to run off into the *monte* with a man. A fine example you're setting for her."

It was nothing that Amalia hadn't spent the past day telling herself, but she tried not to let any of them see the wave of guilt washing over her. "Anything I've done has been for Lucía's sake, which is more than I can say about you, Tio. Tell me, how much is Victor here paying you for her?"

Victor's faintly amused expression didn't so much as waver, but her uncle reacted as if she'd thrown lamp oil at a fire. "How dare you suggest such a thing?" he hissed, rounding on her. "As if I haven't given up my entire life to raise you ungrateful—"

Don Reynaldo cleared his throat, and the sound doused Tio Francisco's temper almost immediately. Visibly pulling the shreds of his self-control around himself, Tio Francisco tightened his mouth briefly before saying, in a much more measured tone, "I was hoping you'd decided to do the right thing and step aside so that your sister could make a decent match. The Fuenteses are a respectable family and if anyone stands to gain from the alliance, it's Lucía."

Amalia knew how much Lucía hated confrontation, and how much it must have cost her to say, "I don't want to marry Victor. I just met him last night."

"You're very young. You don't know what you want yet," Tio Francisco said dismissively. "You'll thank me someday."

"Ah, now that's a familiar tune." Julián half sat on one of the sturdy tables, crossing his arms over his chest as he looked at Lucía. "Far be it from a rascal like me to offer anyone advice, but being intimately acquainted with that particular song and dance, it's my displeasure to tell you that future thankfulness rarely materializes."

"Your opinion is as unwanted as it is unsolicited," his father told him shortly. "This affair is none of your concern."

"Isn't it?" There was a challenge in Julián's gaze that Amalia didn't quite understand. His relationship with his father and cousin was clearly adversarial, and had been since he was much younger. But there was something else at work here, and it clearly had something to do with the Troncosos.

"Why *are* you here?" Victor asked.

"I've always liked the Europa," Julián replied lazily. "The food's good and the wine's even better."

"In town," Victor clarified. "You've been carousing your way through Puerto Rico for the better part of a year. Why return now? And why feel the need to intrude in what is clearly a private family matter? After all, I seem to remember you renouncing this family and all it stood for just before you stomped away in a huff."

Cold dread was starting to rise in Amalia's stomach. More and more things were falling into place, because Julián was not the enigma she'd made him out to be; just a very good liar.

"You knew, didn't you?" This was the first time she'd addressed Julián directly since the truth of his identity had come out, and she couldn't miss the way he blanched when her accusing gaze landed on his. "About the engagement. That's why you did all this. That's why you pretended—"

Fury choked off the rest of her words. She'd been grateful—*grateful!*—that he'd agreed to accompany her all the way to Puerto Plata.

The enormity of his deception was crashing over her in waves, as the whole thing was too much for her mind and her heart to comprehend at once. He hadn't just lied to her about who he was. He'd let her believe that he was helping—that he was at her service.

Even worse than that, he'd let her believe that he cared.

The breeze filtering in through the half-closed shutters was heavily scented with flowers and perfume. It turned Amalia's stomach.

Victor's sharp gaze scraped over her like knives. "Don't worry. You aren't, by far, the first woman to fall for Julián's lies. And if I were a wagering sort of man, I'd say you won't be the last."

Don Reynaldo looked at his son with disgust. "Have you a single shred of decency left?"

"That would imply he had any to begin with," Victor put in.

Amalia didn't have to be endowed with superior powers of perception to notice the gleeful twist to Victor's smile. It made her sick to look at it, and not entirely for Julián's sake—this man who seemed to delight in cruelty was who her uncle expected sweet, innocent Lucía to marry? Did he even care how it would ruin her life?

His arrangement with the Fuentes family must have been very profitable indeed.

She turned to glare at Tio Francisco, only to be met with a triumphant expression. "You see, Amalia," he said, trying to sound like the kindly uncle he had never been, "this is why I ask for your obedience. All I have ever tried to do is keep you and Lucía safe from those who would use you for your fortune."

Julián scoffed. "I have no need for Amalia's money."

"Perhaps not," Tio Francisco said, "but you used her all the same."

His words fell into the thick silence with the force of a cannonball. Already uncomfortably aware of all the eyes on her, Amalia did her best to stifle a loud gasp—or was it a sob?—as she felt the inescapable truth of it drive itself into her seizing heart.

Julián hadn't just lied to her. He'd used her.

Julián had long since given up hoping for any shred of approval from Don Reynaldo Fuentes. But from the moment he'd walked into the hotel's dining room to see Amalia face-to-face with Victor, he'd been holding himself in such rigid control that even his father would have been proud.

All it took to crack it was one remark from her uncle.

No—that wasn't right. It was the look on Amalia's face when she came to the realization that Don Francisco was right. Julián *had* used her. Not for the reasons they all thought, and his interest in her wasn't entirely mercenary, but well, there it was.

Amalia didn't just look hurt. She had that dazed look of someone who'd just had the floor pulled out from under her. He couldn't have hurt her more if he'd deliberately set out to do it.

Julián's heart—if he had such a thing, and if it hadn't already shriveled beyond recognition—felt like it was splintering.

And there would be no putting it back together. He had already seen Victor glance down at the ring Amalia still wore. The sharp narrowing of his eyes when he recognized it made Julián's stomach sink. He knew what was coming. He'd seen Victor do it once before, almost a year ago now, and he wasn't about to give his cousin the chance to do it again.

Shielding Amalia from Victor's machinations was going to be impossible now. But at least Julián could soften the blow. Unfortunately, the only way to do that was to make Victor and his father believe that he had little interest for her beyond what he could get out of her. So instead of throwing himself at Amalia's feet and showering her with apologies, Julián was going to do his best to break her heart.

And the remains of his with it.

It was for the better. He'd vowed to himself that he

would never put himself in a situation where someone he cared for could be used against him. Not again. Never again.

Julián summoned up one of the insolent smiles he knew irritated his father beyond all reason. "*Used* is such an ugly word," he said lightly, forcing himself to look directly at Amalia. "Especially when our journey from San Pedro proved so pleasurable. Dare I say mutually so?"

There was a split second in which Amalia's eyes were wide and unguarded and raw with the shock of his betrayal. Then they shuttered, and grim determination hardened her generous mouth.

Less than an hour ago Julián had laid claim to those lips. He had reveled in the dips and hollows of that sumptuous mouth, thinking that it would be his— maybe not forever, because he knew better than to aspire to that much happiness, but for a little while at least. Long enough for him to commit her taste to memory.

"I doubt she would describe any time spent in your presence as *pleasurable*," Victor said.

Amalia didn't bother to hide her irritation. "I can speak for myself," she told Victor, before turning to Julián. "Whatever it is you're trying to imply—"

"I'm not implying anything," Julián said, knowing how much the interruption would annoy her. He felt a bitter sense of satisfaction. Whatever his father believed, Julián was good for one thing at least. "I'm saying it outright—we had our fun on the ship, but I thought you knew better than to expect anything else from me. I was perfectly clear when I told you that my dalliances never last long if I can help it."

"Trust me when I say I don't expect anything from you," Amalia said with chilly politeness, and Julián found that much more gut-wrenching than if she'd given in to her anger.

He shrugged. "Then we can dispense with the re-criminations and the questioning about what I may or may not have known, or who I may or may not have used. That's bound to get tiresome, and I have better things to do with my time."

Don Francisco was making a halfhearted attempt to sputter out something about his niece's honor, as if he hadn't gone and ruined her reputation by telling half of San Pedro that she'd run away with a stranger.

"I think we've had enough of your contemptible behavior, Julián," Victor announced over the older man's bluster. "Clearly, you've only returned to embarrass us, as you've always done. Or because you think that ruining my future happiness will somehow make up for the mistakes you yourself have made in the past."

Future happiness? Victor hadn't so much as glanced at his fiancée since Julián had joined them. The girl was still clinging to Amalia's arm, looking anxious. Julián felt a dart of pity—she was entirely too young to be caught up in his family's schemes, much less find herself tied for life to someone like Victor.

Less than a month ago Julián had returned from Puerto Rico with no other purpose than to get to the bottom of his family's involvement in his relationship with Concepción. There was something more important to be done now—keeping Amalia's sister away from them at all costs.

"Go back to your life of debauchery," Victor added,

his eyes glittering in the low light. "Nobody wants you here."

The corners of Julián's mouth lifted into something that wasn't quite a smile. "What's the matter, Victor? Don't tell me you're still jealous that women like me over you. Or are you worried that you'll never be able to find a woman who wants to marry you without being paid by my father?"

"Only you would put women and payment in the same sentence," Victor snapped.

"I've been gone a whole year and you still haven't developed a sense of humor." Julián pretended to sigh. "What a shame."

Amalia made an impatient gesture with her hand. "If the two of you are done with your little squabble, there are more important matters at hand." She shifted her gaze to Victor. "I don't know what my uncle promised you, but if you'd care to renegotiate your arrangement, I can offer you better terms."

Devil take him, but Julián relished the note of defiance in her voice.

He saw the flicker in Victor's eyes a fraction of a second too late. "Would those be the same terms you offered my cousin?" he said nastily.

Julián's muscles bunched with the urge to pummel the sneer off his cousin's face. Only the knowledge that he couldn't show his hand, not now, kept him still.

Victor's lip curled. "I'm afraid I don't have his taste for—"

"Victor," Julián's father said sharply, before Julián could give in to the violent impulse coursing through him.

He realized with a start that his fingers had closed

around one of the knives on the table next to him. With difficulty, and hoping that no one had seen his instinctive gesture, he loosened his fingers and laid his hand flat on the tablecloth.

Heeding the rebuke like the obedient little boy he'd always been, Victor wiped the sneer off his face and addressed Amalia with scrupulous politeness. "There's nothing you can offer me. You have no control over your and your sister's property, and no ability to dispose of any of it. You may be an heiress, but you have nothing." He glanced at Julián. "Not even my cousin's friendship, if that was what he offered you."

Don Reynaldo's voice was like the crack of a whip. "That's enough. Might I remind you all that we've guests just outside?" He nodded at the dining room's half-closed shutters. Through the slats, Julián could see glimpses of the milling crowd, interspersed by the waiters' more purposeful movements as they navigated their way around the courtyard bearing salvers crowded with champagne flutes.

Even if no one had told him the party was being held by his father, Julián would have guessed, purely from the lavish display. However much of a sham Victor's marriage to Amalia's sister might be, Don Reynaldo never missed an opportunity to make a social splash and have his name in the papers—or to display his wealth.

"You will leave," Don Reynaldo continued, pointing at Julián, "without a single word to any of our guests. I don't know what you were hoping to accomplish by coming here today, but I will not let you ruin the young lady's happy day."

"You're ruining her life and you haven't bothered

to learn her name?" Once upon a time Julián would have paid dearly for the impudent remark. His father had never been violent, but his cold silence was punishment enough when all Julián wanted was a little paternal comfort.

His father looked profoundly weary. "I will have you dragged out if you don't leave immediately, Julián. This affair is none of your concern. As for everyone else… I have to ask that you rejoin our guests."

Evidently thinking there was nothing more to be said, Don Reynaldo began to turn away.

"Wait," Amalia said.

She twisted the ring off and held it out to Julián, jerking her hand away when it brushed his palm. The look in her eyes would have killed him, if he hadn't already felt like he was beyond even death. But it was still not as bad as when she turned to his father, asking, "Has the engagement been announced?"

"Not yet," Don Reynaldo said warily.

"Then I will ask you one thing. Spare Lucía," Amalia said, her voice clear and her gaze fierce. "Spare her, and I'll marry Victor instead."

Chapter Eleven

Julián went home.

Not to the sprawling estate where he'd once lived with his father and cousin, but to the light blue house he had bought when he realized that he'd rather become a wastrel than keep trying and failing to meet his father's expectations. Both its stories were so luxuriously appointed as to make the Troncosos' home look like a pauper's den, especially the set of rooms on the second floor where Julián romanced all of his conquests.

His own bedroom was markedly plainer, if no less comfortable—a feather mattress in a handsome wooden frame, an upholstered armchair by the window and no fussy drapes to block out the sunlight. At the foot of the bed was the leather trunk full of things that had once belonged to his mother. Next to the armchair, a small round table with a lamp and a decanter that he usually kept filled with French brandy. A mahogany armoire and a matching chest of drawers contained his expansive wardrobe, mostly made up of Italian leather shoes and bespoke suits and shirts he'd had tailored during his travels around Spain.

The whole house was modern and bright with electric lights, and with the exception of the married couple he employed to see to the interior and grounds, utterly deserted.

He lost two days to his smoldering resentment. He could feel it festering inside him, as well as the old urge to drown it in drink and women. But his usual pursuits no longer held much appeal. Playing the dissolute rake had been his way of getting his father's attention, at least at first. When it became clear that there was little he could do to satisfy Don Reynaldo's exacting demands, Julián opted for distraction instead.

Now there seemed little point to continue inquiring into the damned mess with Concepción. His charade was over, and so was his investigation. There seemed little point to it now.

Julián should have known that Amalia would volunteer to marry Victor in her sister's stead. She would throw herself into a flaming pyre if it meant keeping Lucía out of it. Nor was he surprised that Victor had accepted her impulsive proposal. His cousin had never had any scruples, and he would think nothing of what it would mean for Amalia's or his own future if it meant taking something away from Julián.

Once again, Julián's life was crumbling to pieces and there was little he could do to shore it back together.

When Concepción left him, Julián had been crushed, as breathless with his pain as if his house had fallen around him and he was trapped under the rubble. It was nothing compared to what he felt now, knowing that Amalia not only despised him, but that she was days away from marrying his cousin, as well.

It was the work of an hour to find out what he'd

suspected—his father had put the Troncosos up at the Hotel Europa, which he had purchased while Julián was away. Why not? He owned practically everything else in town.

Julián didn't waste time in wondering what would have happened if he'd taken Amalia somewhere more circumspect. He'd thought about it—a humble set of rooms like the ones he'd occupied in San Pedro, paid for discreetly in cash. The Europa was one of the few places in Puerto Plata where Julián had halfway pleasant memories, and sentimental fool that he was, he'd wanted what little comfort could be scrounged from them.

The hotel was where his mother used to take him every Friday for lunch. Contrary to what he'd told Amalia, he remembered those afternoons with painful clarity. Victor, who was two years older than Julián, had his French lessons on Fridays, and Don Reynaldo was often working, so it was always just Julián and his mother. He could close his eyes and picture her as she'd looked sitting at a table in the courtyard, bathed in golden light as she laughed and teased him.

Julián remembered them as some of the few moments when he'd felt unreserved joy. When he'd felt safe from his demanding father; safe from Victor's little cruelties...

And then she'd died and he hadn't visited the Europa again until he was old enough to continue the tradition on his own. Julián, who spent most of his days and evenings in the company of his cronies and whatever woman was currently tolerating him, had always gone to the Europa alone. Until now—until Amalia—there hadn't been anyone he'd wanted to share it with.

In any case, she and her sister and her uncle would be at the Europa for the foreseeable future, and Julián was finding it damn difficult to stay away.

In the handful of days that followed the absolute disaster of their arrival in Puerto Plata, Julián walked halfway there three times and turned back each time.

Amalia wouldn't want to see him. He'd made sure of that. As for Julián… He obviously hadn't learned his lesson. Even after seeing the speculation in Victor's eyes, that little glint of triumph when he'd worked out that Amalia and Julián had been more than simple travel companions—even after all that, Julián was still considering lurking in the lobby behind a newspaper, if only for a quick glimpse of her.

He should have been used to this howling loneliness. He'd never stopped feeling it, even when he surrounded himself with the loudest, wittiest, most amusing people. It had all but dissolved in the two days he'd shared with Amalia. Now it was clinging to him again, more unbearable than the suffocating heat.

Every once in a while he would take the necklace Amalia had given him to pawn out of the pocket where he kept it, and the sight of it would remind him of all the strength and courage that ran through her small frame. Thinking about all she had gone through made his own loneliness less desperately unbearable.

It wasn't until the fourth or fifth day that Julián realized that he had one valid excuse for paying the Troncosos a visit—he'd left his carpetbag with Amalia's luggage. He didn't care about the clothes in it, but there was some money there as well as the documents he'd taken from her uncle's desk. Julián snagged his hat from the stand by his front door, and set off for the Europa.

He asked for the Troncosos' rooms at the front desk and was unsurprised when he was told that the family was out for the day.

"I'll wait," Julián said and marched over to the seating area before anyone could tell him he wasn't welcome.

According to the clock set behind the front desk, barely ten minutes had passed before Amalia's uncle strode into the lobby. Julián was up like a shot, intercepting Don Francisco before he could reach the staircase toward which he was heading.

The older man's glance of irritation changed into a scowl when he recognized Julián.

"I was under the impression that you would not be troubling us again, young man." Don Francisco's side whiskers, liberally streaked with gray, were almost quivering with outrage. "Your father assured me—"

"My father has no say in what I do," Julián said as evenly as he possibly could. "He doesn't keep me caged, as you do Amalia and her sister."

Don Francisco's expression remained twisted with obvious dislike. "I would ask you what you want, but it's painfully clear. My niece does not want to see you. Now that your shameless dishonesty has been revealed, I sincerely doubt that she ever will. So if you will kindly step aside..."

Julián had no intention of doing anything of the sort. He stood his ground and said, "She has something of mine and I want it back."

"You ought to have considered that before you inveigled her into doing whatever it is you had her do on your journey here."

"You and I both know that Amalia does exactly what she wants and nothing more. It's a nuisance for you, I expect. What with your flagrant attempts to rob from her and her sister. But I happen to think it's glorious." Julián watched the other man flinch and smiled. "Whatever you tell yourself—or society—about your dealings being all for the benefit of your wards, I hope you're aware that I know the truth. You're robbing them of everything they've got, including their youth and freedom."

Don Francisco remembered his indignation. "How dare you accost me with such lies? The hotel's manager has been instructed by your father to have you hauled away if you so much as stepped inside. I need only call for help."

Julián may not have been a true bandit, but he certainly knew how to behave like one. Lowering his voice into a silky whisper, he said, "My father and cousin are not the only powerful Fuenteses in town. You do anything to hurt Amalia or her sister, and I will make you regret it, Don Francisco. I can promise you that."

Then he spun on his heel and walked away.

The sky was a pure, uninterrupted blue, and Amalia was wishing for rain.

Her limbs were twitching with inaction. She'd done nothing but rest for the three days she and Lucía had been confined to the suite while Tío Francisco and the Fuenteses hammered out the details of her marriage to Victor. Nothing, that was, but desperately try to think of a way out of it.

She and Lucía were sitting in the long, narrow balcony that stretched along their four-room suite. It was a well-appointed set of rooms with upholstered armchairs and costly Tiffany lamps. Lace curtains framed the windows, and the round, marble-topped table by the entrance held an ostentatious bouquet bearing a note from Victor.

To my spirited new fiancée. Looking forward to the wedding.

Amalia wanted to knock it over.

The sound of carriage wheels traveled up from the street below, loud enough that she almost missed Lucía's words when she spoke.

"I hate to think that you've made yourself miserable for my sake."

Lucía was the one who looked miserable, huddled in her chair with a small booklet of sheet music on her lap. Amalia had twined Lucía's hair into a braid that morning, since they had no plans to leave the suite, and the hairstyle made her sister look even younger than her seventeen years.

Amalia leaped up from her own seat, flinging aside the newspaper she had been staring at with sightless eyes.

"I would commit crimes for your sake," she said fiercely. "Move mountains. Glare the sky into submission if thwarting a storm would make you happy."

Lucía bit her lip. "I wish you could. You've had thunderclouds hanging over your head since you got here, and I don't blame you. The very prospect of having to marry that Victor…" She shuddered.

Amalia wanted to swear out loud. The thing hanging above her head wasn't thunderclouds—it was a tempest. And Amalia wanted to rage with it. At her uncle, at the Fuenteses and even at herself, for not having figured out what was happening sooner.

"I can't help but think it's not just marrying Victor that's got you all twisted up, bad enough as that would be," Lucía ventured. "What happened between you and his cousin? I know you said that he escorted you here, and he implied some shocking things, but..."

Shocking. That was one word for what Amalia and Julián had done—not just aboard the ship, but in the two days they'd shared. Amalia was half inclined to call her lack of sense shocking, too.

It had been so easy to let herself get swept away by the thrill of being around him and doing things she'd never imagined she'd be able to. That, Amalia decided, had been Julián's main allure. Her rebellious nature couldn't entirely be chalked up to her circumstances—she'd always gotten a kick out of doing the forbidden. That was the only reason she'd let her guard down around Julián. Not because she'd felt anything for him.

Amalia waved away the thought with a flick of her wrist as she went to lean against the wrought iron railing and peer at the goings-on below. Puerto Plata, or what little she had seen of it, seemed as busy as San Pedro, and the Hotel Europa was clearly a favorite with both the travelers conveyed into town by the great steamships and those from the interior of the island who came for weekend jaunts on the express trains.

Watching people stream in and out was one of the few ways to pass the time, since Tío Francisco would rather she and Lucía not wander around an unfamiliar city, and Amalia was trying hard to appease him by feigning obedience until she worked out her next move.

It had nothing to do with being on the lookout for a dark-haired man.

Amalia frowned. "Julián Fuentes is a liar. And he was just a means to an end." Turning toward Lucía, she explained her reasoning behind the fake kidnapping. "I'm sorry I didn't tell you. It was damn heartless of me to make you worry, but I didn't want you to be in trouble with Tío Francisco if he found out. If I'd known he would be glad to have me out of the way—"

"You didn't know," Lucía said quickly. "You couldn't have. To be honest, I don't think it would have made a difference—he would have found a way to keep you in the dark about what he was planning. He's scared of you, you know. Of what you might do or say."

"Good," Amalia said grimly. "I hope he's terrified. What he's doing to us isn't right, no matter what Papá's will says. We're not his pawns to do whatever he wants with and even if we were, he's terrible at chess. I won't let him ruin both our lives to satisfy his greed."

"It didn't look like Julián was happy about it, either," Lucía pointed out. "If you ask me, I think he almost went into apoplexy when you said you would marry Victor. I saw your face when you looked at him, too. Whatever Julián is to you, you need him more than you think."

"I don't need *anyone*," Amalia said fiercely. "Except for you."

"And I think you liked him more than you care to admit," Lucía continued, with more determination than Amalia thought her sweet, quiet sister had in her. "If he hurt you in some way—"

"He couldn't have," Amalia said, raising her chin. "You have to care for, or about, someone for them to hurt you and I wouldn't give three whistles for Julián Fuentes."

Lucía was giving her a scrutinizing look. "Sometimes I think that the more you like someone, the harder you try to push them away. You do know, Amalia, that everything Tio Francisco says about people only liking us for our money isn't really true. I'd say that especially applies to Julián."

It had taken very little effort—and a couple of conversations with the maids who'd come in to tidy the suite—for Amalia to find out that the FUenteses were railroad tycoons, with a fortune to rival Mr. Vanderbilt's in America. They didn't just own the hotel, they owned land and businesses all through the island, and their influence extended just as far. The gold-and-diamond ring Julián carried around with him, valuable though it clearly was, must have been a trinket compared to the jewels that must have hung around his mother's neck.

"He may not have tried to get close to me for my money, but he still used me," Amalia said tightly, adding, before Lucía could remark on the sudden brightness of Amalia's eyes, "In any case, Julián doesn't matter. I don't plan on ever seeing him again." At Lucía's puzzled look, she elaborated. "I'm not going to marry Victor. I'm going to get my hands on some money, even if I have to rifle through Tio Francisco's pockets or pawn his watch and its gaudy chain. And then you and I are going to get as far away from here as we possibly can."

Lucía looked as if she didn't dare to hope such a thing was possible. Then she glanced over Amalia's shoulder, her eyes widening. Amalia followed her gaze and saw her uncle striding toward them.

Heart racing, Amalia moved back into her chair. He couldn't have heard her speak all the way from the doorway, could he? His expression held nothing more than his usual dourness, though, and Amalia forced herself to relax.

"How were the negotiations?" she asked airily. "Did you trade me for pigs or for sheep? No, wait, I forgot—you're much too business savvy to accept anything less than a herd of cows."

There it was, the furrow that tended to appear between his brows whenever he and Amalia had any kind of exchange. "If you're asking after the health of your betrothed," he said pointedly, "I'm pleased to tell you that he's very well—and that he has extended an invitation for the three of us to join him and Don Reynaldo for dinner at their home."

Amalia immediately resolved to cut the evening short by feigning a headache. "He wouldn't have if he knew what I could do with a fork," she muttered, ignoring the puzzled glance that earned her.

Tío Francisco eased himself into an armchair. "I really hope you'll be sensible on this matter, Amalia—none of your contrariness. I wouldn't have had to go to the lengths I did if you had acted right from the beginning."

"I could say the same," she told him. "If you ask me, I'm getting tired of this little waltz."

As usual, her uncle mistook her meaning. "I'm glad to hear that. Cooperation is all I've ever asked. All I do is for your sakes, you know."

He said it often enough, but Amalia had wondered more than once if he truly believed it.

Knowing that he was five seconds away from a lecture on docility and gratitude, and knowing just as well that in her current mood it would only end in her doing something wildly inadvisable, Amalia rose from her seat. "If you'll excuse me, I'm going to look through my clothes to see if I can find something suitable for dinner. Lu, will you help me?"

Looking happy to abandon their uncle to his own company, Lucía hastened after Amalia. "You're already trying to work out how to skip the dinner, aren't you?" she asked when the door to the bedroom they were sharing closed behind them.

Amalia grinned. "I would, but I wouldn't want to leave you alone with all those snakes."

Her luggage had been unpacked by the hotel's maids, who had folded and hung up her clothing in the large wardrobe in a corner of the room. Neatly stacked below her gowns were her valises and hatboxes—and Julián's ratty old carpetbag, which was a testament to how accomplished a liar he had turned out to be. He hadn't missed a single detail.

As Lucía perched on the bed and continued to peruse her sheet music, humming under her breath, Amalia yanked out the carpetbag and set it on the bed. Ordinarily, she would have never dreamed of going through someone else's things. Under the circumstances, however, she felt justified.

Unsnapping the old clasp, Amalia opened the bag to see that Julián hadn't packed a great deal of clothing. At the time Amalia had imagined he hadn't had more. She knew better now—Julián probably had wardrobes upon wardrobes full of bespoke suits from the best tailors in the country, if not the world.

There were only a couple of neatly pressed shirts in the bag, and some folded linen garments that she set aside hastily, heat rising to her face.

Amalia's embarrassment faded almost immediately as her gaze fell on two stacks of banknotes as thick as a brick, bound together with twine and a paper band stamped with an insignia that she recognized as that of the National Bank.

The money gave her pause. There was enough in there for her and Lucía to live comfortably on for a year or more in a nice little garret in Vienna. Those stacks of bills would solve all their problems. Or if not all, then certainly the most important ones.

But Amalia wasn't a thief.

Pushing the money out of the way, she continued her exploration until she found a sheaf of papers nestled at the bottom of the bag. She would have thought nothing of it, save that the first few lines of handwritten text bore her uncle's name. Amalia pulled out the papers, going through them slowly. They were all letters, and all addressed to Tio Francisco. Julián must have pilfered them from his desk when she'd been distracted looking for Lucía's note.

It only served to remind her that at every step of the way, whether he was proclaiming that he was at her service or kissing her senseless on the steamer's deck, his little errand had always been on his mind. He had used her—Tio Francisco had been quick enough to point that out the day before. He'd also lied. But the most unforgivable thing Julián had done was that he had made her trust him.

And he'd made her forget that nothing good ever came from trusting men.

Her hands were shaking slightly as she put everything back into the carpetbag. *Seek and you shall find.* Wasn't that what they always said? If there was an equally apt saying about throwing your lot in with bandits, Amalia didn't know it.

Her resolve hardened as she stared down at the papers. She was going to confront him—and she was going to make him tell her what these papers were all about. She wanted answers, and she wanted them now.

With a decisive snap, she closed the carpetbag and seized the handle. Sneaking out of the suite wouldn't be easy with her uncle just outside, but she'd done it at home plenty of times. "Lu, will you tell Tio that I've got a headache and will lie down for the rest of the afternoon?"

Lucía looked up from her music, her brows drawing together in apprehension when she saw Amalia holding the bag. "You're going out?"

"Yes, but don't worry, I'll be back in time to dress for dinner."

"Where are you going?"

Amalia gave her sister a grim smile. "To pay a bandit a visit."

Chapter Twelve

It had been far too easy for Julián to slip into his old habit of rising well past noon and sitting down to eat hours after most people had enjoyed their midday meal. He couldn't remember the last time he'd sat in front of a plate of beefsteak with only the ticking of the clock for company. He'd briefly thought about going to one of his usual restaurants, but he couldn't stomach the thought of sitting at a table full of fashionable people and listening to their gossip and stories and jokes and having to pretend to find it all amusing.

A sudden banging at the front door propelled Julián out of the dining room. He reached the entrance before his housekeeper could so much as peek out of the kitchen, which was located at the very back of the house.

Julián was grateful for that when he opened the door and found an heiress on his doorstep.

"Amalia?"

"Were you expecting someone else?" she asked tartly.

She was breathtaking in a dark olive skirt with black

squiggles made out of some sort of braided material and jet beads that matched the trim on her white shirt-waist. Beneath the brim of her straw hat, her gaze was so dispassionate as to be almost cold.

Julián rarely lost his composure, but a smooth greeting was beyond him at the moment. "How the devil did you find out where I live?"

"I followed the scent of *eau-du-liar*," she snapped, and Julián couldn't hold back a grin.

Amalia was beautiful at the best of times. Anger made her resplendent. Part of him wanted to tease her just for the fun of it, but Julián was more aware than ever that he still needed to put distance between them.

"I went to the Europa earlier," he said over his shoulder as he led her to the front room. "Had a nice chat with your uncle. Did he tell you I stopped by?"

Instead of answering, or sitting, Amalia dropped something heavy onto one of the side tables. His carpetbag. Stomach sinking, Julián threw himself on a cane-backed chair. It was too stiff for a proper lounge, but Julián tried his best to strike up the proper insouciant attitude.

Not that Amalia was paying him any attention. She reached inside the bag and flung a stack of papers onto the table with enough force that half of them skidded on the polished wooden surface and cascaded to the floor. "Is this why you came to the hotel? To look for these?"

"In part, yes," he said with a calm he knew she would find maddening. "Much obliged to you, Your Highness. Anything else I can do for you, or would you rather rifle through my wardrobe?"

She placed her hands on her hips. "I'm tired of being lied to. Far be it from me to demand honesty from *you*, but I want you to explain to me exactly what's going on. I tried to read the letters, but there doesn't seem to be anything about business in them. So I'm asking you to tell me—why are our families so determined to see this marriage take place? What do they have to gain by it?"

The shell of anger around her cracked at the last question, letting Julián see past it and into the despair that had been driving her from the moment he had pulled her into his saddle and pretended to abduct her.

Julián wasn't the reason that Amalia and her sister had gotten involved in this mess, but nonetheless he felt like he owed her an explanation. After all, it wasn't like anyone else was going to offer her one.

"It's a very long story, and I've just now begun to piece it together." Julián cocked his head. "Do you think you can stand being around me long enough for me to tell it?"

Amalia crossed her arms. "I'll manage."

Julián, on the other hand, had serious doubts about his ability to be this close to Amalia without letting all the things he shouldn't say tumble out into the space between them. To quell the urge, he went to the decanters set out on a sideboard and poured himself a double whiskey. He thought about the *aguardiente* in the tin mug from the shack, wishing he and Amalia were still there and that the past few days hadn't happened.

"I joined my father's company as soon as I turned seventeen," he began, flattening the long-seated anger out of his tone. "Victor already had, a few years earlier, and he was acquitting himself excellently in my father's eyes by the time I came along. I didn't think I was doing too badly myself—I was never very studious, but I did have a head for figures."

Julián drained the last of his drink with a second deep swallow and immediately poured himself another glass, walking with it over to the window for the simple reason that he needed something as sturdy as the frame around it to prop him up. "I had this absurd notion of making my father proud. But I quickly found out that I didn't have the stomach for the way he and Victor do business. They're ruthless to the point of bloodthirstiness and they think nothing about destroying the life of whoever stands between them and their profit. Victor especially seems to get a thrill from it."

"Just the kind of people my uncle loves to associate with," Amalia said tightly.

"My father's company was awarded the contract to lay the railroad track between Puerto Plata and Santiago around ten years before I started working with him. He made a fortune importing steel, even with import duties being so high, but it didn't take him long to realize that the real money was in the lands the government was purchasing. After President Heureaux was killed in ninety-nine, my father began trying to use his influence with the new government to extend the railroad all the way to San Pedro. He hadn't been successful—until now."

"That must be why he wants our lands so badly," Amalia said, guessing in instants what it had taken Julián days to work out.

"And they'll stop at nothing to get them, not after all they've already done. They have ruined lives for this railroad deal. Including mine. Last year..." Julián's throat was suddenly so tight it took him a few seconds to get the rest of his words out. "I was courting a woman."

Something, perhaps recognition, flickered in Amalia's gaze. "Your young lady from Seville?"

Julián nodded. "She inherited a great deal of land from her grandfather—land that my father knew would be bisected by the new railroad. He wanted to buy it, but the price was more than he could afford."

It flared up again, the rage and the grief that had driven him for the past several weeks. And yearning. There was yearning, too. Not for Concepción, not anymore, but for the life Julián might have led had her affection for him not been stolen away.

A series of thoughts always came on the heels of that one. That maybe nothing had been stolen from him. That he'd never had Concepción's affection. That the affair was always going to end with Julián alone and brokenhearted, because Julián had never done anything to deserve more than that.

If his own father couldn't bring himself to love him, why would anyone else?

As he'd done so often over the past year, Julián tried to drown out his feelings with another sip of whiskey.

"Victor used my proximity to Concepción to get information about the other offers she and her mother were entertaining. And then he and my father hatched a plan to drive the value of her lands down and offer to buy them for a pittance. My father has never been able to countenance having his wishes thwarted, and he knew I would do anything in my power to keep them from cheating Concepción—I'd been a thorn in their side for years by then. Victor arranged it so that my father walked in on me and Concepción in bed. My father pretended not to have known about the affair—and that he was irate that I had seduced a young woman from a good family."

That particular wound was no longer as raw as it had once been, but Julián still recalled the sting of it. "I had been drinking and carousing a little too heavily, and it provided him with another excuse to send me away. Honestly, I was half convinced that someone like Concepción could never truly love a rascal like me, and I was relieved at the excuse to leave before she came to her senses." Julián lifted his shoulder into a shrug, though he knew that Amalia would see past his attempt at appearing unconcerned. "They had to make sure I didn't realize what they were doing because they knew I would try to stop them. So I wasn't there to keep them from driving Concepción and her mother to ruin."

"Why return, then? Why didn't you stay in Puerto Rico?"

"An acquaintance of mine told me that Concepción and her mother had been forced to leave the country and stay with relations in Seville. I wrote to her, and when she didn't answer, I wrote to one of her friends. That's when I found out that Victor had used my departure to turn her against me—to make her believe that I had never cared for her and was only working on my father's behalf."

"Only you did care for her," Amalia said. "She was the only woman you've ever loved."

Her words hung heavily in the air between them. Julián found himself unable to dispel them with one of his smart remarks. It was true, after all... Wasn't it?

With something of a start, he realized that he didn't think about Concepción as often as he once did. Hadn't thought about her, in fact, beyond his speculation of what his father and Victor had done.

Julián had held on to the pain of losing Concepción for close to a year. He hadn't just let it drive him. He had been well on his way to letting it consume him. And maybe it was just that the events of the past few weeks had offered him a distraction as much as a purpose, but he was a little disconcerted to find that the resentment he had harbored for so long had…maybe not faded, exactly, because he still felt strongly about the injustice that had been done to them both. It had changed.

And so had he.

"Right," Julián responded after a lapse of several moments.

It wasn't until he saw Amalia's mouth drawing into a tight line that he realized that she'd been looking for an entirely different answer. And even though he hadn't meant to hurt her—not this time, at least—it was just a matter of time before it happened. No one who got close to him escaped from getting hurt, after all, and why should Amalia be any different?

And in any case, if she really was going to be forced to marry Victor, the more she despised Julián, the less ammunition Victor would have to use against her.

He made himself cock his head. "Oh, Amalia," he said softly. "I thought I had made myself clear. I'm not looking for love, or for marriage, or for anything more meaningful than a night's pleasure."

For a moment Amalia looked like she was contemplating striking him. But all she did was toss her head back, her voice crackling with fury as she said, "Surely, you're not referring to what happened on the ship? That was nothing more than a dalliance. Not even that. It was—" she waved her hand in the air "—nothing more than a momentary lapse of judgment."

A lapse of judgment. Well, she wasn't the only woman to tell him that. And she very likely would not be the last.

"And yet, you're angry with me," Julián said, quirking up his lips into a suggestion of a smirk.

"I'm not," she said. Her upper lip was shaped like an archer's bow and in Julián's opinion it was just about as lethal. When it curled, it was like an arrow flying into his midsection. "If I'm angry at anyone, it's at myself— for believing that I could count on you, and for expecting that you would be any different than every man I've ever known. You're not a good man. You told me so yourself, Julián. You said it over and over again and I refused to listen. But you were right, weren't you?"

Slowly and deliberately, mostly so that she wouldn't notice the slight shaking in his fingers, Julián drained the last of the whiskey from his glass and set it aside. "I hope that made you feel better," he said casually. "It's nothing I didn't already know, though—you'll have to do better than that if you really want to hurt me."

Beneath her frilly blouse, Amalia's breasts were heaving up and down with shallow breaths. A handful of steps put Julián so close to her that she couldn't fail to notice his insolent gaze on her shirtfront.

Her expression shifted, and he curled his lips into a smirk. "If you have nothing more to say, may I suggest that you go back to your hotel? Unless you were hoping I would take you upstairs, in which case I would be more than happy to oblige."

She gazed at him and he knew she felt it, too…the

desire spanning between them that made the air crackle with heat.

The moment stretched, tension mounting between them until Julián had almost convinced himself that she was a second away from falling into his arms. The thought was followed by a rush of anticipation that he had difficulty quelling, though he knew that she would never give him the satisfaction. Not after everything he had just said to her.

And sure enough, Amalia broke the moment not with a kiss, but by giving him a look that by all rights should have withered him on the spot.

"You're despicable," she said, and with one last furious glance at him, turned on her heel and left.

Maybe it was a good thing that every single second they had spent together was engraved in Julián's mind, in luxurious detail, as there was no chance that Amalia Troncoso would ever willingly touch him again.

Enraging. Julián Fuentes was the most enraging man Amalia had ever met.

Now that he had gotten what he could out of her, he had abandoned all pretense of politeness. In fact, it almost seemed like he was doing his best to push her away. If he was, he was clearly doing it to be insufferable—one had only to see Julián around his father and uncle to notice how much pleasure he derived from being contrary.

Of course, anyone could say the same about her and her uncle. But she didn't care to find any common ground with a scoundrel like Julián.

She'd told him the truth when she said she wasn't angry with him. She wasn't even disappointed. If she had been thinking clearly at any point during the past several weeks, she would have seen past the rage and worry and exhaustion filling her and realized that she was breaking one of her cardinal rules.

Don't trust men.

Then again, knowing that he was a liar hadn't kept her from feeling like she would give anything for the pleasure of burrowing into his arms. She had grown too used to relying on him for everything, including comfort. Another minute and she might have found herself giving in to the urge.

Standing outside Julián's door, Amalia took a moment to gain control of the emotions raging inside her chest. A fortnight ago Julián had been nothing to her. Another couple of weeks, and anything she felt toward him now would have dissipated like wisps of smoke.

She didn't need Julián. What was more, she didn't even want him.

In a few hours she would sit at the table with his father and cousin and sip their wine and smile at their jokes. Then, while her uncle slept, she would comb through his luggage for anything of value. By the time the sun rose the next morning, she and Lucía would be on their way elsewhere. Maybe not Europe, as they had dreamed, but even a shack in a mountain somewhere would be preferable to being maneuvered and controlled by Tio Francisco and the Fuenteses.

Having a plan made her feel better. Squaring her shoulders, Amalia finished going down the steps.

She unlatched the iron gate at the front of Julián's house and paused when the sleeve of her shirtwaist caught on one of the twigs protruding from the hedge growing inside the fence. Cursing under her breath, she turned to free the fabric—and realized it wasn't a twig, but a man, and a familiar one at that.

She had just enough time to see the thin red line above his collar where Julián had sliced him with the broken bottle. Then the ruffian from the ship grabbed her by the waist, pinning her arms to her sides.

A rough, heavy hand that smelled vaguely of stewed cod clamped around her mouth before she could let out so much as a breath. Amalia swallowed back her scream, wishing for a fork or a knife or any kind of eating implement, even a spoon, as she tried and failed to drive the heel of her shoe into his instep.

The ruffian lifted her bodily off the ground and swung her toward one of the carriages lining the street. Amalia bucked wildly, kicking out ineffectually as she was stuffed into the carriage and the door slammed shut.

Her heart was pounding as she shakily hauled herself onto the seat. She ran her hand over the carriage door to find that the inner handle had been pried off, and the truth of what had just happened shuddered through her.

She was being kidnapped—this time in truth.

Chapter Thirteen

"Amalia, wait!"

The slam of his front door drowned out his words. Julián's body tensed with the need to run after her, but what was the use? He needed to make her hate him and judging by the look in her eyes, he had clearly succeeded.

If there was one thing Julián had always been able to do well, it was making himself disagreeable to everyone around him.

Julián stayed by the window, gripping the frame until his fingertips hurt as he tried to will himself not to care. Not about Amalia, not about the fact that she and her sister were about to be cheated out of their inheritance, and most decidedly not about the giant tear in his chest.

He almost didn't hear a muffled cry coming from the direction of his front gate. Sharply, Julián glanced outside in time to see Amalia being seized by a man in a brown suit.

A string of curses rolled out of his mouth as he vaulted out the window and pelted to the swinging gate. By the time he had shoved it open and thrust himself through it, though, Amalia had been bundled into a waiting carriage. One snap of the reins and the two horses at its head were galloping away.

Julián swore again, though a great deal more breathlessly than he had a moment before.

The carriage was plain black with no distinguishing marks, the horse pulling it, ordinary. He hadn't gotten a good look at the man who'd grabbed her, but he would be willing to bet a large portion of his fortune that it had been the ruffian from the ship. They'd assumed the man had been sent by Amalia's uncle, but now that he knew just how deeply Victor was involved in this whole business, Julián was damned sure who was behind this.

He didn't bother with his hat and jacket. Mounting his sleek, dark horse, which was hitched in front of his house, he galloped to the commercial property that housed his father's offices.

The three-story building occupied one of the busiest corners in town. Above one of its doors, which had been set at a forty-five-degree angle from the two on either side, a painted sign bore the name *Reynaldo Fuentes & Hijo*. The latter part had always twinged unpleasantly through Julián whenever he happened to look at it, as it served as one more reminder that he had never been the kind of son his father wanted. It must have affected Victor a similar way, though Julián had never asked.

Now, though, as Julián flung himself off the saddle and stormed inside, he hardly spared it a glance.

The front room was lined neatly with desks and bookcases stuffed with ledgers; bypassing these without a word for any of the clerks who voiced their protests to his intrusion before they recognized him, Julián thundered upstairs and to the glass-paned door at the end of the second-floor hallway.

"Where did they take her?" he demanded as he shoved open the door.

But it wasn't Victor sitting behind the massive mahogany desk, it was his father.

Looking neither startled nor alarmed at the intrusion, Don Reynaldo flicked his fingers in dismissal and the young clerk who had been taking notes on the other side of the vast desk hastily gathered his things and exited, closing the door softly behind him.

For a long moment the only sound in the room was the *snick* of the latch as it caught. Then Julián's father lifted an eyebrow. "Am I to guess what you mean by bursting into my office, or did you intend to offer an explanation?"

The two wooden chairs in front of the desk were now vacant, but Julián remained where he was. "Amalia Troncoso was just kidnapped exiting my house," he said, shaping each word around the gaping wound left behind by the sight of Amalia being hauled into that carriage like a sack of plantains. "There's no doubt in my mind that Victor is behind it."

"So you came here demanding to know her whereabouts. I wish I could say I was surprised, but you have always been transparent as glass."

And Don Reynaldo was as hard and unmoving as a boulder.

Outside his father's office, Julián could hear the clatter of typewriters, interrupted now and then by the clerks' hushed voices as they went about their business.

Because the world hadn't stopped when Amalia was taken; only Julián's heart.

He had paused to marshal his thoughts into some semblance of order, but now he took a moment to consider his father's expression. It was something Julián had done for as long as he'd had reason—for years he had studied his father with more scrutiny than his schoolbooks, intent on finding the secret to pleasing him. Don Reynaldo was reserved, but Julián had learned to read every slight twitch of his eyebrows and minuscule tightening of his mouth.

"It wasn't Victor," Julián said slowly. "It was you who gave the order."

Only a jerk of his fingers on the leather blotter betrayed the fact that his father was not, in fact, a boulder. "I'm sure I don't have to tell you that this deal with the girl's uncle is as delicate as it is important. Whatever you may feel for the girl—"

"I don't feel anything for her," Julián said, and knowing his protest sounded hollow, added, "but she does for me. She's headstrong and stubborn and will keep making trouble for you as long as her sister is involved. I can assure you that whatever you've asked that ruffian to do isn't enough to hold her back."

Don Reynaldo's eyes narrowed ever so slightly.

"Amalia isn't easily manipulated, but she has grown to trust me, and she dislikes Francisco. If I marry her, I will be better positioned legally to get rid of him. Bypass him altogether and you won't just have the lands you need—you'll have her entire fortune. Which, as I understand, includes plenty of property for development. I'd want seventy percent, of course," he added offhandedly, knowing his father could never resist a negotiation.

"Thirty," Don Reynaldo said automatically, and Julián held back a triumphant smile, "as I'd have to put up the capital."

The elder man sat back in his chair, fingers steepled together in thought. Julián knew he shouldn't push, or seem too eager, but every second that ticked by was one more second in which Amalia was alone in the company of that brute.

"It's not a bad scheme," Don Reynaldo said, and his eyes seemed to bore into Julián's. "Though I'm not altogether convinced that your reasons are purely mercenary. She is a very attractive girl, after all."

Everything in Julián revolted at the implication. He would have liked to slam out of that room—maybe he would have, if he hadn't been so worried for Amalia. This time, however, he was going to play his father's game. And he was going to win.

"The journey from San Pedro wasn't a chaste one, if that's what you're referring to," he made himself say casually. "I wouldn't object to sharing her bed in the long term." Sauntering to the desk, he laid both palms against its gleaming surface. "I can carry this off far better than Victor, and you know it. Force is effective in its own crude way, but it *is* a risk. Do things his way, and you open yourself up to speculation, at the very least, or a social outrage—Amalia will make sure of it. Make her believe I'm working on her behalf, and we have her full cooperation."

Don Reynaldo gave a thoughtful nod. "Victor is obedient and moldable. But he's not nearly the asset you would be if you weren't so softhearted. Triumph in business, as well as in life, requires a certain ruthlessness. You've never had it, Julián. What makes you think you have what it takes now?"

Julián gave his father a slight, humorless smile, glad that he had waited to confront him over Concepción. "I lost my head over Concepción, and paid for it by spending almost a year in exile. I like to think I've grown up since then. I know what it is to stand in your path now, and I'm not fool enough to think that a woman is worth the consequences."

His father didn't say anything, just looked at him. Julián had been on the receiving end of those looks long enough that he knew not to try to fill the silence with exhortations, promises or explanations. He emptied his body of all thoughts and simply gazed back.

"I had hoped you'd learned a thing or two," Don Reynaldo said finally. "It seems like perhaps you have."

Julián jerked his head into a nod. "I do have conditions, of course. If I've learned anything else over the past year, it's to never give anything for nothing. The first is that you sell me the Europa. In its entirety. I want to be the sole proprietor. The second..." He hardened his voice. "Get rid of Victor."

A slight twitch of his father's lips that could have been the beginnings of a smile made Julián turn around. It was only then that he realized that at some point during the conversation, the door behind him had opened. It wasn't a clerk at the doorway, but Victor, standing still as a snake that hadn't decided how to strike.

Julián turned back to his father, who had a clear view of them both. Don Reynaldo had always played them against each other, perhaps believing that would make them stronger. Julián, who had seen the way

Amalia cared about her sister, couldn't help but think that his father had been deeply mistaken. Maybe, under different circumstances, he and Victor might have been able to be friends.

"Is that your way of saying that you agree to my terms?" Julián asked his father, who looked faintly amused.

"Show me that you're serious about it," Don Reynaldo answered. "And I'll consider it."

Julián couldn't fail to notice that Victor hadn't said a word. "Where is she?"

To his surprise, his father answered. "The train station."

That was all he needed.

Victor didn't step aside as Julián exited, so he shouldered past him, walking out with his stride unbroken.

For once in her life Amalia was doing exactly what she was told.

Granted, it was only because of the knife being pressed against her lower back, but she still felt like she deserved some credit.

"You do know," she told the ruffian who'd abducted her, in as conversational a tone as she could muster when her heart was racing inside her chest, "that the boning in my corset will probably bend that cheap knife of yours if you tried to stab me with it."

There was nothing cheap about the heavy blade and the ruffian must have been clear on that point, because all he did was grunt.

He had been about as gregarious on the carriage ride to the train station where they stood. She had seen the single-story building from the carriage when she and Julián first arrived in Puerto Plata. It was hard to believe only a scant few days had passed since then when so much had changed. She'd lost Julián, or the person she had believed him to be, and now she was on the verge of losing what little hope she'd had of getting away with Lucía.

The station was crowded with families in a flurry of departure and uniformed porters rushing to and fro with carts laden with luggage. Quite a few people had already boarded the train, and the open windows of each car were full of travelers waving goodbye to those they were leaving behind.

All save for the car toward which the ruffian was guiding her. Dark blue curtains with tassels shielded its interior from prying eyes, so it wasn't until Amalia stepped inside, past a man standing to one side like a guard and through a narrow, carpeted corridor, that she saw that instead of a row of seats, it contained an opulent parlor.

Paneled in gleaming mahogany, with brass fittings and tasseled curtains at the window, it held an imposing desk on one side below a large oil painting in an ostentatious gold frame, and a seating area in the other. The furniture was finely crafted, the upholstered seats plush and comfortable.

The man sitting stiffly on one of the armchairs, on the other hand, looked out of place and ill at ease.

"So it's true," Tio Francisco said heavily as Amalia was pushed the rest of the way into the car. "You defied my orders about staying in the suite—and to go to Julián Fuentes, of all people. I didn't want to believe it, but I've learned to be cautious when it comes to you."

Amalia heard the *snick* of the door shutting behind

her, and she felt her shoulders relax at the relief of no longer having a knife against her back. "You didn't tell me he'd come to the hotel."

The air inside the car was stale and smelled vaguely of cigar smoke. There were plenty of places for Amalia to sit, but she felt better standing. A small part of her wanted to take a page out of Julián's book and lounge insolently against the paneled walls, just to see if it would get a rise out of Tío Francisco.

"He didn't come for you," her uncle said curtly. "He doesn't care for you, and if you think he's going to look out for you instead of himself—"

"I don't," Amalia said crisply, but she could tell that he didn't believe her.

"Amalia," he began, and she tensed at the patient, reasonable tone that he employed when he wanted to imply that she was being the exact opposite. "I'm not an unfeeling sort of man. I remember what it was like to be young. And I understand that my efforts to shelter you and Lucía from the ravages of fortune hunters and other opportunists have been so zealous that neither of you has had the opportunity to learn much about human nature. Julián Fuentes is not a good man. His own father despairs of him. He's trying to sow discord within his family and he's using you to do that. Whatever he may have said to put you up to this—"

Amalia's eyes narrowed. "If by this you mean saving Lucía from an unwanted marriage, I can assure you that Julián had no part in it."

Tío Francisco gave her a brief, infuriating smile. "I'm sure that's what he's led you to believe. You needn't feel embarrassed about falling for his manipulations. Men like him always know to target naive young—"

"What is this about?" Amalia demanded impatiently, noting in satisfaction her uncle's irritation at being interrupted yet again. "Did you have me kidnapped and forced aboard a train just to give me a lecture? You could have saved yourself the trouble—I was on my way back to the hotel to get ready for the blasted dinner with your new friends. I'm doing everything you've asked of me—"

"You've been planning to abscond with your sister," Tio Francisco snapped. "I heard the two of you plotting earlier. You had no intention of marrying Victor, and I would appreciate if you stopped lying about it." He took a deep breath, as if to gather his patience. "Women like you and Lucía have a responsibility to your families. I have tried my hardest to raise you to consider more than just yourselves—it would be the height of selfishness for you both to insist on a love match."

For a long moment Amalia couldn't do anything but stare at her uncle. Selfish? He thought they were selfish for not wanting to submit quietly to a life they hadn't chosen? She couldn't tell if he truly believed that, or was only saying so for her benefit.

Maybe it didn't matter. Both were bad enough.

And in any case, he hadn't raised her—her parents had. When her father died, a year after her mother, Amalia had been thirteen and more than old enough to look after her sister. All Tio Francisco had looked after was their money, which he clearly prized more than his nieces.

"A union between us and the Fuenteses is mutually beneficial," he continued, firm under her incredulous gaze. "This arrangement will make you and Lucía very rich women indeed. You'll be able to do anything you like…buy anything you want."

"*You* certainly will," Amalia bit out, finally finding her voice. Tio Francisco didn't understand—he never had. More money didn't always mean more freedom. It meant more obligations and never knowing if someone liked you for yourself. "I hope you're being paid well for this. I hope you're getting everything you ever wanted. Because we're not your property to sell or trade as you see fit, and one day I will give you cause to regret having ever treated us as such."

Amalia half expected her uncle to launch into his usual performance designed to show her that she was being unreasonable—he stifled sighs, pinched the bridge of his nose, massaged his temples as if to ward off incipient headaches and, something she found supremely annoying, he injected a hint of scorn into his tone to convey just how absurd he found her.

He didn't do any of those things. If anything, he just looked furious. "I've given you girls *everything* and that's never been enough for you. And now you're doing your best to poison your sister's mind."

"Lucía has a mind of her own," Amalia snapped. "She's been very clear about not wanting to marry Victor, or anyone else. If you go through with this, I'll do what I should have done from the start. I'll go to the gossip papers. I'll tell everyone I know—everyone *you* know—that you put your greed above your nieces' happiness."

Tio Francisco's face, normally a pale brown lighter than Amalia's own, reddened until he looked like he was going to burst.

Amalia had never seen her uncle like this. Irritated beyond reason at one or another of her exploits, yes. Even angry. But he had never glowered at her with such virulent dislike. He leaned forward, his eyes on Amalia's, his voice low and hard.

"And who would believe you? I have been nothing but devoted to the two of you, and all of San Pedro society would attest to that fact. Whereas you have only done what pleases you, with little regard for how it reflects on your family. Are you willing to damage your sister's reputation as well as your own, just for the sake of getting your own way? Will she thank you for that? When she's cast out of good society, starving in some garret and forced to play her violin on street corners for crusts of bread, will she be grateful or will she resent you for ruining her life?"

Amalia reared back, feeling as though she'd been slapped.

Her uncle wasn't finished. "I'm done trying to reason with you, Amalia. You have tried to undermine me and my plans from the moment your father left me in charge and it's clear you're never going to stop. I spoke with Reynaldo and Victor earlier, and they have agreed to release you from your engagement. I'm sure you understand why I can't allow you to return to the hotel."

Amalia clenched her fists so hard her nails left bloody half circles on her palm. "Will you at least tell me where I'm being taken?"

"This is the express train to Santiago. The journey won't be long, and you will be made comfortable once you're there." Tio Francisco stood. "I'd instructed my men to keep you there until the wedding is over—but if living by my rules is so intolerable, then I should probably consider finding you permanent living arrangements elsewhere. You did say something about Europe this afternoon, if I recall correctly."

"You can't do this." She struggled to sound defiant through the anger and frustration coalescing inside her. Amalia Troncoso didn't cry. She *never* cried. "I won't let you."

"I regret the necessity of doing this, Amalia, but you have forced my hand. The men won't harm you—unless you give them cause."

With those ominous parting words, Amalia's uncle let himself out of the compartment, closing the door firmly behind him. Amalia didn't bother to try it. Even if it wasn't locked, she knew that the ruffians would be waiting on the other side.

A few moments later the train began to roll away from the station, taking Amalia far away from her sister and any hope of getting her out of this mess.

Chapter Fourteen

If the hardy horse Julián had bought in San Pedro had been fit for a bandit, the thoroughbred he kept in Puerto Plata was perfect for the son of a railroad tycoon. Sleek and beautiful and expensive, it was also fast.

And Julián was desperate.

The train whistled just as he arrived at the station. Julián looked wildly at the windows, hardly daring to hope—

There. He caught a glimpse of her a fraction of a second before the air between them was filled with steam. She was in the third car from the end, which had long ago been designated as his father's private car. Through the window's filmy glass, Amalia looked as he had never seen her—utterly discouraged.

Julián's heart lurched. And in a split second, he made his decision.

He never wore spurs, out of principle, and he had no need of them now. A single nudge to the racehorse's flank was enough to make him explode into motion. He bent down low over the saddle as they leaped nimbly over a low fence and galloped after the train as it started to slowly pull out of the station.

It was much smaller than some of the great locomotives he'd seen in other parts of the world. The last couple of cars were made out of wood, and probably held luggage and some sort of cargo.

The roar of the train had become the roar of his own heart. As its engine belched coal into the blazing sky, Julián's entire world narrowed to one of the two iron poles jutting out from the back of the car. He had a single attempt and only a few moments to do it—once the locomotive reached its full speed, there wasn't a scrap of chance that he'd be able to overtake it.

Fail, and he'd break an arm or a leg or both and be of no use to Amalia or himself.

Another nudge and his horse put on a burst of speed, unflappable even as they neared the locomotive's chugging wheels. Julián stood up on the stirrups, holding the reins in one hand and reaching for the pole with the other. His fingers brushed the iron, a mere centimeter too far for him to grasp it.

Just a little farther—

The moment the palm of his hand connected with the pole, Julián flung himself off his saddle and onto the small platform at the back of the cargo car.

He slammed hard against the sun-warmed wood. The impact, or the leap, or the utter foolishness of what he'd just done, snatched his breath away, and he had to lean back against the car for a few minutes until his worry for Amalia forced him back into action.

As quickly as he could, Julián clambered to the top of the car and made his way past the hair-raising gap between each car to where Amalia was being held. Julián hadn't traveled with his father in years, but he remembered the layout of the car well enough, as well as his father's preference for keeping his staff separate from himself so that he could conduct business in private.

He also remembered the accident that had led to his father installing a hatch on the roof of his car.

The late-afternoon sun was beating down on his bare head, sending rivulets of sweat streaming down his temples in spite of the warm breeze that buffeted the damp hair around his face. The desperation and audacity that had allowed him to leap aboard a moving train was quickly fading away, and memories were rushing like waves over the sand to fill in the space they had left behind.

The sickening jolt. The weightless sensation of being flung into the air. And—worst of all—the sound of crunching metal, underlaid by the screams of agony he still heard in his dreams.

Julián sagged to his knees. The locomotive was no longer a roar in his ears, but a live beast charging beneath his braced hands, ready to buck him off at any moment.

With fingers that had grown suddenly clumsy, he scrabbled for the hatch—the hinges had been set so that it could be pushed or kicked open from the inside. He grasped the latch, yanked it to one side and then he was sliding through the opening and dropping onto the compartment's thick carpeting.

He landed on his feet, but the jostling of the train cost him his balance and he found himself pitching right into Amalia.

Her curves provided him a cushioned landing. He slid down her body until he was kneeling between her thighs in a position that was quickly becoming a familiar one.

The devil himself knew there was nowhere else he would rather be.

He took one look at her wide, panicked eyes and covered her mouth with his palm to silence the scream that would bring her captors running. And then he made himself grin, because it was either that or let out his own howl.

"Missed me, Your Highness?"

Above his hand, Amalia's face was a study in shock. Her breath was quick and hot against his palm as he released her mouth and skimmed her cheekbone and the line of her jaw, telling himself he was only making sure that she was unharmed. Her creamy brown skin was unblemished and unbroken, as perfect as it had been on the day he'd met her. But her eyes were rimmed with red, and that proof of her distress was enough to make him vow to rain down vengeance on Victor, his father, her uncle and everyone who'd ever wronged her.

Reaching down, Amalia twined her graceful fingers in the fabric of his shirt and used it to pull him toward her. For the space of a breath, maybe two, they stared at each other, swaying slightly along with the train as it raced on.

"I'm sorry," she said in a rush. "I'm so sorry for what I said. I didn't mean it—and I thought I'd never see you again to tell you so."

And then their mouths were meeting with violent desperation. Greedily, Julián drank in the taste of her lips, the soft plushness of her thighs beneath his spread hands.

Amalia was clinging to him like he was one of the life preservers he'd seen hanging on the deck of the

S.S. New York. And Julián was holding on just as tightly, half-afraid that he would drown in the waves of desire as he stole kiss after kiss from her.

But it wasn't stealing, was it, when it was so freely given?

Julián's heart seized with a pleasure that felt almost like pain. He'd never expected her to direct another word at him, much less for something like this to happen. Another man might have taken it as his due, especially after what he'd just done, but Julián knew that kissing Amalia Troncoso was a privilege—and that he would do much more than jump into a moving train for the right to do it again and again.

Amalia made a little sound in her throat. Her grip on his shirt tightened for one long moment. Then she flattened her palms against his chest and pushed him away.

She did it lightly enough, but Julián responded at once to the repudiating touch and cast himself backward, forgetting about the armchair behind him. All the furniture had been nailed to the floor, so it didn't budge, but he did crack the back of his head against its wooden frame.

He swallowed back a curse at the sudden pain flaring through his head, then remembered it was Amalia in front of him and went ahead and cursed out loud. Another woman would have probably shot him a disapproving glare, but Amalia merely looked interested at this evidence of his prodigious vocabulary.

His hair was already so disheveled that rubbing his head made little difference. "My apologies," he said, even though he hadn't been the one to initiate the kiss. "I was overcome with emotion."

He hauled himself into the leather armchair, feeling

every muscle in his body protest the slight effort—he led a more active life than most, but even his body had its limits. "For what it's worth, I'm the one who should be sorry. I was trying to hurt you. And I—"

"Succeeded," she said and clamped her lips together, casting a glance toward the door.

Julián answered her unspoken question. "They won't hear us over the sound of the train. My father had the compartment soundproofed so that he could conduct business in here without worry of being overheard."

Amalia acknowledged it with a nod. "How in the world did you get up there?"

He shrugged. "Did some acrobatics—isn't that how all the fashionable people board trains these days?"

Her frown made it clear that she didn't appreciate his attempt at humor. "How did you find me? How did you know where I was?"

"A bandit has his ways," Julián said. He tried to punctuate his flippant remark with an equally offhand smile and failed miserably. He was so tired of dissembling and pretending and turning everything into a joke. "I went to my father. He told me where you were in exchange for me saying everything he's always wanted to hear—that I was finally ready to stop being such a wretched disappointment and pull my own weight in the company."

"Did you mean it?"

Julián shook his head. "I was lying through my teeth the whole time. I'm very good at that, as I'm sure you'll remember."

That earned him—not a smile, exactly, but something approximating one.

"Well," she said a little grudgingly. "You may be a lying scoundrel, but you are brave."

"Brave?" Julián's head ached. For that matter, his thighs and biceps were also in agony. The motion of the train—or maybe just the knowledge that he was in one—was making him want to pitch himself out the window. The hell with trying to pretend that he didn't want her. "I'm a wretched coward, Amalia. If I'd truly been brave, I would have let you walk out of my life. I would have stayed away from your hotel and refused to let you inside when you came to my house this morning. Or even better—I would have turned around when I saw Victor follow you and your sister into the hotel's dining room instead of bursting in there and making everything worse. Everything I've done, from the moment you glared at me when I gave you that glass of *aguardiente* when you'd asked for water, has been out of fear of losing you."

She'd been staring at him as he spoke. With a little hitch of her breath, as if she'd realized she was staring, she looked away. "That was a very nice speech," she said in a tone chilly enough to fuel an entire ice factory. "Pardon me for not swooning."

"I didn't expect you to. And I don't expect you to forgive me." Julián scraped his hair back. "I know I went about it all the wrong way. I should have told you everything from the beginning and I should have never hidden my identity from you."

She cocked her head and let another arrow fly from those bow-shaped lips of hers. "That would imply there's ever a time when you're truly yourself. Do you have any idea of who the real Julián Fuentes is?"

This wasn't the first time she had laid him utterly

and uncomfortably bare with a single look. "I don't know," he said after a moment. "But I do know that whoever that person is, the closest I've ever come to being him has been when I'm around you."

Amalia didn't know what to say. Was he being manipulative, or had he actually decided to try honesty for once?

Even now, after everything that had happened, she longed to experience what she had on the night they'd spent together—that surge of power and strength that had come from surrendering herself to his embrace.

But for every bit of her that wanted to throw herself into Julián's arms, there was a much larger part screaming at her to hold back.

As warm as it was inside the compartment, the temperature had risen noticeably with his presence. He had literally dropped in, windblown and dashing and looking every inch the bandit in his shirtsleeves, without a hat or even a necktie. Amalia's surprise at the sudden—and not altogether unwelcome—intrusion had gone to her head. That was the only reason she'd kissed him.

That, and the hot, undeniable, inescapable desire that had flooded her as soon as his body had come into contact with hers.

She took a steadying breath, trying not to notice how the scent of Julián's cologne, underlaid by faint traces of his exertion, cut through the stale, cigar-tinged air of the compartment. Then, instead of trying to find a way to answer his declaration, she opted to change the subject.

If he was a coward, then so was she.

"Any ideas on how we're going to get out of here?"

"I'm not going to jump out of a moving train with you in tow, if that's what you're asking," Julián returned, looking like an arrogant young aristocrat as he sprawled back on the leather upholstery. The man could do many things, but sitting upright did not seem to be one of them. "It'll be dark when we get to Santiago— it won't be too hard to slip away then."

"There are two men outside the compartment," she said. "They—"

"Have pistols, yes. I expected as much," Julián said. "I'm entirely unarmed, save for my dashing smile, and somehow I don't think that'll be enough to keep them from shooting at me."

Amalia stared at him, feeling disconcerted. "You're unarmed, and yet risked your life coming in here."

"I couldn't let them take you away," he said simply. "I would have done much more than that for you."

"Why?" she burst out. She could understand it when he'd been a bandit waiting for his payment. But surely, he had gotten everything he wanted from her.

"Because I would rather die than be one more in the long list of men in your life that have done you wrong. Because I—"

"Don't, Julián," she said quickly, tamping down the champagne-bubble flutters rising into her chest. "Don't say another word. I don't want to know how you feel— I don't *care*. I have things to do, and I can't afford to let you distract me more than you already have. This would have never happened if I hadn't gone to your house today."

"None of this is your fault, Amalia," he said, looking flinty.

Amalia had gotten so used to his calling her *Your*

Highness that her heart gave a little jump at the sound
of her name as it tumbled from his lips. Her eyes lingered on them for a brief moment, watching them
tighten.

"But it is my fault," she said. "I convinced them that
I was willing to marry Victor, though I never planned
to go through with it. I had it all worked out—I was
going to sneak money out of my uncle's wallet and
spirit Lucía away. But I *had* to go to your house instead of sending a messenger. I told myself there was
no other way to find out the truth, but what difference
does knowing what they wanted make? And now I've
ruined the last chance I had of preventing them from
carrying out their damned plan."

Amalia realized she was trembling. Taking a slow,
deliberate breath, she pressed her palms onto the seat
on either side of her skirt.

Julián was shaking his head. "My father had no intention of letting you marry Victor—he thinks you're
too difficult to control. They only pretended to accept
as a ploy to keep you quiet while they worked out how
to get you out of the way. And now that they suspect
how much you mean to me..." He leaned forward in his
seat. "I'm not sure you understand quite how powerful my father is, or how far his reach extends. Or how
ruthless he can be when he really wants something."

Amalia tilted up her chin. "My uncle said I won't
be hurt."

"That may be what he thinks. But don't you see?
It's my father who's in charge here and he wouldn't
hesitate to do anything to get you out of the way. And
he knows it won't be enough to keep you out of town
for a day or two, not when you've proven that you're

willing to make trouble for them at every step of the way. You're just as much a thorn in their sides as I ever was," he added.

"You really have a way with compliments," Amalia muttered.

But Julián didn't seem to have heard her.

"My father won't stop," he continued intently. "He will never stop. And I can assure you that he is prepared—even willing—to flatten any obstacles in his way. As for Victor…" His lips compressed into a thin line. "He wouldn't hesitate to compromise your sister ahead of the wedding if it would ensure that no one would object to it."

Amalia recoiled. "You really don't think he would do such a despicable thing."

"He's done worse," Julián said flatly. "Victor is the kind of person who reads *The Prince* a couple of times and fancies himself as cunning as Machiavelli. He likes to think he's a great strategist and a manipulator, but he's just a nasty little *lacra* who has grown too used to trampling over everybody."

His words filled her with a dawning horror. Suddenly, Amalia couldn't keep still. Leaping to her feet, she began to pace on the dark green carpet. "I have to get out of here. We have to get out of here."

She had already roamed around the compartment, poking into corners and opening the desk drawers, and had found nothing but an old newspaper, a half-empty box of matches and a withered cigar. She went through it all again, though what she was hoping to find, she didn't know.

"He never keeps anything important in here," was Julián's contribution from the other side of the compartment. "Though he and Victor are the only ones who ever use this car."

"I'm really not looking for anything. I just—"

Feeling suddenly stifled, Amalia yanked at the tasseled curtains until they parted enough to let her open the window. Letting the warm breeze tug her hair into disorder, she leaned her palms on the window frame and looked up. It must have been later in the afternoon than she thought, because shades of orange and crimson were starting to stain the pure blue of the sky.

The rolling landscape was bright in the golden light, save for the dark outlines made by the clusters of palms jutting out from fields of crops that Amalia would have probably recognized if they were on her plate as opposed to hidden behind leaves.

"You're not going to hurl yourself out the window, are you?" Julián asked behind her.

"I'm considering it," Amalia said curtly.

She pulled the curtain open farther, letting in a wash of brightness, and turned in irritation as Julián made a small noise.

It was only as her gaze fell on him that she noticed his shallow breaths. He had crossed his legs, but his grip on the armrest was tight and his chiseled jaw was clenched so hard, it was a wonder it hadn't snapped.

She had noticed the strain in his eyes earlier, and had assumed it had something to do with the conversation. But it was evident now that what she had taken for annoyance was actually something closer to panic.

It came to her as suddenly as a crack of lightning— on the deck of the ship, he'd told her that his mother had died in a railroad accident. "You were there," she blurted out. "When your mother was—"

Julián's face went blank—the expression of a man who'd trained himself not to reveal any weaknesses. Then his head jerked into a nod. "I was there. And I didn't—I wasn't able to—"

Amalia felt her heart constrict as she guessed at the words Julián didn't seem able to say out loud. Could it be that he felt guilty—or had been made to feel guilty—for not having done more to save his mother, even though he'd been so young when the accident happened? Having met his father, she didn't find it difficult to believe that he'd been capable of blaming his six-year-old son for whatever had happened then.

"I'm sorry," she said instead of giving voice to her thoughts. "I wouldn't have opened the curtains if I'd known." She gave the curtains a hasty yank to close them and was dismayed when the fabric tore away from the brass rings, leaving half a windowpane uncovered.

Julián's jaw tightened as he averted his gaze from the landscape speeding by. "I'll be fine. I just…need a little distraction."

The thoughts that went through Amalia's mind at the word *distraction* made heat rush immediately to her face. Her skin was too dark to show it—she hoped—but Julián had an irritating aptitude for reading the most minuscule changes in her expression.

Abruptly, she stood up again, holding out a hand. He glanced at it, clearly puzzled.

"You won't feel the motion as much if you're also moving," she explained and gave her hand an impatient shake. "I'm not asking you to waltz, Julián—pacing up and down will be enough."

His hand slid into hers. His fingers were long and elegant, but she could feel the roughness of the calluses that had formed where reins rubbed against his palm. It may not have been the hand of a bandit, scored with evidence of a hard life, but neither did it belong to an arrogant young aristocrat.

Maybe his real self was somewhere in between.

After tucking his hand into the crook of her elbow, Amalia towed him along as she resumed her earlier pacing. He walked with his usual leonine grace, but his grip on her was tight.

"I never told you why I decided to pretend to be a bandit," he said suddenly.

She made a noise that sounded suspiciously like a snort. "You never told me a lot of things."

"Fair enough." Julián raised an eyebrow. "I used to climb a lot of trees when I was a boy—mostly to get away from Victor. I was so small for my age I used to be able to shimmy up to the very tops of the palm trees in our estate. It helped, for a while, until Victor decided to throw stones at me one day. I fell and broke my arm and couldn't climb until it had healed."

Looking at him now, with his head almost brushing the compartment's upholstered ceiling, Amalia found it hard to believe. Her own head didn't reach much higher than the distracting curls that brushed the top of his collar—which meant, she couldn't help but notice, that the hollow at the base of his throat was exactly at her eye level.

"Is that where you got…?" Amalia's fingers fluttered near Julián's temple as she gestured to his scar.

He shook his head. "I didn't get that until a few years later, and that was mostly due to my trying to show off in front of a girl." He gave her a rueful smile. "Beautiful women have always been my downfall."

Amalia harrumphed, and Julián's smile widened.

"In any case, back then Victor was much bigger than me, and had longer legs, so I couldn't outrun him. One day it got so bad I ran into the horse paddock and climbed up on one of my father's racehorses, determined to get as far away from Victor as I could."

"Did you?"

"Almost fell and broke my other arm," Julián replied. "I would have, if it hadn't been for the head groom. Miguel had seen Victor tormenting me, and had been wanting to intercede on my behalf but hadn't known how to do it without reprimanding Victor—he had a nasty habit of making trouble for anyone who dared reprimand him."

"Typical," Amalia remarked.

"I could ride well enough, but Miguel had fought in the War of Restoration, back in sixty-three, and he knew all kinds of wild tricks. Soon, I was rushing out to the horse paddock once the tutor released Victor and me from our lessons and spending entire afternoons with the grooms, goading each other into performing one outlandish stunt after another. I'd never experienced that sort of camaraderie, and before long my visits to the horse paddock ceased to be about escaping Victor and more about enjoying their company."

They reached the end of the compartment for a second time and turned back to retrace their steps. Talking did seem to be getting Julián's mind off his discomfort, though Amalia knew that talking about his past always seemed to cause its own distress. Having met Victor and Don Reynaldo, Amalia could certainly understand why.

"How nice," Amalia said softly.

"It was—for a time. Victor told my father, of course,

and it went just about how you'd imagine it. Miguel was sent away, and the others had their pay docked for wasted time. My father made sure I knew that I wasn't their friend, just a nuisance they tolerated to keep from losing their jobs. And then he told me it was my fault he'd had to dismiss Miguel—that if I had behaved as I'd ought to, he wouldn't have been forced to take away the man's livelihood. I was nine years old," he said without a trace of bitterness in his tone, only sorrow, "and I knew that to have a friend, or to care for anyone, was to condemn them to certain misfortune."

There was a long pause in which Amalia tried and failed to find something to say that could provide Julián with just a fraction of the comfort he'd needed as a boy. Don Reynaldo wasn't just cold and distant—he was as cruel as Victor in his own way.

Then Julián said, hardening his tone, "That's the kind of man my father is, Amalia. He takes anything that's good in your life and turns it against you."

"That's what he did to you and Concepción, isn't it?"

Julián nodded. "And what I was afraid he would do to you if he knew…"

Hardly knowing whether or not she wanted him to complete his sentence, she caught her breath and held it.

"I know you don't want me to talk about my feelings for you," he said. "And I mean to respect that. I just need you to know that I meant it when I said I was at your service. Not because I want to thwart Victor and my father, though I do, or even because I feel like I owe it to you after I involved myself so callously in your affairs. I want to do everything I can to get you and Lucía out of this because it's the right thing to do. I'm not asking you to like me, or to forgive and forget everything I've done. I just ask that you accept my help."

Her desire to believe him was so strong, it gave Amalia pause. "You're not just asking me to trust you with my life. You're asking me to trust you with Lucía's."

"I'm not asking you to trust me at all, Amalia. I'm asking you to trust yourself to make the right decision."

Julián paused and Amalia, whose arm was still linked with his, was forced to stop as well, shifting so that she was facing him.

"I've never believed I had much to offer a woman by way of a relationship or a future," he said. "But I do have something to offer *you*—an alliance. Let's band together to rescue your sister." His other arm rose to grip her shoulder. "And when that's done, we can go our separate ways if that's what you truly want."

"You would do that for me?" she asked softly.

He tucked a strand of her hair behind her ear. "I would do so much for you, Amalia. But this… This is what I should have done from the moment I met you, instead of hiding the truth about myself."

Amalia felt herself teetering on the edge of a choice. To trust Julián again and risk being hurt a second time. Or to return to relying only on herself and chance failing her sister—and falling back into a loneliness she hadn't known she felt before meeting Julián.

She opened her mouth to speak, but was interrupted by a noise from the entrance of the compartment as the sliding door was jerked to the side and the large, bulky ruffian who abducted her appeared in the opening.

Chapter Fifteen

There were two men—the large one he'd cut on the ship and behind him, a younger, wide-eyed man with a pistol. In Julián's opinion, there were very few things more alarming than a pistol being wielded by someone too young and too scared to keep themselves from doing anything reckless.

Subtly edging in front of Amalia, Julián addressed the large ruffian. "What the devil do you mean, interrupting our conversation?"

The other man seemed unimpressed by Julián's bluff. "Seize him," he told his companion.

To Julián's luck, the younger man only licked his lips. "Don Francisco said we weren't to harm them."

"Her," the ruffian corrected. "We weren't to harm her. He said nothing about him."

Julián lifted his chin, infusing his voice with cold arrogance. "You do know who my father is, don't you?"

A glint came into the ruffian's eyes. "You mean the man who told me that I shouldn't hesitate to use force on his worthless son? He knew you'd be showing up, though how you managed it, I'll never know. I searched every nook of this train before it left the station."

Something cold and bitter washed over Julián. He should have known that fooling his father wouldn't be so easy. Reynaldo Fuentes hadn't built up the largest fortune on the island by being a fool, much less where his son was concerned.

He twisted his lips into a smirk. "It's a special talent. Second only to my flair for hairdressing."

Julián's arm was still around Amalia. Without releasing her, trying to look as if he was guiding her to safety, he moved them over to the window. He was completely unarmed, and there was nothing in the carriage he could use as a weapon—save for the curtain rod.

"What in the world do you think you're doing?" Amalia said loudly after a sidelong glance at him that made it clear that her words were more a ploy for distraction than real anger. "I've seen you do a lot of low things, Julián, but using me as a shield?"

"If you hadn't noticed, Your Highness," Julián ground out, playing along, "I'm trying to protect you."

"You heard what the man said—I won't be harmed. So let go of me this instant, you wretched coward."

"Have it your way," Julián snarled, and released her.

In the instant that Amalia wrenched herself away from him—and directly toward the ruffian—Julián reached for the curtain rod and ripped it off its brackets. He flung the curtain itself at the man with the pistol, startling him long enough to get in a good blow.

For her part, Amalia was whisking herself away from the enraged ruffian, as lightly as an heiress in a ballroom.

Julián grinned at her as he used the brass rod to knock the pistol clear to the other side of the compartment. If it was discharged in the compartment, a bullet could pierce the walls and strike someone in the next car—which on Sundays was usually full of families returning home from their weekend holidays. Julián's blood ran cold. "Get the pistol," he told Amalia. "Throw it out the window."

"Don't you tell me what to do," Amalia replied at once, but she did put on a burst of speed.

Julián used his makeshift weapon to keep both ruffians occupied long enough for her to dispose of the pistol. He felt marginally more at ease when it was gone, but only for a second—ducking suddenly as Julián swung the rod, the younger man got around him and shoved him from the back.

There wasn't much room to maneuver with the furniture fixed to the floor getting in the way. Julián twisted as his shoulder struck the paneling and grappled with the men to keep the rod from being wrenched out of his grip. Sweat streamed down Julián's face as he slowly lost his hold on his one weapon.

A muffled shriek from the other side of the compartment made Julián's blood curdle. Grunting as one of the men's fists connected with his chest, he cast a wild glance over his shoulder.

There was a third man.

He had gotten hold of Amalia and had lifted her a few inches off the floor as she kicked at him. The heel of her shoe connected with his kneecap with a sound that was audible even over the locomotive's chugging wheels, but his grip on her didn't loosen. Julián saw Amalia's eyes go wide, and it took him a second to realize it wasn't in reaction to her captor.

"Julián!" she screamed raggedly, and he turned his attention to the other two ruffians just in time to catch the glint of a knife slicing down in the direction of his chest. He dropped to the floor at once, avoiding the knife but not the men, one of whom stomped a booted foot on Julián's back as he tried to dive toward Amalia. They pinned him down like an insect, Julián's cheek pressed against the plush carpet so that he could feel the miserable, nauseating motion of the train as it sped on and on.

Julián was no match for three men, much less ones accustomed to this kind of violence. What the hell made him think he could protect Amalia from them? Or from her uncle or his father or anyone else for that matter? Abject defeat coursed over him, heavier than the boot planted in the middle of his back.

Raising his eyes from the patterned carpet, he watched as the newcomer flung Amalia at one of the other ruffians and reached into his pocket. With heavy strides that made the floor shudder under Julián's face, he approached Julián and knelt, saying, "With compliments from your cousin."

A starburst of pain bloomed in the side of his head as the man struck him with something hard and metallic. Julián inhaled sharply, feeling the acrid scent of gunpowder settle in the back of his throat.

Amalia swore out loud, making Julián's lips twitch into the ghost of a smirk.

"He told me to make it hurt," the man said as he struck Julián on the opposite side, making his vision go black in spots.

Julián tried to toss his head to the side to avoid another blow, but the boot grinding just below his shoulder blade made it almost impossible to move. "Whatever he promised you," he said through a groan, "I can give you double."

The man gave him a nasty smile. "Before I toss your carcass off the train, I'm to make sure you know that you have never had what it takes. You'll never be half the man he is." The man bent even closer, lowering his voice as if he was about to confide a deep secret. "And he said to tell you that the girl will never be safe—and there's nothing you'll be able to do about it."

It was as if someone had tossed an entire bottle of liquor into a flickering fire.

Letting out a roar of pain and anger and frustration and denial, Julián bucked hard enough to make the man stepping on him lose his balance. He tried to stagger to his feet, and rose just enough to knock his head against the underside of the third man's chin, hard enough to make his teeth rattle.

A howl came from the other side of the compartment, where Amalia had just freed herself. She rushed toward Julián, swinging the curtain rod at Victor's henchman. It connected with the back of his head and bounced clean out of her hands, thudding harmlessly on the carpet and rolling under the love seat.

Julián knocked him aside with his elbow and made himself get up from the carpet, grasping Amalia to keep his balance as dark spots danced in front of his vision.

"Go," he gasped out, following her through the open door of the compartment. Yanking it closed, he plunged a hand into her curls for a hairpin, which he jammed into the locking mechanism.

"That won't hold them long," she said as the men reached the door.

"I know," Julián replied grimly, shaking his head to clear it.

Taking her hand, he pulled her toward their only

hope—the door at the end of the short corridor. He un-latched it, and as he pulled it open to reveal the land-scape rushing by, he turned to look at her.

"I won't let anything happen to you." He had to shout to be heard over the roaring of the train and the rushing wind.

She shook her head, clinging to the open doorway. "Surely, you don't mean for us to jump. We can't jump, Julián!"

"There's no other way."

Stubbornly, she held on to the doorway. "We'll be killed."

There was a loud, sharp retort behind them—a pistol being fired. It was followed by the unmistakable sound of splintering wood.

"It has to be now. Trust me, Amalia," he said, soft-ening his tone so that his words sounded less like a command and more of a plea.

Her hesitation was written all over her face. He knew how much it would cost her to put her trust in yet another man, especially one who had already dis-appointed her.

Especially when he was asking her to do something as dangerous as jumping out of a moving train.

The three men were barreling toward them. Amalia didn't glance back at them—she didn't take her gaze off Julián as she put her hand in his and gave him one hard, decisive nod.

Together, they took the leap.

Amalia found only breathless exhilaration in the brief moments when she and Julián were suspended in the air, as light as birds.

Then reality—and the ground—rushed to meet them.

It wasn't the cushiest landing. Amalia's left shoulder and hip were throbbing, though Julián had curled around her to absorb most of the impact.

Her pulse roaring almost as loudly as the locomotive that was receding into the distance, she ran her hands over his chest and biceps and down to his hips to reassure herself that he was whole. When her searching, anxious gaze met his, she was stunned to discover his remarkable self-possession crumbled away, leaving only a worry so profound, it made tears spring into her eyes.

"Are you all right? Amalia, are you hurt?"

Impatiently, she blinked away the sting and pressed her lips fiercely to his. Julián took her face into his hands and returned her kiss with exquisite tenderness, tracing the outline of her upper lips with his own and lingering in the deep indentation there.

It was a kiss that demanded nothing and gave everything.

It was a reassurance—that they were alive and whole and for the next several moments at least, no longer in danger.

And it was a promise—that they would continue to survive together.

Amalia couldn't resist letting her hands roam over his body again, this time in leisurely exploration. The muscles of his chest were so defined she could feel them through the fabric of his shirt, his thighs so hard they could have been molded from steel.

Then her knuckles brushed the placket of his trousers and he started.

Breaking the kiss, Julián pressed his forehead to hers. "Please tell me you're not injured."

"I— No." She licked her lips and tried again. "I'm fine. Just a little bruised and scratched. I think the boning in my corset must have protected me from most of the damage. And you, of course."

The reassurance seemed to bolster him. He squeezed his eyes shut then nodded, sitting up. "If anything had happened to you…" Julián let out a careful breath, then Amalia watched as he forced his lips into a crooked grin for his benefit. "I would've had to become a bandit *and* an outlaw after I chased down the men on that train and made them jump off a very steep cliff. Can you walk?"

Her legs felt fine, if a trifle shaky, though Amalia suspected that was entirely due to the kiss. "I think so."

"In that case, we ought to get moving. It'll be night soon, and I'd just as soon not get caught out here in the dark," he said grimly.

"Where would we go?" she asked, looking around at the greenery surrounding them. In one direction the fields ended in what looked like an impenetrable tangle of vegetation. In the other stretched the mountain range that separated Puerto Plata and Santiago. There was very little blue left in the sky above its peaks, and Amalia felt a shiver at the prospect of being out here once the last of the light had fled from the sky.

There were no wild beasts or poisonous creatures on the island, but Amalia was all too aware that the dangers she and Julián faced were all human.

"Whoever tends to these crops must live nearby," Julián said.

He offered her a hand—Amalia was about to take it

when she noticed first the long scrape along the right side of his face and then the slight wince when he moved his right arm. The sleeve covering that arm, she was aghast to realize, was shredded.

"You're hurt," she exclaimed, scrambling to her feet under her own power.

"It's not too bad," he said quickly. "Just my shoulder. I think it's just a sprain."

"And I think you're lying to yourself," Amalia said and started to unbutton her blouse.

It was a shame that old-fashioned petticoats with their many ruffles were no longer in fashion. Fortunately, her formerly white blouse was made so sheer by the lace panels inset into its front that she'd worn a plain white linen cover over her corset.

"What are you doing?" Julián asked, staring.

"Making you a sling out of my undergarments."

She handed him the blouse, which might as well have been a rag for how filthy and torn it was, then wriggled out of the sleeveless corset cover.

It was almost mortifying to note how often Julián had seen her in dishabille, especially taking into consideration that they really hadn't known each other all that long.

Julián, who must have gazed upon dozens of half-dressed women, looked distinctly dazed. "Amalia…"

"Are you shocked?" Amalia raised an eyebrow. "I was under the impression that you've seen dozens of women in all states of undress."

"None of them were you," he said flatly. "I'll turn away if you want me to."

She cast him a teasing glance. "Could you?"

"I'd try if I had to," he said. "I've done all sorts of

difficult things in my life, Your Highness, but voluntarily looking away from such a sight is beyond me."

Under his devouring gaze, Amalia found herself arching her back just the tiniest bit, angling herself to show the contents of her chemise to better advantage. She felt shameless, in the best possible way, liberated from the embarrassment she would have felt with anyone else. She wanted to strip off every layer, and revel in his appreciation.

The thought of undressing for him, here in the full sunshine, filled her with so much heat, she was surprised that the garment in her hands hadn't ignited.

The thin cotton tore with a satisfying rending sound. Amalia tied the two ends together and started binding Julián's arm to his side. It should have been a swift process, but the filmy fabric kept slipping from her fingers as the combined sensation of the warm breeze on her bare shoulders and her awareness of Julián's body conspired to make her fingers clumsy.

As she finished tying the last knot, the fingers on his uninjured side rose to graze the naked skin of her shoulder. Amalia's breath caught and her eyes fluttered shut as he followed the lace edging on the neckline of the chemise she wore under her corset.

"Your skin is the loveliest shade of brown." His fingers reached the green velvet ribbon whose ends trailed between her breasts. "It has a luster to it, as if you were an oil painting come to life."

Amalia held her breath as she felt the warmth of a fingertip playing over the knot at the center of the bow the ribbon was tied in. With her eyes closed, and with the last of the day's sunlight beaming down upon them, Julián and the fields were replaced with a crimson haze. His finger hooked over the knot and he tugged it lightly before dropping away.

Reluctantly, Amalia opened her eyes.

"We should get going," he said and turned away, though not before she saw her own disappointment mirrored in his face.

Amalia made quick work of her buttons. As soon as she was as neatly dressed as her ruined blouse allowed, they set off through the fields, toward the thick cluster of vegetation.

Amalia had never been good at reining in her impatience, and even though she knew that getting back to Puerto Plata before the next morning was close to impossible, what with the state of the roads and the darkness that was about to fall, she couldn't quiet the sense of urgency that almost made her groan out loud when Julián stopped at the edge of the path.

She had barely spared a glance at the banana and plantain grove that was at the edge of the field, but Julián headed directly toward one of the short palms. With a quick wrench of his wrist, he separated a couple of bananas from a hanging bunch.

He passed her one and kept one for himself. "You must be hungry by now."

"Aren't they a little green?" she asked doubtfully, looking down at the curiously small thing in her hand. "I like them when they're speckled."

"They're plenty ripe," Julián said, pulling down another one, having already eaten the first in two bites. "Go ahead and give it a try—you won't be sorry."

Amalia bit her lip. If she trusted Julián enough to go along with him when he asked her to jump out of a moving train, what harm could there be in eating one of these tiny bananas?

She peeled it slowly, then took the top edge between her teeth and bit down.

"Oh!"

The sweetness that burst into her tongue was as intense as it was unexpected. The rest of the small banana was gone in two bites and she was reaching for another.

"Ready to admit that I was right?" Julián was watching her, his lips curled into a smile so smug, she wanted to stroke her tongue over its insolent curve.

"I'd rather eat dirt," she said swiftly, mostly out of habit.

He smirked. "Pairs well with fruit. Here. Have another one."

Amalia nibbled the top of another banana, and she was surprised anew by how its exterior had belied its richness of flavor. It reminded her of Julián, actually. Not because he had an unassuming exterior—even standing in a plantain grove with his shirt shredded to pieces and streaks of dirt up and down his body, he looked every inch the powerful man that he was.

But because she would never have believed in the sweetness of his interior if she hadn't sampled it for herself.

"Your Highness?"

Amalia glanced up to see Julián looking at her with concern. Their traipse through the fields had darkened his nose and cheekbones into a light bronze tinged with red. Against it, his brown eyes looked as soft and warm as wax from a lit candle.

"Are you sure you weren't injured?"

She shook her head. "Just thinking." As happened

all too often around Julián, she could feel the previously solid ground shifting beneath her, and reforming into something different.

Heedless of the sticky dirt clinging to it, Julián leaned against the palm's short trunk and looked at her as if he had all the time in the world to listen to her half-formed thoughts.

She started slowly, struggling to articulate what was going through her mind. "I was thirteen when my father died and Tio Francisco came to live with us. Lucía and I had lived charmed lives until then, even though we'd lost our mother. Then all of a sudden, there he was, telling us to be careful about who we spoke with and forbidding us to so much as go out into the garden without someone to accompany us. He made it seem like people were lining up to take advantage of us—and that the only reason anyone would want to get close to us, or even offer us friendship, was to use us in some way."

"If it's any consolation, I'm interested in you for your body, not your fortune," Julián remarked impertinently.

Amalia smiled and flicked the peel at his uninjured arm. "I know you are, you scoundrel. I can't help but think that if my uncle had really been interested in keeping us safe, he would have taught us how to recognize and deal with those situations instead of driving away anyone who showed the least bit of interest in us."

Briefly, she caught her lower lip between her teeth. "I have spent so much of the last twelve years rebelling against my uncle, in all ways but one—I've been as distrustful as he has taught me to be. I look back at all the moments when I held myself back, or away from someone who could have been a friend, and I feel so much regret. I had even begun to think that you had proven him right." Julián opened his mouth to say something, and Amalia held up a hand. "Don't you dare apologize again. I think what I'm trying to say is…yes. I accept your offer. I want you as an ally. Just…please don't disappoint me again."

"Unfortunately, Your Highness," Julián said with one of his crooked smiles, which Amalia was starting to realize hid a wealth of pain, "disappointing people is all I ever do."

She frowned at him. "I know that's what your father believes—or what he wants you to think. But you and I both know that's not true. You could be capable of so much good, Julián, if you only allowed yourself to believe that you are the decent, honorable person I know you can be."

Julián let out a hollow laugh. "No one's ever accused me of being decent and honorable before."

"Maybe it's time they started."

Amalia held out her hand for Julián's banana peels and piled them neatly with hers beneath the palm. Then she started walking again, her pace fast and purposeful.

"My uncle has given me plenty of causes to dislike him," she said.

"I have a number of things to add to the list," Julián remarked.

"But the worst by far is how he acts as though he should be showered with accolades for agreeing to be guardian to his brother's children. It always irritated me, but it wasn't until a few years ago that I realized it was his way of making us feel like we should be grateful for what he's done, and to keep us from questioning his decisions. I think that your father does something very similar to you. The more he starves you of affection, and the more unworthy he makes you believe you are, the more likely it is that you'll do anything to please him."

At her side, Julián was silent and thoughtful.

"The worst part," she said, "is that he's made you think that love is something you have to earn. But it's not, you know. Love that isn't freely given, that comes bound with obligations and requirements and conditions—I don't believe that's love at all."

"I don't think he knows that, Your Highness. He's… I won't make excuses for my father, but he had a hard time when he married my mother. She was the coddled youngest girl of a very wealthy family and her relations made it clear to my father that he didn't deserve her. I think he's spent the past thirty years trying to prove them wrong—and to earn her love, not knowing that all he had to do was make time for her. Her death didn't stop him and I doubt his own will." Julián snorted. "He had a monstrously expensive mausoleum brought over from Italy—made out of Carrara marble and crafted by some celebrated sculptor or another. Had it placed right across from theirs so that he could lord it over them even in the afterlife."

"That's no way to live your life," Amalia remarked. "Certainly not the way I'd want to live mine."

"How would you? What will you do when all of this is over?"

"I hadn't thought that far," she admitted, then broke out into an impish smile. "Now that I've gotten a taste for jumping out of trains, I can hardly go back to needlework and garden parties. I don't have a vocation, like Lucía and her music, but I'm determined to find something that thrills and interests me, if I have to search the entire world for it."

"I have no doubt that you'll find it," he said softly.

"And you? How will you live your life?"

As the question fell from her lips, Amalia experienced a sudden tug of wistfulness as it occurred to her that she might not be there to see it.

Julián pushed aside a thin strand of vines dangling from an overhead branch. "Maybe I'll give up banditry and try piracy instead," he said lightly, then sighed. "I really don't know. Returning to my old life doesn't seem all that appealing to me, either. Maybe I'll travel."

Or maybe he would marry. Why wouldn't he?

The thought suffused Amalia with an irrational sense of panic. She kicked a fallen palm frond out of her way.

"What are you thinking that's making you huff like a little locomotive?" Julián asked.

She glanced up at him. "Marriage," she blurted out, then added, "Or rather, the wedding. Do you think they're hauling Lucía into the registry office as we speak?"

Julián looked thoughtful. "It's possible, but I don't think they will. Knowing my father, he'll want the wedding to be a lavish affair with plenty of guests. Partly because he delights in any opportunity to show off his wealth, and partly because that would make it harder for you or anyone else to contest the legitimacy of the marriage. You can hardly accuse them of a secret conspiracy to defraud you when it's all being done in front of hundreds of people, after all."

Julián reached out with his good hand and tangled his fingers through her hair. "We'll get there in time.

And when we do, will you allow me to loan you the funds to take Lucía to Europe? I have plenty of money, and little use for most of it. The two of you could be on your way to Vienna as early as tomorrow evening."

"We will," she said with far more confidence than she felt. "Once we get her away, though, there's still the matter of my father's will."

"I could have my lawyers look it over and see if there's anything to be done. Or..." His lips spread into a grin.

Amalia raised an eyebrow as little shoots of excitement began to unfurl in her stomach at the sight of Julián's expression. "Or?"

"We could perform one more act of banditry."

Chapter Sixteen

Night was starting to fall when they reached a large hacienda. Its occupants proved more than happy to put them up for the night when Julián explained that he and his wife had been en route to Santiago when they were set upon by bandits who had robbed them of their carriage, luggage and even his necktie and hat.

With no one of Amalia's acquaintance here, Julián knew they could have very well dispensed with the pretense they'd been forced to use on the ship. But after the day they'd just had, he'd be damned if he'd risk her sleeping alone in an unfamiliar house with strangers. Amalia had agreed—more than that, she had reached for his hand and kept hold of it as their hosts, a planter and his family, clucked over their ill fortune.

He watched her fidget all through dinner, obviously anxious about her sister's fate. When the family retreated to the porch after dinner with tiny glasses of liqueur, Amalia excused herself, claiming that her head ached after the day's events.

After a few minutes' wait, Julián went after her.

They'd been put into the bedroom that belonged to

the planter's daughters, who had been relocated for the night. A wooden armoire and a four-poster bed spread with a crocheted coverlet took up most of the space, but a little dressing table with a flowered skirt had been tucked into a corner. Amalia sat in front of the oval mirror in her borrowed nightdress, yanking a comb through her wet hair, her frustration evident in each short stroke.

They were too far from any town for the hacienda to be reached by any of the electrical grids that had recently been installed throughout the island. In the dancing glow cast by the oil lamp on the table, she looked even more like someone out of an oil painting. The warm light painted her profile, highlighting her stubborn chin and the glint of determination that always shone in her eyes.

It wasn't just that he was drawn to her. It was that he felt as though he would expire on that spot if he didn't touch her, or kiss her, or contrive a way to feel the warmth of her skin beneath his palm.

"We could borrow a horse," she blurted out when she met his eyes in the mirror. "And a lantern. And—"

"And we'd be set upon by bandits—real ones—long before we got back to town." Between the bad roads and the roving bands of men ready to cause mayhem at the slightest provocation, few people of Julián's acquaintance would venture out into the wilderness after dark, even with guards at their side. Julián gave her shoulders what he hoped was a comforting squeeze. "I know you're worried about your sister. I promise you I'll get you to her as soon as possible. But risking your life isn't going to do her any good."

As if to further underscore his point, raindrops began

to beat a tattoo against the wooden shutters. Within seconds the light patter turned into a roar that muffled the faint sounds coming from beyond their door.

"I know," Amalia muttered, rubbing her face. "And I'm sorry for being so impatient."

"There's no need to apologize for being anxious."

Amalia gave a fretful nod and once again began attacking her curls with the comb.

Unable to hold back a wince, Julián held out his hand. "Here, let me help. My hairdressing skills are celebrated and unparalleled, as you might remember."

"I'd settle for plain competency at the moment," she said, surrendering the comb and sighing as she stretched her shoulders. "My arms are beginning to ache. Lucía always does this at home. It's such tedious work—my hair tangles something fierce and it's far too long."

Julián was of the opinion that her hair was, in fact, perfect, but he resisted the urge to say so out loud.

The hair at the nape of her neck had tangled into vicious little knots. Julián, who would have never described himself as a patient man, took his time teasing out the snarls while Amalia offered suggestions on how to get back to Puerto Plata that very night, each more outlandish than the last.

Julián could tell that she wasn't serious, though; just talking through her nerves. Figuring she could use the distraction, he encouraged her by adding impractical suggestions of his own and trying not to laugh when she came up with a convoluted plan involving a submarine, a hot water balloon and a contraption he suspected she had read about in a Jules Verne novel.

Almost a quarter of an hour later, Julián set aside

the comb. Her hair was beginning to dry in the balmy air, the heavy strands shrinking and curling into a riot of light-touched waves. Lightly, he threaded his fingers through the strands, then dove through them to rub her scalp with gentle pressure.

Letting out a contented little noise that went straight into Julián's rib cage like an arrow, she leaned her head back into his touch. He was amused to see her toes curling under the hem of her nightdress.

"I've been wanting to do this ever since that time in the carriage," he said softly as he stroked the short little curls at the nape of her neck. "Your hair is like the sea."

"Blue and wet?" she asked with an arched eyebrow.

He laughed, lifting a strand to admire the way it coiled. "Beautiful. Full of movement. I could drown in it."

Their eyes met in the mirror again, and Julián knew he wasn't the only one who was feeling the thrum of possibility charging the atmosphere until it felt like standing outside a second before a strike of lightning.

She rose from the small chair in a single fluid motion, like a sea goddess rising from the water, and moved the spindly legged chair aside with a slow thrust of her hip that sent a sudden rush of heat over Julián.

"Were you planning on dancing around the subject all evening, or will we talk about it before daybreak?" she asked.

"Talk about what, Your Highness?"

"Your sharing my bed."

She cocked her head, and the challenge in her eyes kindled a slow smile on Julián's lips. "Been thinking about it, have you?"

"From the moment you told the planter we were husband and wife," she said, taking a step that made the front of her billowing nightdress brush against him. "I was hoping you'd done it because you intended to sleep next to me."

"I said it because I want you safe—and the only way I can make sure that you haven't been snatched in the night is to keep you with me."

"Is that the only reason?" she asked, reaching up to fiddle with the buttons on his borrowed shirt.

Maybe Julián wasn't as much of a scoundrel as he considered himself. He pressed his hand to hers, trapping it against his chest. "It is if you want it to be."

In answer, she rose up onto her tiptoes and brushed her lips to his throat, just above his collar. That slight touch seared him.

"I know that we'll part soon," she said. "But we still have tonight."

As if that was enough. As if that could ever be enough.

He had to bend to touch his forehead to hers, breathing out her name. "I used to live my life as if pleasure was one thing and emotion another wholly separate thing, and the pursuit of one did not really require the other. I spent years having one meaningless dalliance after another. It has been so long since I was satisfied by those shallow affairs because it wasn't affection or even companionship that I found with them. It was oblivion—a distraction from all the things I felt I could never have, or even be. I don't want oblivion anymore, Amalia. I don't want a night's worth of amusement when I could have a lifetime."

"What *do* you want?" she whispered.

Julián inhaled the floral scent of hair oil rising from

the top of her head and felt her respond to his tightening grip by shifting closer into his embrace. "You."

The sound of her breathing filled the space between them. Amalia didn't say a word. So he spoke for them both.

"I want more of you than I have any right to. I want to have an endless string of nights in your bed and at your side, because the very thought of being without you drives me to my knees."

"I don't love you." Her voice broke, and her next words came as a whisper. "I can't love you."

Julián rubbed the pad of his thumb over her enticing lower lip. "There is nothing you can't do, Amalia. You've proven that twenty times over in the short time I've known you. Time after time you have done the impossible."

He had always believed that it *was* impossible for anyone to love a worthless wreck like himself. But Amalia was the kind of person who was undaunted by the impossible. If there was anyone in the world who could love him, it was this wild, headstrong, fierce heiress.

Here it came again. That heady, breathless moment when the possibility of a kiss hung suspended between them, as bright and shining as gold. He knew better than most not to take it for granted—possibilities often turned to ashes, and a next kiss was never assured. There was every chance that Amalia would turn around and leave the room.

She was the first one to move, surging up onto her tiptoes to reach him. Their mouths collided and all the passion and need that Julián had ever felt coalesced into that one kiss. And he thought that maybe he *would* expire from the terrible joy of loving this woman.

Her skin was the rich, warm brown of molasses and honey, and just about as sweet. He drank in her taste and her scent, the way her body felt against his. He could have stood there forever, just holding her, relishing in her.

But time, tide and daylight waited for no man, not even him.

Releasing her reluctantly, he went to the spindly chair she had vacated.

"All right, Your Highness. Have your way with me. Use me for your pleasure."

Sitting back, he folded his uninjured arm behind his head and watched her through slitted eyes. If he'd thought that Amalia would grow uncertain, he was wrong. A determined look that was quickly becoming familiar to him came into her eyes and she went to him at once, stepping between his parted legs as she reached for his braces.

After washing earlier, he had replaced her makeshift bandage with one provided by the planter's wife. He hadn't had the heart to throw away the remnants of her chemise, though, and had tucked it into his pocket.

She unwound the bandage and eased his shirt over his injured shoulder. When she pulled the sleeve down his arm, Julián was struck by a thought—no one had ever treated him with such care. Not any of the dozen women who had shared his bed, and certainly not his family. It staggered him that this rebellious, strong-willed woman should be the one to offer him tenderness.

Amalia undressed him with as much confidence as

if she'd done it dozens of times before. As each article of clothing fell away, collecting into an untidy pile on the tiles, Julián felt his skin break out into gooseflesh that had nothing to do with the sultry breeze stealing through the open shutters. He had never seen a more heart-stopping sight than the clearly visible outline of her body as lamplight shined through the fabric of her nightdress, turning the long garment into the robes of a temptress.

She hitched up her hem and placed her folded leg on his thigh. The gathered fabric floated over the bare skin of his abdomen as delicately as the fingertips she was pressing to his jaw. Even sitting while she stood, he was taller than Amalia by two or three centimeters, but he enjoyed the novelty of not having to stoop to reach her lips.

Her kiss was as bold as a bandit's, stealing his breath away as she thoroughly plundered his mouth. The hand she had braced on his good shoulder slid around him and all of a sudden, the light touch of fabric was replaced with a heavier weight as she leaned against him, head inclined so that her glorious, fragrant hair fell like a curtain around them. The world beyond the open shutters faded away as the soft strands grazed his shoulder.

The tight buds of her nipples were hard against his chest. He clasped her by the waist and held her close, following the curve of her hip with one hand. His lips hadn't left hers—he dragged them down her throat, coaxing breathy little moans out of her.

The soft sounds reverberated through him like thunder.

If there was any resistance left in his body to the

idea that he was utterly and deeply in love with Amalia, it vanished when he reached the hollow of her throat. Her hands were resting on his shoulders, her leg on his thigh, her hair all around them—she was entirely in control and he was all too happy to surrender himself to her.

"Your Highness," he murmured. "I'm not just at your service—I am entirely at your mercy."

Amalia reached for the placket of Julián's trousers, remembering what he'd said on the ship about wanting her to feel like a present being unwrapped. Undressing him was like unwrapping a present, too—an all too brief moment brimming with the anticipation of pleasure.

She'd always been the kind to impatiently tear at ribbons and colored paper, but she meant to take her time with Julián.

The top button of his trousers slid out of its place with a twist of her fingers. Before she could reach for the next, Julián's hand shot out and seized her wrist. His grip wasn't painful, but it was firm.

Amalia's gaze flew up to meet his. "What's wrong?"

"I changed my mind, Your Highness."

For a heart-pounding moment, Amalia thought he meant to leave. Then, in a single swift movement, he rose and lifted her by the waist with his good arm. She hardly had time to wrap her arms around his neck before he was walking her to the bed and sweeping aside the mosquito netting to lower her onto the intricately crocheted coverlet.

Then his hot mouth was on her neck and on the swells of her breasts, still covered by the cotton nightdress, and it was overwhelming in the best way possible.

Turning her gently so that she lay on her side, he curled his long body behind hers and continued exploring the delicate skin of her shoulders with his mouth. The jaw that had been perfectly smooth when he'd found her on the train had sprouted bristles in the course of the evening. Amalia couldn't help letting out a moan when Julián rubbed his rough chin against her neck.

"I will never stop craving you," he murmured and her body trembled in sync with the vibration of his voice.

His questing hand found her fabric-covered breasts. She arched her back in a silent plea for more, though her movement had the added benefit of putting her lower back in contact with that interesting bulge in his trousers.

It was a singular sensation, being pressed against a man's body with so few layers between them. Too much and not enough, all at once.

Grasping the ribbon that held the neckline of her nightdress gathered into a drawstring, she pulled it open with a single jerk, exposing her skin to the warm night air and his relentless touch. Heat washed over her breasts as he thumbed the stiff points, flooding her until she felt incandescent.

I don't love you. She'd said that to Julián, willing it to be true. Love had never served her. The things done to her in its name had only brought her grief. But just like she had decided to reassess her mistrust of people, knowing Julián was making her want to reconsider everything she had always believed of love. The thought was terrifying, and she had to bite down on her lip to keep her impulsive self from blurting out something she might regret later.

In any case, Julián was doing a very good job of distracting her from her thoughts. He had raised her nightgown and his warm mouth trailed scratchy kisses down her spine, blazed a path over the curve of her hips—and then, when he turned her gently on her back, did unspeakable things to the thin skin of her inner thighs.

Under his encouragement, Amalia let her legs sprawl open, her pulse quickening as he dipped the tip of his tongue into the crease of her thighs. Liquid heat pooled between her legs, spreading up her midsection in languid waves.

Amalia had never been a very patient person at the best of times, but this slow teasing was nothing short of agonizing. She writhed into the bedsheets, pleading for release through breathless pants. Julián only laughed.

"Was it Napoleon who said, *'Dress me slowly, I'm in a hurry'*?" he asked, shaping the words against her skin in a way that made her stop writhing and start trembling.

"Who the devil knows?" Amalia snapped. "And who the devil cares?"

Julián chuckled again. "We have so little time together… I intend to go as slow as possible and savor every second."

"I can appreciate that—in theory. In practice, though…" Amalia gave him a subtle nudge with her hips, loving how wanton she could let herself act around him. "I need you."

Dipping his head, he captured one of her nipples in

his mouth, tonguing it until it grew tight and hard, then retreated just enough to blow cool air over it.

When he had her breathing unsteadily again, he raised himself up to bring his mouth to hers. His lips tasted like the mint liqueur they'd had after dinner, and the cool fire of it filled her, racing along her limbs. She had once compared kissing him to champagne bubbles, little knowing that spirits were much more exciting than the pale fizz.

But Julián wasn't like genteel liqueur, either, or at least not entirely—he was *aguardiente*, as searing as liquid fire. And he was hers, if only for one more night.

Amalia never wanted it to end.

And she didn't want to think, or make any more plans, or do anything but sink into this heady rush of sensation. She was going to fall apart at any moment, and she wanted to enjoy every second of her dissolution.

Then Julián sank into her, slowly and gently and rolling his hips in a way that had Amalia muffling her cries against his shoulder. And she realized that she had gotten it wrong.

This wasn't falling apart. It was coming together.

The warm glow from the lamp kissed Amalia's bare curves as she lay on her side. Stripped of her lace and frills and velvet ribbons and pearl earrings, clad only in lamplight and plain cotton sheets, with her long, dark lashes fluttering as sleep tugged on her eyelids, she was beauty itself.

Julián had always thought that it wasn't fair to compare women to each other, much less those who had been kind enough to share his bed. Even if he was to disregard his rule, it would be impossible to compare Amalia to anyone else, purely because she was beyond comparison. She reminded him of something his mother used to say, about big surprises coming in small packages. Or was it big gifts? Amalia was both those things.

Julián was exhausted, and his shoulder bothered him more than he wanted to admit, but he couldn't seem to stop running his hands over the deep indentation of her waist long enough to drift into sleep. They were both slightly sticky with sweat, and the humidity in the room had given her curls volume and a life of their own. They tumbled wildly over her shoulders and the crisp white pillow, sticking to her skin in places. Gently, Julián gathered it all in a bunch and twisted it away from her neck.

She murmured something incomprehensible, giving a little sigh of relief when he blew cool air toward her nape.

"Where are you going?" she asked drowsily when he stood up.

"Nowhere, Your Highness."

He went as far as the washstand in the corner. Dribbling some water onto the towel she had used earlier, he returned to the bed to wipe her down with care, rubbing the fabric over her body as if he was polishing a bronze statue.

"That's lovely and cool," she said, voicing her pleasure with a breathy moan.

Turning onto her stomach, she slid her arms under the pillow and hugged it to her chest.

Julián pressed a kiss to the small of her back, and then another one on the nape of her neck, for good measure. He tugged the crumpled blanket out from under her hip and covered her up, tucking it securely around her. The coverlet was heaped on the floor at the foot of the bed, and Julián left it there—the night was too hot and humid for another layer.

"Get some rest," he said, though she was more than halfway into sleep. "Tomorrow's going to be a long day."

He went over to the chair to spread the towel over its back so that it would dry by morning. Then he blew out the lamp and got into bed next to Amalia.

She rolled over to face him, eyelids at half-mast and lips curled into a lazy curve that was barely visible in the moonlight streaming through the shutters. Even in the faint light, her eyes sparkled as she asked, "No midnight secrets tonight?"

"I have no secrets left, Your Highness," he told her, smoothing back one of the curls springing over her forehead and bending his face down to hers. "And nothing to confess. Not anymore. I think you've seen all the way into my soul."

She kissed his throat, hitching up a leg and tucking it between his thighs. "If I have, I've liked every bit of it."

He felt the warmth of her breath as she exhaled against his skin—once, twice and then she was melting into the bonelessness of heavy sleep.

And Julián... Julián was feeling, once again, what it felt like to fall from a great height. He wasn't just smitten, as Doña María had said over breakfast only a few days before. He was well and truly in love with this woman. Desperately so, with a hunger and a tenderness that made him ache to take her into his arms and brush kisses over each of those tantalizing curves.

Julián had always known that love wasn't meant for

men like him. Love was for the stalwart and the upright, not for worthless scoundrels like himself. He had never done anything to deserve such a thing, but for the first time in his life, he wanted to—even if it came at the expense of his own heart.

Chapter Seventeen

Amalia had never arrived anywhere early in her life, and her sister's wedding was no different.

Upon their return to Puerto Plata, it had taken them a matter of minutes to find out in which church the wedding was being held. Leaving Julián outside, Amalia had bent low over the saddle and touched her heels to the horse's flank, guiding it into a straight gallop up the church's steps and right into the nave.

The gasps of over a hundred people almost drowned out the thundering of hooves on tile as they raced to the altar. Along with the reins, Amalia held the pair of pistols Julián had bought from the planter that morning. Without so much as a waver, she kept one trained on Victor and the other on the pew where her uncle sat next to Julián's father.

"I do hope you weren't planning on starting without me," she said, shooting her sister a reassuring grin.

Lucía, whose mouth had fallen open in a gape, recovered enough to smile back at Amalia.

Out of the corner of her eye, she saw Don Reynaldo stand. "What is the meaning of this?"

"This," Amalia said evenly, "is a kidnapping. Give me the girl and no one gets hurt."

"Amalia?" That from her uncle, who had been a trifle slower on the uptake. "But how—?"

"If you're asking me how I escaped your own attempt to have me abducted by ruffians," she said in a loud, clear voice, relishing in the instant murmurs from the crowd, "I can tell you it was easier than you might suspect. I really hope you didn't pay them in advance."

Tío Francisco's eyes narrowed. "I don't know what you mean by this, young lady, but I suggest that you—"

Nothing could have persuaded Amalia to let him finish that sentence. "It's as you told me yesterday," she said. "I have an obligation to this family. It just doesn't involve selling myself or my sister in order to fill your pockets."

Tío Francisco's face was turning puce with fury. "You want to ruin your sister's prospects, and her life with it? Do it, then. I won't stand in your way any longer. I wash my hands of you."

Her nerves were taut—no, they felt stretched to their absolute limit, as if they would snap any second. She couldn't keep her foot from jiggling in the stirrup, though it made the horse snort. "I don't just want my sister. I want our money, too."

He blanched, but recovered quickly enough. "So you can spend it all on dresses and hair ribbons?" he snapped. "You know nothing about managing finances or property."

"You're right—I don't know anything about it. Which is why I plan on hiring an estate manager who can run things while Lucía and I learn how to do it ourselves."

"Do you know how many people are cheated by unscrupulous managers? You'll be fleeced."

"And fortune hunters will ply us with poetry and flowers, and pickpockets will run off with our bags." Amalia shrugged. "I feel sorry for you, if that's what you truly believe the world is like. If you truly think that people are lining up to take advantage of you."

Julián's father, who had stood up from his spot in the front pew next to her uncle, made an impatient gesture with his hand. From what Julián had told her, nothing would have angered him more than being embarrassed in front of his fashionable friends. And she was definitely giving them cause for gossip. "I've had just about enough of your insolence. I command you to remove yourself and this filthy beast from this church at once."

"Happily. As long as my sister comes with me."

"Touch a single strand of her hair, and Francisco will have you charged with kidnapping," Don Reynaldo said. The gray in his temples glinted like steel in the light pouring in through the stained-glass windows. "You and my son both, though I can't help but notice that the scoundrel has finally done what he does best—give up."

"You don't know anything about what your son can and can't do," Amalia told him. "Lu, will you come with me? There's nothing here for you or for me."

Tossing her bouquet to the floor, Lucía took a step toward the horse—and was stopped in her tracks as Victor's hand closed around her arm.

"My betrothed is not going anywhere," he said coldly. "Much less with you. I swore to protect her from harm, or I will very shortly, and that includes bad influences like you."

Lucía tried to tug her arm out of his grip, but even from her perch Amalia could see that he held her too tightly. "My sister's the only person who's ever looked after me," she protested.

Amalia felt her heart squeeze with guilt and remorse and a hot flash of anger. "Let go of her, you brute."

She swiveled the barrel of the pistol a fraction of an inch, but Victor had placed himself so that Lucía stood between him and Amalia. The damn coward.

It was a good thing neither of the pistols had a single bullet in it.

"I'd just as soon it doesn't discharge by accident," Julián had said earlier when he'd checked the chamber. "And in any case, neither of us has a taste for violence."

"Speak for yourself," Amalia had growled, but Julián had been right. She wasn't going to shoot anybody, not even Victor, no matter how much he deserved it.

And oh, how he deserved it.

Moving quickly, Victor had seized Lucía and was holding her in front of him like a shield. Lucía hunched her shoulders against the unwanted touch, but she didn't move away, making Amalia think Victor must have some sort of weapon.

The question was, what sort of weapon? Did a man like Victor wear a knife? That was the one thing she and Julián hadn't counted on when they'd made their plans.

She didn't have any time to figure it out before Victor started talking. "What do you think will happen if you try to ride out of here with my fiancée? Do you really believe that my uncle won't send the entire Civil Guard after you both? How far do you think that poor beast can carry you?"

For all that he was hiding behind Lucía, he had managed to inject a calm, almost smug tone into his voice. He sounded just like Amalia's uncle did when he was trying to reason with her, and as always, the sound only made Amalia feel even more furious.

"I had a lot of time to make plans when my uncle and your father had me abducted," she bit out.

All too aware of the dozens of guests filling the pews who were watching their exchange in rapt silence, Victor raised his eyebrows. "As far as I can tell, Amalia, the only person trying to kidnap anyone here is you." He softened his tone. "It's all right, Amalia. I know that my degenerate cousin has put all kinds of ideas into your head. He's led you to believe that he's trying to help you. But Julián has never served any interests other than his own. He's accomplished enough at making young women think he loves them, but the truth is that he will never love anyone more than he loves himself."

A glint came into Victor's eyes. "He's been lying to you this whole time. I heard it all—he plotted with my father about how to win your trust by getting rid of Francisco and persuading you to marry him. All so that he could hand over both your hands and your fortune to Tío Reynaldo. Seventy percent," he said casually in the direction of his uncle. "That's what you agreed on, right?"

Amalia looked into Victor's eyes and all of a sudden, it was a little harder to breathe. She could see in his expression that he believed what he was saying. And even though Julián had told her something similar, she was dismayed to discover that the flicker of doubt she had felt that morning hadn't been entirely extinguished.

Out of the corner of her eye, she caught a glimpse of a figure moving soundlessly behind the arches that separated the nave from the side aisle. As they had agreed, Julián had taken advantage of her attention-stealing entrance to slip into the church unseen. She cast an involuntary glance toward him, taking her eyes from Victor for only a split second.

It was a second too long.

Victor had a pistol, too, and his was loaded.

Pointing it at her over Lucía's shoulder, he didn't even hesitate before firing. The report echoed inside the church, and as the guests began screaming over the sound of shattering glass, the horse spooked and reared and Amalia found herself flying off the saddle, her arm exploding into agony.

One moment Julián was watching the proceedings from the back of the church and thinking that Amalia, at her boldest and brashest, was a sight to behold. Then she was being shot and thrown off a horse and he—

Well, the truth was that Julián had no clear memory of the next several minutes. The interval between the gun being fired and his arriving at Amalia's side was lost to the burning haze of his rage.

Amalia's sister had ripped off her veil and was using it to stanch the blood pouring from her arm.

It was every nightmare Julián had ever had—someone he cared about getting hurt because of him.

Not just someone. Amalia.

He looked her over quickly but thoroughly, a detached part of his mind matching up the single shot he'd heard fired with the runnel it had carved through the fleshy part of Amalia's upper arm.

Most of the guests seemed to have fled, but a few men had remained, and two of them were holding Victor back. A third was declaring something about having the Civil Guard fetched, though most looked uneasy at the thought of involving the law in what was clearly a family affair.

That, Julián thought, was exactly how Victor had come to be the man he was. The world they lived in made men like him think they were above justice, or even consequences.

"Has someone gone to fetch a doctor?" Julián heard himself say, his voice cold and distant.

He didn't hear the answer, focusing instead on Amalia.

Her eyes had fluttered open, and though her face was ashen, the snapping fire in them made him almost faint with relief.

Julián bent to brush his lips against her forehead. "I told you, Your Highness—everyone who gets close to me ends up hurt."

"There you go again," she said, looking irritated, "blaming yourself for something that is most decidedly not your fault."

He let out a laugh that could have passed for a sob. "You're going to be all right."

"I know *that*," she said. "It's just my arm. Pity you haven't any nice underclothes for a sling."

"I'll give you the shirt off my back if you want it," he said.

A sound from behind him drew his attention to his father. Don Reynaldo looked furious with Victor. Julián couldn't tell if he was angry over the fact that he had tried to shoot a young woman, or that he'd done it in full view of his fancy society acquaintances. At any other time the doubt might have saddened him—but Julián no longer cared.

After making sure that Amalia was all right being left with her sister for a moment, Julián strode to meet his father, who was advancing toward them with a flinty look in his eyes.

"I've had enough of this," Don Reynaldo said when he was close enough, taking care to avoid being overheard by the other men. "I humored your little attempt to pull the wool over my eyes because I was pleased to see you taking initiative for once, but this has gone on long enough. You will abandon your attempt to take the girl, or I will have Francisco declare her sister to be mentally unfit to handle her own affairs. Leave now, and you might still be able to persuade her to marry you."

Julián felt his face going very still, very suddenly. "I'm afraid you didn't understand. We didn't come here to negotiate with you. We're following your example and taking what we want with no regard to anyone else."

His father regarded him with disgust. "I should have disowned you long ago."

"I'm fine with being disowned," Julián said calmly. "Shooting at Amalia, on the other hand—that I have a problem with. Oh, and with being murdered. Although I'm not sure you were apprised of that particular plan of Victor's."

A slight flare of his father's nostrils told Julián he was right. He glanced toward where his cousin was being held back.

"With compliments from your cousin," he quoted, raising his voice so that Victor could hear him. "That was what the man you sent after us said. Would you like me to tell my father all the messages you had him relay? About no one knowing what you're capable of and no one appreciating all you do. He had plenty to say about Amalia, too, and none of it pleasant." He turned toward his father. "Don't tell me you're surprised to know that Victor was doing things behind your back. I thought you liked initiative. Or are you wondering what else he was involved in?"

His father looked at Victor as if he were seeing him through new eyes. "Is this true?"

Victor didn't look at him. "Look at you," he spat at Julián. "Roaming around the island like some sort of bandits, riding horses into churches and driving respectable men to desperation. No one can fault me for trying to protect my bride and my business from the pair of you."

"*Your* business?" Julián's father said in a low, dangerous voice that made the men holding on to Victor's arms take an unconscious step backward.

Victor seemed to realize his mistake. "Tio Reynaldo," he said and licked his lips. "It's not as it sounds. You know I would never dream of—"

Julián's father turned away. "Call the Civil Guard," he said over his shoulder. "I'm done with this business."

Julián would have sworn that the snarl that followed that remark had been made by an animal. His mouth fell open as he watched Amalia's uncle burst into sudden motion, seizing the pistol Victor had dropped and pointing it first at Julián, then at his nieces, as if he couldn't make up his mind who to shoot first.

"I'll be damned if I let you ruin this for me," he said in a hard voice.

He won't have me hurt. Amalia had said that, over and over again. Clearly, she'd been wrong.

Julián's eyes narrowed and he began to stride forward, directly toward the wavering barrel.

"Go ahead and shoot me," he said, advancing quickly toward the older man. "Just know that if you do, you had better kill me on the first try, because the second I get my hands on you, I will make *you* wish that you were dead."

Dropping the hand holding the pistol, Francisco tried to edge away, but all he did was back directly into a column. Julián put on a burst of speed and closed the distance between them, pinning Francisco to the column with nothing more than the menace in his stare.

"Come to think of it," Julián said, "that's one way to get past the will, isn't it? I wonder what provisions their father made in the case of your death."

"You won't kill me," Francisco said, but his eyes were wide and his chest heaving with one unsteady breath after another.

"Probably not," Julián agreed. "But like I told you a few days ago—I will make you regret everything you've ever done to your nieces. My lawyers will be paying you a visit later today. You will work with them to sign everything over to Amalia and Lucía."

"But—what am I to do?"

"Have you considered a job?" Julián said dryly, watching with amusement as true panic flashed over Francisco's face at the prospect. "I discussed the matter with Amalia, and she is prepared to give you a yearly allowance."

Greed flickered over his expression. "They owe me—"

"We," Julián said severely, "owe you nothing. Not even gratitude. Everything you've done has been for your own financial gain. Not for their father. And definitely not for them."

Francisco took a swing at Julián.

Nimbly, Julián stepped back from the older man, leaving him to crumple to the floor. Nobody went to help him up, and the church was very quiet as Julián strode back to Amalia's side.

Chapter Eighteen

Amalia must have drifted out of consciousness. She was aware of people around her, and of being gathered up into a pair of strong arms. Then there was nothing but disorienting flickers of something that might have been dreams, interspersed by an amorphous darkness.

When she managed to force her eyes open, she was so relieved to find Julián at her side that she let out a sob.

At the sound, Julián immediately lifted his head. "You're all right, Amalia. You've been seen by a doctor and your arm has been bound. You lost some blood, but he says you're going to be all right."

"I thought you had left me," she tried to explain through her tears.

"You can't get rid of me that easily, Your Highness," Julián said, the corners of his eyes crinkling with humor though he still looked worried.

Amalia tried to sit up, and found that she was able to haul herself upright without too much effort. Her entire body felt bruised, and her upper arm was in agony, but that was all. They were still in the church, and she had been laid on one of the pews. Julián was kneeling on the floor beside her, Lucía sitting at her feet.

Shifting her gaze behind them, Amalia saw a resisting Victor being hauled away by a pair of men in Civil Guard uniforms. Don Reynaldo appeared to have vanished.

And her uncle...

"Don't let him leave," Amalia told Julián. "I have something to say to him."

Julián helped her to her feet, which to her surprise were fairly steady under her. Tio Francisco, who had resentfully been talking to a guardsman, turned to watch her approach with obvious dislike in his eyes.

Amalia looked steadily back; after a moment his gaze slid away from hers.

"What is it?" he asked sullenly.

"I was thinking the other day, that it was a curious thing that you never married. I'm sure plenty of women would have liked to be courted by a man who commanded so much wealth and power, even if it wasn't his own."

"What of it?"

"Nothing, really, only I wondered... Were you so intent in keeping us isolated that you didn't dare bring another person into the household for fear that she would take our side? Or do you just abhor parting with money so much that you would have rather stayed alone all these years rather than support one more person?"

He shrugged. "Why would I need a wife when I already have everything?"

"And now you have nothing." Silence stretched between them as the truth of what she had just said sank into him. "Was it worth it?" she asked softly.

"I don't have to explain myself to you. I did as my brother asked me, and no one, not even your paramour, can claim that I have been profligate or careless with your inheritance."

Amalia's lips twitched mirthlessly. "That's always been the problem, Tio. You've always thought that managing our inheritance is about tallying up columns on some ledgers and watching numbers grow into inflated figures. But it was never about the money for us. All we wanted was our freedom."

Looking at her uncle's expression, Amalia realized that her explanations were pointless. He was never going to understand what she and Lucía had needed all these years. And he was never going to care about them the way they wanted to be cared about.

There was no more to be said. Amalia stepped back, searching out Julián, who was standing next to her sister like a guard, though his eyes were firmly on Amalia.

Maybe Amalia was slightly more overcome by her wound than she'd admitted to, because her knees went suddenly weak and she found herself being gathered gently into Julián's arms.

In the course of the next hour or two, he had not only managed to procure them a carriage to convey them to his house, he had also sent someone to the Europa to fetch their luggage, and had called for a doctor to attend to Amalia's arm.

The sun was still high in the sky behind the dark shutters when Julián helped Amalia into a freshly made bed whose carved posts were twined with mosquito netting. Her arm was freshly cleaned and bandaged, and the tonic the doctor had administered was making her eyelids impossibly heavy. So it was very likely that she imagined the glint in Lucía's eyes when her sister proclaimed that she needed to freshen up and hastened out of the bedroom, whisking the door closed behind her.

And then it was just Amalia and Julián. She reclined exhaustedly on the lace-edged pillow while Julián tugged a light cotton blanket over her.

"Have you always been this—this—"

"Handsome?" Julián filled in helpfully as she groped for a suitable word. He was as disheveled as Amalia felt, his shirt smeared in blood and grime, and his hair in complete disarray. "Dashing? Irresistible?"

"Competent," she said, offering him a drowsy smile. "For someone who continually calls himself a useless wastrel, you certainly know how to get things done."

"Allow me to let you in on a little secret, Your Highness—sometimes I have been known to make myself useless on purpose. Mainly to avoid anything having to do with my father's business. Though perhaps if I'd been obedient and diligent like Victor, my father would have appreciated me more."

"Affection shouldn't be earned through obedience, and you, Julián—" she reached for his hand "—you should be loved for your own sake, not for what you can do for other people."

"I'll try to keep that in mind," Julián said, the corners of his lips twitching upward as if Amalia had said something amusing. Or as if he didn't believe her.

Amalia frowned. At least, she thought she did. As important as she knew it was to convince Julián of the truth of her statement, the tonic was proving to be too strong and she could feel herself drifting into what promised to be a heavy stupor.

"Will you stay with me?" she murmured, making a valiant effort to keep her fluttering eyelids open.

The mattress dipped as Julián climbed in beside her. Amalia's head landed heavily on his shoulder, her eyes already closing.

The last thing she heard, before sleep finally pulled her under, was Julián's voice as he spoke softly into the shell of her ear. "I wouldn't dream of leaving you."

Amalia had been up for over an hour when Julián finally began stirring. She had awakened with her head pillowed in the crook of his arm, their faces close together as if they had sought one another's lips in the depths of slumber.

Sometime in the night Julián had kicked aside the light cotton blanket they had slept under. He lay sprawled over it now, the long, lean planes of his body golden against the bedsheets even in the faint blue light of early morning. Still asleep, he turned his head slightly, and Amalia saw that his arrogant profile was softened by the suggestion of a smile.

She loved him.

The thought came as suddenly as a lightning bolt.

She loved him with such a sudden, fierce strength it felt as though she *had* been struck by lightning— seared and electrified and dazed.

Julián's eyes blinked open, and he smiled in earnest when he saw her.

Her body's response was as swift as it was strong— unbridled delight danced through her limbs, and she couldn't hold back her answering smile. She would have kissed him—she wanted to, so deeply her heart clenched inside her chest—but she had a feeling that kissing Julián would no longer be the fun, reckless lark it had once been.

After everything that had happened, kissing Julián would be nothing but a straight descent into the near desperate need and longing she had spent most of her life trying to avoid.

He, on the other hand, was looking at her as if there was nothing remarkable about waking up next to a woman.

Because it wasn't, Amalia reminded herself. Not for someone who was always embroiled in one affair or another.

"Good morning, Your Highness," he said in a raspy voice that made the knot in her stomach tighten, reaching to run his fingertips over her cheekbone. "How do you feel? How's your arm?"

"I'm all right," she said, letting her gaze roam over the room as if by doing so she could escape his scrutiny.

Two mahogany wardrobes, their doors inlaid with mirrors, flanked a chest of drawers whose surface was littered with small bottles of hair oil, cologne and what looked like a sepia-tinged photograph in a silver frame. By the shuttered window was an armchair, a folded newspaper forgotten on its seat, and next to it a small table laid with a silver tray bearing a decanter and a single glass. It occurred to her that this must be Julián's bedroom—and his bed.

Whatever foolish fantasies Amalia might have once harbored about spending another night in Julián's bed vanished abruptly in the reality of the situation.

The sudden prickle of tears behind her eyes made Amalia sit up and swing her legs over the side of the bed. "I should make sure Lucía's all right," she said with her back to Julián.

"I don't know where you think you're going," he told her, his voice rich with amusement, "but I don't think you'll get very far."

Amalia cast an annoyed glance at him over her shoulder and found herself averting her gaze at the sight of his bare, muscular back.

To her profound irritation, he was right—she was still unsteady enough on her feet that she was forced to let him help her first to the washstand, and then down the stairs and into the dining room. Lucía, who had always been an early riser, was already at the long table with a cup in one hand and a bun in the other.

She bounded up from her chair, insisting on helping Julián as he lowered Amalia into a padded armchair. Amalia felt her heart soften as she let her sister dote over her.

The table was piled with a platter bearing all kinds of pastries, as well as a porcelain pot full of hot chocolate spiced with cinnamon and ginger, a silver one with coffee and smaller containers that held milk and sugar. Lucía puttered around it, putting together a plate for Amalia and exchanging teasing remarks with Julián as if he was the older brother she'd never had.

Back in the Hotel Europa's courtyard, when she had learned the devastating truth about his identity, Amalia had watched Julián transform before her very eyes. But what she had taken for him dropping a pose had actually been him assuming one—the cynical, amused, detached mask that he presented to his father and cousin. There was no trace of it left now as he made Lucía giggle into her *café con leche*.

Maybe Amalia did know the real Julián, even if he didn't.

He *was* handsome and dashing and irresistible. Or maybe it was just that Amalia didn't want to resist him, though she could think of a dozen reasons—maybe more—why she should.

Her father had done his best to protect his daughters, and all he'd accomplished was locking them in a gilded cage. Julián himself had tried to keep her from being hurt by their association and broken her heart in the process. However well intentioned their actions, they had both caused her pain.

But the difference between her father and Julián was that Julián was still here—and, having seen how she had suffered, he knew better than to trample over her opinions and wants and dislikes. He was the kind of man Amalia had never known existed, the kind she never knew she could want.

And now that she knew, how could she give him up?

Her gaze shifted to her sister, and Amalia felt her resolve firming. She'd give up *anything* to avoid thrusting them back into the situation they had fought so hard to escape—including Julián.

"I hope you know how grateful I am for everything you've done for us," she told him later, when Lucía had wandered into the kitchen to beg some honey for her bun from Julián's housekeeper. "I'm afraid we'll have to impose on you a little longer, at least until we're able to finish settling matters with our uncle. And then..."

"And then?" Julián echoed, lowering his cup.

As much as she wanted to keep her gaze fixed to the

painted flowers decorating the rim of her saucer, Amalia had never been a coward. With some difficulty, she looked into Julián's eyes. "And then Lucía and I will leave for Vienna."

She tensed, half expecting Julián to try and change her mind. All he did was nod slowly, though, and say, "I'll be happy to help you in any way I can."

The emotion that unfurled inside her wasn't relief, but disappointment.

She pulled herself together long enough to give him a carefully blank smile and thank him politely. Then she pled a headache and asked to be returned to bed.

Chapter Nineteen

"The first thing I'm going to do when we get to Vienna," Lucía said dreamily as she gazed out the carriage and up at the steamship she and Amalia would be boarding in a quarter of an hour, "is buy sheet music and sit in a café in the Ringstrasse and eat *sachertorte* and *apfelstrudel* and—"

"And give yourself indigestion," Amalia said, giggling. "You do realize we're going home to San Pedro first, right? It'll be a few weeks until you'll be able to while away your days in cafés like a Viennese *fraulein*— or eat like one."

To Amalia's amusement, Lucía refused to let this shred of logic dampen her dreamy smile. "I will dream about cakes every day until then."

Amalia snapped open the clasp on the powder blue leather traveling case she had purchased the day before. "You won't have to wait that long."

She lifted out the small box she had nestled in the blue silk lining, alongside their steamer tickets and money for the journey. Lucía looked intrigued as Amalia lifted the lid and showed her its contents: half dozen little cakes that looked like jewels, topped as they were with glittering sugar crystals, glazed nuts and pieces of candied pineapple and ginger.

It had only been ten days since the two of them had left Julián's house and settled into a hotel. Amalia would have charged into a steamship immediately after the events at the church, but Lucía had begged her to spend a few days recuperating. Amalia had always found it hard to deny her sister anything, but in truth, the main reason she'd agreed to it was Julián.

He had been the rock she and Lucía had never had—he'd spent the past few days dashing around the city, fetching doctors to see to her healing arm, and lawyers to start dismantling their father's will and even magazines and newspapers and endless sheafs of sheet music to keep them entertained. He'd accompanied them on shopping expeditions and to concerts and shown them the sights of the town, including the colonial-era fort he and Amalia had glimpsed from the ship on their arrival.

Through it all, he had made no demands, or asked any questions, or indicated in the slightest that he wanted anything from her. But Amalia couldn't help but be aware of the unresolved business hovering overhead.

He hadn't come to see them off this morning. Amalia couldn't blame him for wanting to avoid the awkwardness of parting.

That was a lie.

She had waited until the last possible second, blinking back the sting in her eyes as the clock above the front desk counted down the minutes until she had to leave. She'd been seething by the time she had finished distributing tips to the bellhops and climbed into the hired carriage that was conveying her and Lucía to the port.

Maybe she *should* have felt relieved that he was sparing them the difficulty of having to say goodbye. But all she could think of was all the things he had said that night at the planter's hacienda, about never wanting to be apart.

He had meant it—she knew that with all the certainty in her body. She no longer had any doubts about his intentions, or of her feelings toward him. So what, then? What had stopped her from asking him to come along with them?

Was it just that she wasn't as brave as he wanted to believe she was?

The coachman guided the carriage into a spot next to a cart loaded with wooden crates. Amalia felt the carriage move as he jumped down from his perch and began unloading their luggage.

What the devil was she doing? Was she really going to leave without Julián?

"Lu," Amalia said suddenly, turning to her sister, who was absorbed in sampling each of the cakes. "Would you mind terribly if I asked the coachman to turn back? I think I may have forgotten something—"

"Something? Or someone?" Lucía asked, looking impish.

Amalia nodded wordlessly, feeling her throat constrict with emotion.

Lucía dimpled as she raised a finger to point at the crowd milling outside their open carriage. "Looks like he hasn't forgotten *you*."

Amalia followed Lucía's finger, her heart leaping.

It *was* Julián, walking toward them at a vigorous clip that made him stand out from the milling crowd.

She turned back to her sister to see Lucía's gaze on hers. "Don't deny yourself love, Amalia. Not for my sake."

Then Lucía was hopping down lightly from the carriage, saying that she would oversee the porters as they transported their luggage into the ship. Before Amalia could follow her, Julián climbed into the seat Lucía had just vacated.

He was in a very fine suit, the kind he had worn all through the past several days. But he was bareheaded even though the midday sun was at its fiercest, and his hair wasn't smoothed back with pomade like the other men's. Amalia drank him in, lingering on the details. His chiseled jaw was shaded behind at least two days' worth of bristles. His tiepin looked like it cost more than her entire considerable wardrobe. And there was no denying that his longish hair, curling around his collar, was badly in need of a cut.

Neither bandit nor aristocrat, he looked wholly himself.

Hurricane-force winds couldn't have held back Amalia's smile. "What are you doing here?"

"I realized I still had something of yours, and I couldn't let you leave without it."

Amalia's smile faltered. "Oh?"

She'd supervised the packing herself and made sure that the things she and Lucía had brought to Puerto Plata—not to mention the many, many they'd bought since then—were neatly placed in their trunks and valises. She'd been very meticulous about it, out of a desperate need for distraction from the confused snarl of thoughts about Julián and her future.

Julián was reaching into his inner jacket pocket. "I never intended to keep it this long. I meant to return it as soon as we got to Puerto Plata."

Amalia glanced down as Julián took her hand, though not to clasp it, but to place something on her palm.

"My mother's necklace," she said softly. "You didn't pawn it."

"How could I, when I had more than enough money to pay for our passage and I could see how much it meant to you?"

"Thank you for keeping it safe for me." Amalia slipped the bright links into one of the small velvet pouches in her leather case where she kept the rest of her jewelry. As grateful as she was to Julián for not having forgotten about the necklace, she felt a little hollow. Was that the only reason he'd come?

"I know it was only in my custody for a handful of days, but it became something like a talisman," Julián continued. "Looking at it made me think of your courage. You didn't just part with something that belonged to your mother and clearly held a lot of sentimental value—you used it to fight for a better future for yourself and Lucía. I'm ashamed of how many years I spent wasting my time and my life because I didn't think I could change my circumstances."

Julián leaned forward. "I meant to be at the hotel to see you off this morning, but I had to stop by my father's office first. He asked me to run his company this morning. Not out of any excess of appreciation toward

me, I don't think, but because Victor is now useless to
him and he needs a second-in-command."

"What did you say?" Amalia asked.

"I told him that if he had changed his mind about
disinheriting me, I was still more than happy to disown
him. In the short time I have known you, Amalia, you
have shown me a side of myself that I never wanted
to admit existed. It was too easy to dismiss myself as
a scoundrel and a wastrel when it seemed so unlikely
that I would ever get what I wanted. I don't want to be
like my father or Victor, but neither do I want to be the
man I was before we met."

"Oh, Julián." Amalia reached for his hand. He held
hers in his larger one, thumb idly stroking her knuckles.

"This is the right path for me. If I'm to make something of myself, I'd rather do it on my own." He took a
deep breath, and Amalia's heart began to pound. "But
not by myself." He traced a fingertip over her cheekbone, his touch so soft it was like being stroked with a
rose petal. "I want you, Amalia. Not for a dalliance, or
a moment's pleasure. For always. And though I would
never dream of telling you not to go, I am asking if I
can come with you."

Amalia didn't have a chance to answer.

"I know you already gave me an answer. That night
in the planter's house, when I begged you to love me,
and you said you couldn't. And I respect it. I also
haven't forgotten that you swore off marriage," he added
in a rush, his hand tightening on hers. "I'm offering myself to you with the understanding that I won't make
demands of you. It doesn't matter if you won't marry
me, or if you don't love me, as long as you don't make

me live without you. It's been a long time since I've actually wanted a future for myself, and I'll be damned if it doesn't include you, Your Highness."

Placing her other hand on top of his, Amalia said, "I think I could be persuaded to make an honest man out of you."

Julián looked startled. "You changed your mind about marriage?"

"Not entirely." Amalia threaded her fingers through his, saying lightly, "But I have recently come to the realization that I would be bored to tears if I had to go through life without you." She offered him a tentative smile. "I love you, Julián. Loving you is one of the most terrifying, exciting things I have ever done. Who's to say that marriage won't be as exciting as it is terrifying?"

"Are you sure about this, Amalia? Because I wouldn't dream of—"

"What was it that you told me a few days ago? That there is nothing I can't do? Well, I'm determined to prove you right."

Julián looked stunned.

"Also," Amalia said, because it seemed that, at the moment, speaking was beyond Julián, "I have everything I could ever hope for now, save for a bandit of my own. Would you be interested in being mine?"

He caught her into a crushing kiss, heedless of the crowds moving around the open carriage. Amalia could hardly lay a claim to propriety after everything that had happened, so she let herself be deeply, thoroughly debauched.

He lifted her bodily from the seat and placed her on his knees. A surge of joy rushed over her as she wrapped her arms around his muscular shoulders and caressed the back of his neck.

The rasp of his whiskers filled her with an equal measure of lust and delight. His mouth was languorous and unhurried as it ranged over hers, his tongue gentle when he probed the indentation on her top lip. It was the kiss of someone who knew he had a lifetime's worth of them left, and that made it all the more precious to Amalia.

Julián was smiling when they finally pulled apart, their hands clasped tightly together. "Well, then, Your Highness. Only one thing is left. What would you say if I officially, formally, asked for your hand in marriage?"

"That I could imagine nothing more thrilling than to spend the rest of my life at your side," Amalia said at once.

"Then I have something else for you. It was going to be a parting gift if you refused me, but either way, I've known from the moment I saw it on your finger that it was destined to be yours."

Amalia caught her breath when he pulled out his mother's ring. It was just as lovely as it had been when she'd first seen it, diamonds glittering like ice as they caught and reflected the morning light.

She forestalled him by raising a hand. "Not now." He froze and she hastened to add, "You can put it on me tonight—when we ask the captain to marry us."

Amalia caught a quick glimpse of the gleam in his eyes before he bowed his head. She couldn't resist drawing it to her and holding him against her. Brushing back the dark, untidy curls tumbling on his forehead, she placed little kisses around his hairline.

"That was almost more terrifying than leaping out of a moving train," Julián mumbled.

"I found it invigorating, actually," Amalia remarked. "Wouldn't mind doing it again."

Julián lifted his head and grinned at her. "That, Your Highness, is exactly one of the reasons why I love you. Allow me to enumerate the rest."

He actually started to do it, and looked like he could have spent the rest of the day at it. Shaking her head, Amalia seized his hand and pulled him down from the carriage.

They were halfway to the ticket office when Julián bent down to whisper one last item in Amalia's ear. "And above all, I love you because when you're near me, nothing seems impossible."

They were married by the captain as soon as the ship had been steered out of the bay and into open waters— Julián was ready to insist on being married the instant he, Amalia and her sister were on board, but he grudgingly allowed that the captain did have more important things to attend to.

The sunset blazing behind them, the deep blue waters of the Atlantic Ocean spreading before them, Julián and Amalia stood on the deck and pledged themselves to each other.

Amalia was wearing another ensemble that looked like it had been made in a Parisian confectionery; this one a pale, muted green with a froth of lace, garnished with gold jewelry and topped with a modish hat. Just before they'd boarded, Julián had pressed a small fortune into the hands of a steward who had procured an indecent amount of flowers. Amalia and her sister had covered themselves with blooms, weaving them into their hair and tucking them into their clothes, and dozens more waited in the luxurious cabin Julián had arranged for himself and his new bride.

The wedding reception took place in the dining room, where Amalia's sister and the rest of the ship's passengers, all strangers, celebrated their union with flute after flute of champagne.

"An unconventional wedding for an unconventional bride—and groom," Lucía said as she toasted them, her dark skin flushed with champagne and good cheer.

Julián turned to look at his wife—he would never tire of that word. She sat with her back to the dining room's window, the countless lamps reflecting on its pane making her look like the embodiment of the light that had come into his life when he met her. Julián took her hand and kissed it, and when she turned her sparkling, luminous eyes toward him, he kissed her lips with his heart in his mouth.

At long last, Julián managed to spirit his vibrant, beautiful wife into their private cabin, where he meant to whisk her straight into bed.

First, however, he spared a moment to enjoy her delight. The same gardenias, camellias and tuberoses that adorned her hair and dress were crowded into the silver-and-faceted crystal vases on every surface. They had turned their cabin into a fragrant garden, but their perfume was no match to the delicate saltiness clinging to her skin.

Julián swept Amalia into his arms and nibbled at her neck, recalling the last time they had stood together in a ship's cabin.

"Remind me to take you into the bath later," he murmured into her ear. "So that I can lick every drop from your skin."

"Oh?" she asked, sounding intrigued. "Please say more."

He shook his head, tightening his arms around her. "Later. I want to devour you first."

Taking her hand, he kissed each one of her knuckles before turning over her hand and laying another kiss on her palm. Then he twined his fingers through hers again and tugged her toward the bed.

Lying back on the satin coverlet, she reached for the fastenings on her dress, but Julián brushed her hands away.

"It's my turn to undress you, Your Highness," he told her and turned his head to press a kiss to her thumb when she stroked the side of his face.

"Undress me slowly," she quoted, leaving off the second part of the sentence because there was no need to hurry anymore, not now that they had forever.

He took his time with every hook and ribbon, tracing each lace-edged border with his tongue and caressing each inch of skin as it was revealed. He tasted the salt that had collected in the hollow of her throat and the slight dip behind her ears, returning again and again to the sweet warmth of her mouth.

It was where he belonged.

"I have never loved anyone as much as I've loved you," Julián told her. "I will do everything I can to deserve this trust you've placed in me."

Amalia laid the back of her hand against his cheek. "You already have. I hate that I ever doubted you, even for a second."

"I think we needed every one of those seconds, Your Highness. To find our way to each other and to ourselves."

"I had no idea I was marrying someone so wise," Amalia said teasingly as she reached for his shirt buttons.

"Not wise. Just…in love."

"And lovable," she added, sliding his shirt off his shoulders. "And deserving of love. Not because you're useful, or obedient, or because you're handsome or clever or good at business, even though you are all those things. But because you're you, and that makes you worthy of all the affection you have ever needed and longed for."

Braced on his forearms, Julián let her slowly and thoroughly strip him bare, both in body and soul. If Amalia had once worried about losing control if she married, to Julián it was an opportunity to surrender himself to her and make her the guardian of his body and his heart.

Hours later, as the dense night began to lighten into dawn, Julián was drifting into sleep when he felt Amalia rise from the bed. To his chagrin, not even the tantalizing thought of licking droplets from her smooth shoulders could make his heavy eyelids stay open—but he managed it several minutes later when she opened the door of the lavatory, softly so as not to disturb his sleep, and paused to turn on the electric lamp.

Her fine lawn nightdress billowed down to just an inch above the floor. It was suspended by a delicate tracery of lace or crochet—Julián couldn't tell the difference from a distance—that left the length of her arms bare.

And then there was her hair. It rippled down her back like a miniature ocean, cresting and swelling with dark waves, all the way down to her waist.

Feeling as dazed as if he'd been struck upside the head, Julián watched from the bed as she padded to the vanity and poured a few drops of some sweet-smelling oil onto her hairbrush. She cast a glance at the bed, and Julián saw her mouth curve when she noticed he was awake. "You wouldn't mind helping me, would you?"

Julián let out a laugh as he walked toward her. "Are you trying to flirt with me?"

Amalia smiled up at him. "Did it work?"

"Always."

Gently moving her hair to one side, he dove into her neck for one kiss after another, making her squeal. He didn't pull back until they were both breathless with laughter.

Her sterling silver hairbrush was part of a set, with a swirling botanical design on its back that matched the small hand mirror she had laid on the vanity next to a leather jewelry box. Julián drew the brush through her curls, watching as the strands separated and reformed in the wake of the bristles.

Only a few minutes went by before Amalia spoke again. "I have something for you."

After opening her jewelry case, she extracted a folded scrap of paper from beneath the curled links of a necklace and half turned to hand it to him. "When I met with your lawyers several days ago, I asked for their help finding someone. They sent a messenger with this just before I left the hotel this morning."

Julián set down the hairbrush.

"Miguel?" he asked, gazing down at the words written in the neat hand of a clerk. "You had them track down Miguel?"

He'd thought about doing the same thing so many

times over the years, but he'd never quite dared—out of worry that the horseman wouldn't remember him or worse, that he would resent Julián for costing him his job. And heaven only knew if that was the only thing his father had done to the man.

"I hope I didn't overstep. The way you talked about him… I thought you might want to get back in touch with him. I want you to have people in your life who care about you, Julián. Other than me, I mean."

"You have no idea how grateful I am." Julián folded the piece of paper like the valuable thing that it was and tucked it into the pocket of his jacket, where it would be safe. He'd scrounge up some stationery and write to Miguel the next day. "I don't know if I'd ever have had the courage to try and find him, but as always, you're so much braver than I could hope to be."

"Your and my childhoods were similar in a lot of ways, but at least I had Lucía," she said, looking earnestly up at him. "For Miguel to have been one of the few people to have shown you kindness, and for you to have been blamed for his being cast out—the way you were both treated fills me with rage. I wish I could make right all the times your father wronged you, Julián."

"I don't think even he can do that," Julián said, kneeling between her legs and sliding his arms around her waist. "But I refuse to dwell on the past when for once in my life, I have so much to look forward to. Like renewing my friendship with Miguel and escorting you and Lucía to Vienna and setting up my own business." He dipped his head to kiss her wrist, dragging his lips higher up her slender arm. "And making love to my extraordinary wife. You are incomparable,

Your Highness. And thoughtful and beautiful. And if I'd paid better attention to my tutor, I'd probably have more words at my disposal."

"I know one more," Amalia said, bending over him and touching her lips briefly to his forehead. "Yours."

Epilogue

Less than a fortnight after their arrival in San Pedro, Amalia found herself on her way to another outdoor excursion. She had planned this one as well, though this time her main goal was to provide Lucía's friends with an opportunity to say their goodbyes.

After quick greetings all around, Amalia stepped away from the throng to survey the tables of food she herself had helped set around the *anacahuita* tree. One of the first things she had done upon returning home was persuade her uncle's housekeeper to leave his employ and preside over the house she and Julián had bought together. The older woman had agreed at once, and after a few days back and forth with Lucía, had produced a feast that would not have looked out of place in the Royal Palace of Madrid.

Amalia admired the spread as she nudged silver trays into place and brushed fallen leaves off the white tablecloth.

Her pale green dress, with its ivory trim and panels of delicate lace, was utterly unsuited to an outdoor romp. Though Lucía had twined lilac ribbons through her dark curls, Amalia had chosen to weave hers into a coronet, adorned with tiny white flowers. She was intercepting one of the flowers as it fluttered off her head and toward a tureen filled with hard-boiled quail eggs floating in a pink sauce when she felt someone step beside her.

"Amalia, there you are," said Paulina de Linares warmly, leaning in to press her cheek to Amalia's in greeting.

She had not given up on her gentle but insistent pursuit of a friendship with Amalia, and Amalia couldn't have been more grateful for another chance at letting herself open up to friendship. It felt almost as risky as opening up to love, if in an entirely different way, but Paulina was a motherly soul and she had seemed really concerned over Amalia after the way she'd gone missing from their last outing.

"I was just speaking with your sister. She says you're leaving town soon?"

Amalia nodded in confirmation. "We're going to Vienna so that Lucía can work on her music and I… Well, at my husband's urging, I'm looking into starting a charity to provide legal services to women and children who are in the position Lucía and I were in."

Amalia was a woman of means now, and she also wanted to be a woman of influence. In the meantime, Julián was devoting himself to teaching her and Lucía how to manage their properties and finances. These days Amalia's neatly balanced checkbook was her biggest source of pride.

Paulina nodded in understanding. "If you could keep just one person from experiencing what you and

Lucía—and I—had to go through at the hands of our relations…"

Amalia felt a rush of warmth for her new friend. Of all people, Paulina would understand her drive to help others. They had talked for a long time when they ran into each other outside Don Enrique's store more than a week before, and Amalia had learned that Paulina had gone through an experience similar to hers after her parents had died and left her in the care of her horrible brother.

"We'll have a chance to talk more about it when I stop by tomorrow for coffee," Amalia promised, having spotted a familiar figure at the edge of the gathering. "Will you excuse me for a moment?"

She waited for Paulina's nod and smile before hurrying over to the palm tree against which lounged the bandit who had stolen her heart.

He didn't cover his face with a kerchief these days, and there were few rusty suits in his wardrobe. But his rakish smile made her pulse gallop as hard as it had when he'd raced away with her.

"Enjoying yourself, Your Highness?"

"Not as much as Lucía," Amalia said as she stepped into Julián's arms, tilting her head toward where her sister stood, surrounded by a gaggle of chattering young women. Without their uncle's influence—and without the prospect of marriage hanging over her head—Lucía fairly glowed with good spirits.

"She's in her element," Julián observed.

"Just wait until she pulls out her violin." Amalia's sister had been practicing all week for what she laughingly called her first concert.

Julián smiled, his gaze returning to Amalia. "Will

you come with me for a moment? I have a wedding present for you."

"Another one?" Amalia asked fondly. Every day since they had disembarked, Julián had presented her with baubles or sterling silver hairbrushes or articles of clothing that consisted of barely more than scraps of lace and silk and were not meant to be worn outside their bedroom. "You're spoiling me, Julián."

"No such thing." He tugged at her hand, nodding at the path half-hidden behind the palms. "Come on. They won't miss us for a little while."

Amalia half expected his horse to be hidden among the greenery. The path was empty, though, and they strolled along it arm in arm until they came to a wooden structure that didn't look nearly as dilapidated as it had a month ago.

"The shack?" Amalia asked, tilting her head.

"I bought it, and the two acres of land surrounding it. I thought we could use a little refuge. In case we ever decide to take up banditry again and need to run from the law."

"We own four homes," Amalia protested, laughing. "Five, I think. Or more?"

"Definitely more," Julián said. "And they're all so large and grand. Don't you sometimes wish we had a cozy little hut just for the two of us?" He trailed a deliberately slow finger down her spine, which he knew never failed to make her shudder. "A place in the middle of the wilderness where no one could find us...or hear us?"

His lips met the juncture of her neck.

"The location does have its advantages," Amalia was forced to concede as her knees gave way and she melted against Julián.

"The interior, too," he said, laying a kiss on the corner of her lips. "Come and see."

Amalia didn't know how he had managed to fit a four-poster bed inside the small shack, but she deeply approved of it. Draped with mosquito netting and piled with embroidered cushions and feather pillows, it looked delightfully comfortable.

She sat on the edge, and Julián bent at once to remove her shoes and stockings before joining her on the smooth white sheets. From her vantage point, Amalia could see the shelf on the other side of the room, laden with a private spread he must have filched from the party—and quite a few bottles of *aguardiente*.

Filled with searing, effervescent delight, she rolled over as Julián molded himself against her back. "I'm not casting aspersions on all of your other lovely presents, but I have to admit that this one is by far my favorite."

Julián blew a cool gust of air into the back of her neck, which already felt damp from the morning's heat, and Amalia squirmed pleasurably again. He had been holding on to her waist, but now he relaxed his arms so that they rested on her hips and thighs, and devoted himself to exploring the curve of her earlobe with the delicate tip of his tongue.

Amalia nestled back against Julián, feeling herself growing molten from the warmth of his touch. If she'd been standing, she wasn't altogether sure she would have been able to remain upright.

His fingers dove into her hair, eager as always to release it from its pins. "I'm glad you like it, Your Highness. We should come as often as we can before we leave for Vienna."

"We'll come every day," she promised, rolling over to lightly bump his nose with hers before capturing his mouth in a kiss. She'd asked him not to shave that morning, and she took a moment to nuzzle his bristly cheeks, enjoying the pleasant prickle on her own soft skin.

"Don't be surprised if I have this place disassembled and packed into crates. Europe is rich in history and culture, but I have a feeling it will be severely lacking when it comes to wooden shacks. And after all," he added, "we'll need to find a way to keep ourselves occupied while Lucía is busy with her music lessons."

Amalia had several ideas, and she wasted no time in brazenly whispering them into Julián's ears.

"You, my dear," Julián said, fiddling with the pearl buttons running down her back, "are the most incredible woman I've ever met. Remind me to add this moment to my list."

"One of these days you'll have to let me see this list of yours. If only to prove that it does, in fact, exist."

"Oh, it does," he assured her. His hands had reached the last button at the small of her back and she could tell he was lingering over it. She arched into his touch, inviting his hand to trail lower and knead her bottom.

"By now, it's probably as long as your…arm," she said.

"Wherever did a gently reared heiress like you learn such filthy innuendo?" His attempt to look scandalized gave way to a smirk, and Amalia couldn't resist kissing him through her laughter.

She reached for the placket of his trousers. "You're a terrible influence on me. Then again, you know what they say about keeping company with bandits."

Julián's lips grazed her neck. "I don't, actually. What do they say?"

Amalia grinned. "That it's damned exciting."

* * * * *

If you enjoyed this story, be sure to read
Lydia San Andres's debut

Compromised into a Scandalous Marriage

HARLEQUIN
PLUS

Try the best multimedia
subscription service for romance
readers like you!

Read, Watch and Play.

Experience the easiest way to get
the romance content you crave.

Start your **FREE TRIAL** at
www.harlequinplus.com/freetrial.